RUBICON

Agnar Mykle

RUBICON

Translated from the Norwegian
by Maurice Michael

E. P. DUTTON & CO., INC.
NEW YORK   1967

First published in the U.S.A. 1967 by
E. P. Dutton & Co., Inc.
English translation copyright, ©, 1966 by
E. P. Dutton & Co., Inc., New York,
and Barrie Books Ltd., London
All rights reserved. Printed in the U.S.A.

FIRST EDITION

Published simultaneously in Canada by
Clarke, Irwin & Company Limited,
Toronto and Vancouver

Library of Congress Catalog
Card Number: 66-21314

Published in Norway 1965 by
Gyldendal Norsk Forlag A/S
under the title *Rubicon*
Copyright, ©, 1965 by
Gyldendal Norsk Forlag A/S, Oslo

TO TORIL MYKLE

*"You have heard the old people say:
'in the beginning was the word'.
But I tell you that in the beginning
was the novel."*

RUBICON

DEEP DOWN in Denmark, at the most southerly point of Jutland where Scandinavia ends and the Continent begins, on the very threshold of the wide world, a young fair-headed man was standing one afternoon in June 1939.

The run down had been a journey through fairyland. Early that morning he had come ashore from the ferry at Hirtshals, in the north, with 180 miles of Jutland ahead of him . . . lush meadows, large cows, low wooded hills, pink half-timbered houses thatched with yellow straw, here and there a still, black stream with ducks swimming in it (and the picture of one little duckling that had lagged behind and was rashly swimming along by itself); a small grey church built of round boulders; an excellent minor road, a main road, the great trunk road with signs so obligingly clear you could not go wrong, and also small, rectangular kilometre stones along the verge so that you always knew how far you had travelled; later, he was to remember them as white stones with red numbers, white stones with red numerals half hidden in green grass—it was enough to make you feel quite poetic; and when he saw his first windmill beside the roadside, he had stopped and exclaimed delightedly: "Oh, a windmill!" and some farm children, who could not know that he had never seen a windmill before, came and gazed at him with unblinking, round eyes.

But that fairy-tale ride was over; now he had come to the ogre's castle and the giant who had no heart.

But life was no longer as it had been in his childhood, when, if the picture book he was reading with hair on end became too terrifying, he could drop it and run for immediate corroboration: "It's true, Mother, isn't it: it isn't true?" "What isn't true?" "It's true it's not true that the witch cooked Hansel and Gretel? It's not true that witches cook children? It's true it's just a fairy story" "Yes, it's just a fairy story."

Nor could he do as he had as a boy at the cinema, when the film became more than he could bear. He had invented his own way of dealing with that. When the Thief of Baghdad had been captured and was strung up, stripped to the waist, to be flogged, as the executioner raised his rhinoceros-hide whip and was bringing it down, he had quickly shut his eyes, squeezed his lips together, clenched his fists and with all his might forced himself to think: "It isn't true. It isn't real. It's just a trick. Just a film. It looks as though it's real, but it isn't. Just remember, it isn't real!" In that way he had managed to fight his way slowly out of the horrors, and when finally he had dared to open one eye, Douglas Fairbanks had just landed a kick in the executioner's stomach, or rolled a barrel at him, knocking him over; and then had snapped up the rhinoceros-hide whip in his teeth, picked up the knife in his toes and cut himself free, and then—oh, look at that!—the Thief of Baghdad had tugged the long Persian rug from under the feet of his pursuers, sending them flat on their backs, and the next moment was sitting up on the roof of the nearby mosque waving gaily! And cocking a snook!

But this was true.

Here, at the customs station in the very south of Jutland, on the frontier with Germany, this was real.

And—this was the strangest contrast—it was a sparklingly lovely day.

Summer had come in an overwhelming rush that year. Although it was still only June, it was boiling hot and quite still, as on a day of high summer. The soft scent of clover from the fields and of petrol from the road came drifting on the hot air; flies buzzed on the sunny wall of the Danish customs house: summer had come and the sky was huge and blue.

10

When Caesar stood on the banks of the Rubicon, did it ever occur to him that he could turn and go back, that he was not obliged to cross?

That thought occurred to this young man now.

He slid his great goggles off his face and looked up at the sky mistrustfully. He did not know what he had expected; perhaps the hollow, distant rumble of guns, but it was as quiet as in a vicarage garden. And that sky! Blue, ineffably blue.

It was suspicious. He narrowed his eyes and again peered up at the arching heavens. It was so oddly blue. Was it camouflage?

Was it a trap?

"Norwegian?" asked the Danish customs officer in a friendly voice. The young man started. Then he nodded and with a courteous smile handed over his passport.

As he did so, he began to tremble.

He began muttering to himself scraps of acquired wisdom, for he was a learned young man. In a sort of grim gaiety he said to himself: "That er hræddr madr sem ekki thorir at skjalva!" which is the tongue of the old Vikings and means: "Only a coward is afraid to tremble". but it did not help, or not much. Then he said to himself stoically, in the tongue of the ancient Romans: "Non dolet, Paete!" which means "It won't hurt, Paetus!" but that did not help either; not much. The dead can be wise, can't they?

"And where are you off to then?" asked the Danish customs officer, fingering the young man's passport.

The young man smiled to himself. The question had sounded like a line of verse, had a sort of jovial music to it. Fancy being able to talk like a poet with Germany right in front of you, only a bowshot away.

He gulped.

"France," he said.

The next moment he was afraid that he had spoken too loudly. Perhaps they had heard him over in Germany. And perhaps it was forbidden to mention France there. He shot

11

a quick glance across the frontier, then he leaned nearer the customs officer:

"France," he whispered. The sound of his whisper stirred him. "This is a great day for me," he went on still whispering. "This is my first trip abroad. . . ."

The customs officer took the student's red passport, opened it flat, held it with his left hand against the wall of the building, raised his date stamp and placed it on a blank page. For a short instant he hesitated—and do not all customs officers do just that?—do not all customs officers hesitate for a moment as though to emphasize the extent of the favour that, incomprehensibly, they are doing the traveller? Is not all power, in heaven and upon earth, really gathered there in the customs officer's right hand?

Then the man pressed the stamp. It was like a little metallic animal. The sun glinted on its scissor-legs, it curtseyed in a swift movement that brought its belly onto the paper with a soft click, firm and perfect.

"All in order," the man said crisply, and obligingly handed him his passport back.

The student had to smile. It was as though the man had meant his motorcycle or the world situation. . . .

The young man could not move. He opened his passport and looked at the stamp.

"Out 20 June 1939."

Was that all?

A matter of life and death—and all you got was a triangular stamp in a little book! You had been attended to —like a customer in a shop! You weren't given any more attention than a pig, a dead pig! The carcass had been duly stamped. Given its blue trichinosis stamp!

The customs officer was already walking towards the boom.

The student was seized with panic. He wanted to say a prayer. Everyone has the right to say a prayer before being executed. He did not want to enter Germany as suddenly as this, actually he didn't want to enter Germany at all. It might be quite a good idea to stay in Denmark for a bit. At any rate overnight! Wasn't there an inn here or a Youth Hostel?

Besides, weren't there formalities to be attended to at a customs station? Some sort of palaver and fuss? Call this a system? Wasn't it the man's duty to examine one's baggage? Oughtn't he to question one?

The young man removed a hand from the handle-bars and raised it beseechingly. My dear customs officer, good brother Dane, he wanted to say: don't you see I have a suitcase and a rucksack on the carrier! A very mysterious rucksack! Have you any idea what I've got secreted in it? I might have dynamite, gold, cocaine! A belt of rubies round my waist! A secret compartment beneath the saddle, military plans, the design of a new torpedo, a child's severed hand! You've no idea what sort of person you're dealing with! Don't I look in the least suspicious? What if my mudguards were made of platinum? Don't you want to tap them? Haven't you a little file to take a sample with? I thought all customs men carried tiny files in their waist-coat pockets. Don't you even intend to search me?

It can't possibly be right for you to let a traveller off so easily. You haven't examined anything, nothing at all, and yet you tell me "All in order!" How do you know that? Actually, I ought to report your behaviour to the King of Denmark. The frivolous way you do your job, you must be losing your country millions a year.

Listen, I've got some cigarettes, I tell you, Norwegian cigarettes. If you let me through with those in my pocket won't that be smuggling? Real smuggling?

The customs man was already at the boom.

*

The Danish customs officer put his hand under the heavy boom and pushed it up with amazing ease. The iron frill hung swaying; the links of the chain clinked and a shiver ran down the student's spine.

13

He had to glance across to the German side. The boom pointed obliquely into the air. It reminded him of a guillotine.

He shut his eyes, swallowed hard and started his engine. He opened his eyes when his front wheel was under the boom and looked across at the Danish customs official. Their eyes met for a brief second. The Dane seemed to understand what was going on in the young man's head. But what could two men do? What could two Scandinavians do? The Dane gave him a quick all but imperceptible little nod, almost of encouragement, of solidarity, of sadness and shame, then he half turned away and looked at the ground. There was something about that bowed head that moved the student profoundly. He knew that he would never forget it.

The student looked away. He turned to face Germany and rode on slowly. The other man stood motionless. Neither looked at the other.

Then he heard the boom fall back into place behind him.

Between the two booms at a frontier lies a piece of no-man's land, a lifeless expanse. It may be thirty yards long, it may be three hundred; what he drove across may have been a street, or a bridge, for afterwards he could not remember a single detail of that brief ride. He must have been unconscious.

When he came to, he was standing on an open space surrounded by yellowy-grey brick buildings arranged in the shape of a horseshoe. It was a large space and made of concrete.

He felt himself falling back through time. . . .

*

He was eight and must have been in the second form, when it happened. One autumn morning, a dark autumnal morning, he came in through the gate expecting the familiar bustle, the great, colourful, noisy sea of sound made by hundreds of children. And there was no sound.

The school-yard, that enormous yard, was empty and deserted.

He must be late. They must all have marched in already.

He had never seen the yard empty before.

He stood as though rooted to the spot, could not even breathe. He looked at the high brick buildings: they were dark, cold and without compassion. He was standing outside the headmaster's house. He knew that after that year they would no longer have mistresses. They would have a form-master, nothing but masters. Men. They used canes; they held your hand and hit the tips of your fingers with a ruler, hit you with an iron ruler.

There he was in the empty school-yard. He had not seen it before; but he did so now: it was made of concrete. There is nothing in the world so forlorn, so without pity, as a large empty concrete school-yard. He tried to raise his eyes, tried to see over the big buildings at the end of the school-yard, he looked down through the corridor of time and suddenly, at eight years old, he knew that he was doomed. He saw no hope, no light. Standing there, he knew. All at once, he knew what life was. It was too big. He would never measure up to it.

For a moment, he tried to pray: "Dear God," he prayed, "dear God, make me stay a child. If you can't, then let me die here. I know now what life is like. And I don't want to live it."

"Dear God," he prayed in that deserted school-yard, "let me die here. Next year we have to go to the dental clinic. There are dentists with white coats there. They have needles, crochet needles that they prod the nerves with. They have sharp syringes and electric drills. We aren't allowed to have anyone from home with us. We have to go alone; the dentists hit you if you start crying. It smells of anaesthetic, even on the steps outside. And they have white rubbish bins with cotton wool and teeth and blood in them. I've seen it. Dear God, I daren't grow up. Dear God, let me stay a child, always. Or let me die here."

Then he stood and waited.

God was almighty, wasn't he?

After a while, he understood.

He tried to lift his feet. It was as though his boots were made of lead. Heavily he stomped towards the entrance. He caught hold of the rail, dragged himself up, step by step. He thought, sadly and with a wry smile: I'll get scolded now for being late. . . .

He had been eight at the time. He had thought he had caught a swift glimpse of life's grim horror; he had thought himself doomed. But all the same he had gone on living. . . .

Now he was twenty-three. He blinked up at the sun, perplexed. He was in Germany. At the customs station in Flensburg, on a concrete yard.

Now it was coming.

Why hadn't he turned back! Why hadn't he turned and ridden back, while he was still on the Danish side! Hadn't he once thought of going to Paris by boat? What was he doing in Hitler's Germany? Why hadn't he taken the Bøjg's advice to Peer Gynt and gone round?

Why hadn't he gone by boat?

Cautiously, every sense on guard, he opened his eyes. To his surprise he realized that a sort of animal alertness had taken possession of him: his ears had grown, his skin become electric, the fair hairs on the back of his hand had begun to bristle.

On the Danish side there had been just one customs official, a little man in civvies, but here were two hulking men in gleaming uniforms. Their military coats were green and reached to their knees. It was a grassy green, but not the green of fresh grass, rather that of mown grass, mown and slightly rotten. They had broad, black belts round their waists and bandoleers. Their caps had glossy black peaks and were of a kind he had never seen before. The crowns stuck up and out over the peaks. They were flat, actually more than flat, concave, which meant that in front they went up in a slight curve. They were caps with erections. The effect was spuriously masculine, especially as both men were middle-aged, thick-set and fat: their long uniform overcoats looked like cloaks.

The two customs men (or were they soldiers?) were busy clearing a Swedish motorcar. Their voices were blustering and loud. Too loud. He shot them a cautious glance ready to look away instantly, if they looked at him.

Both men wore broad armbands, white with red swastikas on them. He became strangely agitated. They might at least hide those, he thought; keep them to themselves, keep them at home, in their rooms; they had no need to display them to strangers. Before, he had only seen swastikas in photographs or films. And these men were wearing them as though it was a perfectly natural thing to do. They didn't even seem to be aware of the sort of armband they were wearing! If I were compelled to wear a swastika on my sleeve, the student thought, my arm would drop off; it would detach itself at the shoulder and drop off!

He looked round cautiously, but could see no Germans other than the two customs officials. What had he expected? Battalions? Columns of tanks? He did not know. All he knew was that behind these two policemen in their green uniform coats was a great sombre state with an underworld of cellars and skeletons. A great, sombre nation that had an unredeemed inheritance of night and gallows, Walpurgis and Wartburg, Faust, St. Vitus Dance, flagellants and Black Death, witches and devils, an inheritance of yellow horns and scaly tails. . . .

It was as though Germany—the land in between—had an old caul on it, a slough that it could not shed, could not kick off. It was as though a tight snake-skin clung to its hindquarters, rattling, dragging, clattering, not to be shaken off. Just take the language. Just? Is not language really the expression of a nation's soul? (And their script, their Gothic script. . . .) If one has a light airy language, one dances through life. If one's language is ponderous, then one day-dreams about deeds of violence, of blasting oneself a way to heaven. . . .

When the Germans say "gefährlich", the Scandinavian says "farlig". The lack of the Teutonic prefix "ge", which the Scandinavian has discarded or, perhaps, never had—makes him thirty-three per cent lighter. In the case of the German "gewiss" which in the North is "viss", the Scandinavian is a whole fifty per cent lighter than the German! And weight is the enemy. . . .

"Hans, bist du fleissig und gehorsam?"

"Jawohl, ich bin fleissig und gehorsam."

Those two lines had been his first childhood's encounter with the German language. They were right at the top of the first page of his German book. The word "lydig" is a dreadful one in Norwegian too, as "obedient" is in English, but the German: *gehorsam* is doubly so. Fleissig und gehorsam! It was like hearing the cogwheels of a rack creaking.

The lines were repeated lower down the page, now in the plural: the whole class being included:

"Seid ihr alle fleissig und gehorsam?"

"Jawohl, wir sind alle fleissig und gehorsam."

*

Germany. . . .

For him it conjured up Dürer's horrible engraving "The Knight, Death and the Devil". The devil was depicted as having the head of a wild boar and tiny, piercing eyes. . . .

The student shivered in the blazing sunlight.

Was there, he wondered, a corresponding national symbol in his own country's history? If you wanted to explain to a foreigner what Norway was, what would you say? Thinking back, he could not remember a single knight in armour. Perhaps Norway had not had any Middle Ages? He had to go right back to the age of the Vikings, and suddenly he smiled ... he had just thought of a king, a young king with a golden helmet. There was a tall statue of this king in the market square of his home town—were he to survive this trip, he would certainly go and lay a wreath of flowers at that king's feet. ...

He had walked along his ship's oars when they were overboard, that was the sort of king he was. He had not ridden heavily across the dark earth, but sailed gaily across the blue sea (his golden helmet glinting ...). When this king had nothing else to do aboard his long ship, he had walked overside along the oars!

If I were an engraver, the student thought, or a painter— I would do a picture of that. Not of the knight and his horse, but of the king and his ship!

Of course, Death and his scythe had caught up even with King Olav Trygvason.

Was all that he had heard and read about Germany, true? The barbed wire, rubber truncheons, steel whips? That they thrust red-hot knitting needles under the nails of prisoners they were interrogating?

Suddenly, he could feel the money burning through his pocketbook.

It was perfectly legal money: 20 marks; two 10-mark notes, bought in a bank in Norway. "You can get tourist marks," the clerk had said, "they're cheaper." He had said yes without thinking and was given his twenty tourist marks. He had accepted the offer. He had accepted that shameful offer!

Tourist marks. ...

Tourist—does not that mean that you are glad to be there, does that not mean riding singing through a country while the engine blows little white smoke rings from its funnel, does it not mean singing and waving your hat and blowing kisses to the girls?

But can you be glad, when you know that there are human wrecks being kept in prisons and concentration

19

camps, and when you cannot help them? Is it then physically possible to be a tourist?

They had outwitted him with their tourist marks, caught him off his guard. In a nasty cunning way they had made him an accessory. He was a young man with a tender conscience. And a socialist as well. He would have like to have taken the two 10-mark notes and torn them. . . .

Torn them to shreds. . . .

He was not one who treated money lightly. Money was dreadfully serious; money was the most sacred thing there was. At a stretch a child could be forgiven for *losing* a coin, a small coin; but if a child went and *threw* a coin *away*, that was the most sinful thing it could do: for that there was no forgiveness.

Coming back from school one day when he was nine, he had been crossing a long wooden bridge, called Gangbrua, and right in the middle of it, it had struck him that he had a one-øre piece in his trousers pocket. He had been walking along thinking about the nature of sin. He took out the coin. It was warm from having lain in his pocket. He looked round: he was alone on the bridge. He rubbed the coin till it shone. Just as an experiment, he thought. Just to see if anything happens. After all it was the smallest coin there was. I could get a stick of liquorice with it, he thought. No one had ever said that you could be punished for throwing a stick of liquorice into the river. Could there be a punishment, let alone an eternal punishment, for throwing a one-øre piece into the river? It was only a piece of metal after all. . . . Yet, nevertheless, he shuddered: in some inexplicable way he felt that a one-øre piece was more than just metal. Suddenly he felt angry. He raised his arm. He threw the coin, a quick, hard, high, angry throw. He wanted to measure his strength with God. He saw the coin describe a twinkling arc through the air; then it dropped abruptly and disappeared into one of the big white eddies far below. He felt his heart sink. He had that

20

feeling in his heart for over a week and for two weeks he went about waiting for his punishment. It never came. Then a strange thought occurred to him: the worst punishment is that which never comes!

That way God wins, whatever happens, he had thought. God always wins. . . .

He sat quite still on his motorcycle watching the two Germans out of the corner of his eye. He compared their black, high riding boots with his own. Theirs were stiff, glossy and curved round their legs stiffly. His were soft, dusty and sagged in folds round his ankles. He had bought them one summer two years before, when he was up in Finnmark. He had made a quick trip across the frontier into Finland, to Boris Gleb, where there is a Russian Orthodox chapel and where you could get American cigarettes cheap. He had seen a stall in the market there full of riding boots, they hung looped in pairs, and the whole wall was covered with them. They were lovely boots, and they were for sale. They were astoundingly cheap; shamefully cheap; he had thought: you can't pay a shoemaker only sixteen crowns for a pair of brand new beautiful, soft riding boots. They were good stout boots, of excellent workmanship; new leather boots have an exciting smell of their own, an almost animal smell, warm, good and clean.

At that time he was having an affair with a woman, he may even have made her pregnant; he kept looking at those riding boots; then all at once he bought a pair. As he tucked them under his arm and walked away, he knew that it was an illusion, but he felt morally uplifted, for a moment in imagination he was with the Three Musketeers. . . .

Later, when he went south to more civilized parts, to Trondhjem and Bergen, he realized that he had very little use for boots of that kind. They were too heavy and close fitting for walking tours in the summer, while the folds round the ankles chafed; and in winter you could not ski in them, nor skate. Nor could one wear them to dances; nor to lectures, because the moment you appeared in them one of the others was bound to enquire after your horse, ask whether the gentleman's horse was fit and well, and he did not include a horse among his possessions; and, most certainly, one could not attend meetings of the Students Socialist Society in riding boots: all those Marxist comrades would look at you as if you were a capitalist, an aristocrat, a strike-breaker, a Menshevik, an escaped member of the Tsar's family, a kulak; worst of all, they might think that you were one of those who imagine that they *are* somebody.

Those boots became a burden and a problem: on the one hand he could not use them for walking and, on the other hand, they were too beautiful to sell: they became a cross between a dream and a museum; mostly museum. ... Then one day a letter had come from a woman.

THERE ARE moments in history when people sense that the future is contracting, that life's gates are in the act of closing. . . .

Perhaps it is something we have heard people talking about, perhaps something we have read in the newspaper; perhaps it is just a cloud shutting out the sun . . . but from that moment our lives are changed. . . . War. If war came, then we would all be shut in.

Did we not lie sleepless in our beds straining our ears into the night? That spring, did we not, at night, think we could hear a strange and distant sound, like that of great gates treacherously and quietly turning on their hinges? In the morning, when we got up, did it not seem as if those two great gates there ahead of us had moved a thought closer together? A millimetre? Was it imagination? Had we not caught a brief glint, a dangerous glint, like that of the sun reflected in heavy copper? And did we not, the next night and the one after that, still hear that distant, muffled sound, like that of great hinges being secretly and imperceptibly turned? And in the morning had not those great copper gates ahead of us really slid a shade closer? One millimetre? Two millimetres?

Living was becoming slowly more and more difficult. How long had the world left? One month? Two months? Six months? A year perhaps? After that, Time's corridor would be shut, the copper gates would have closed altogether, the way out would be locked and bolted, there would be no light, it would be siege, siege and confinement; and all would be dark and drear.

Who—while there was still time—would like to make a foray into the green lands? Who—while there was still time—would like to steal a little sunshine against the future?

23

While those copper gates still stand open—who would venture a sortie?

H E BLINKED. He felt it in his throat. He had just seen that one of the policemen had a pistol. A huge military pistol in a black holster fastened to his belt at the hip. And so had the other policeman!

He had never seen a pistol before.

In Norway they had rifle clubs, where you shot at targets. . . . But in Germany they shot at people!

So it *was* true!

He swivelled round in the saddle and looked back. The Danish customs officer had been unarmed, had not had anything but the stamp he used for passports. He had been an ordinary person, not in uniform. Well, no doubt, somewhere inside the building there would have been a service cap, on a chair; but it was sunny and hot, so the good Dane had left it lying there and had gone out bareheaded. Bless him, bless every man who can don his cap when it rains and doff it when the sun shines! That good Dane, quiet, dry, business-like, obliging, calm, civil; he had been polite, encouraging, but also slightly absentminded, wasn't he just what you would expect the village chemist behind his counter to be like? Hadn't his jacket been rather threadbare, too?

But these two! Everything new, bright, glossy, blustering, it all reeked of authority! Two thickly clad NCO's with sun-burned necks (one of them had slipped behind the Swedish car and raised his cap to mop his head; he was bald, how pitifully pale the crown of his head was, submarine white against the lobster red of his neck!)—all padding and spit and polish, two stout, glistening, brutal men, brutal yet attempting a jovial smile, a blink of sunlight from a gold tooth.

The student sat straddling his motorcycle; he eased his

25

behind off the saddle, not quite knowing whether to sit or stand. What was the done thing in Germany? Nor did he know what tone to adopt when his turn came. Ought a democrat to look at a Nazi with demonstrative contempt? A cold, reticent, cutting look with eyes narrowed? Should he look over the man's shoulder, instead of at him? Or look right away? Or should he stand stiffly and be dumb, not say a word? Should he mumble incomprehensible sounds out of the corner of his mouth? Or should he give the Nazi a great, broad, juicy smile, clap him on the shoulder and give his ear a friendly pinch? Which would be right? What role should he play?

Whatever he did, he wanted to avoid doing anything wrong. A wrong word here on the frontier, a thoughtless smile, a cough at the wrong moment—and not only would he land in a concentration camp, but he might start another world war!

He had read about the shot fired in Sarajevo: and he had no wish to go down in history as the perpetrator of the Flensburg cough!

To soothe his nerves he pulled out a packet of cigarettes. The next moment a great shadow appeared beside him, two heavy heels clicked together, and a dark voice close to his ear shouted:

"Heil Hitler!"

The student swallowed smoke the wrong way and dropped his cigarette. He could not afford just to stamp on it, so he bent down and, trembling, picked it up off the concrete, nearly tipping his motorcycle over as he did so. He bit his lip: then he replied:

"Guten Tag."

He could see that the policeman was piqued. But the next moment the man had recovered and, raising his eyebrows, attempted a smile. He looked at the student, then let his gaze travel over his motorcycle and baggage. He gave a little cough, thrust his tongue into his cheek making it look fat and crafty, then he drummed his fingers on the lid of the student's suitcase and said, quite genially:

"Und wo haben Sie die Kontrabande?"

"Kontra-b-bande?" said the student. He cleared his throat. "Nichts," he said.

"Nix?" said the policeman. He thrust his lower lip forward and looked at the student.

The young Norwegian did not like that. "Nix" is pidgin-German. When he said "nichts", which is High German, the man should not have come and taken it down a notch. That was to deprive him of his education! Again the German let his gaze wander over him and his baggage, scrutinizing. Perhaps he ought to have returned his "Heil Hitler" after all, the student thought: now he's going to pay me out. . . .

"Wo fahren Sie hin?" said the policeman.

There, the student thought, the interrogation has begun. "Nach Frankreich," he said, and added: "Bin Student."

He began searching for his passport. He even had a letter of recommendation from a university lecturer in Norway. Actually it was in French, but perhaps it would help. . . . The German stood looking at the motorcycle. It was a Zündapp 250 cc.

"Deutsches Fabrikat," said the policeman, giving the student a significant look and proudly tapping a mudguard with a knuckle.

"Ja," said the student, relieved, "sehr."

He had meant to say something quite different; that it was a good motorcycle, a really first-class motorcycle. . . . After all he knew German, he was very good at German, at school he had even played the lead in an amateur performance of a German comedy, *Der Onkel aus Honolulu*, and earned the praises of the entire staff for his pronunciation, even of the Head himself. He had been the school's bright boy in German; and now here in Germany he was tongue-tied and inarticulate. How on earth had that idiotic "Sehr" slipped out? He wanted to correct it, but felt it was too late. The word just hung there in the air. He felt himself blushing.

27

The German wanted to know what he had in his rucksack. He laid a pressing, groping hand on the top flap. For one reason or another the student objected to that hand. The man should have been content to ask questions.

He told him that it contained personal things: clothes, shoes.

"And in this suitcase?"

"The same. Reise-Effekten."

"Sie haben kein Fleisch—Butter—Fett?"

"Nein," said the student in amazement, "nichts."

If the man had asked about furs, cigars, opium—but who had heard of a traveller trying to smuggle a case of margarine?

"Bitte machen Sie den Koffer auf."

The student gaped. Was he expected to open his suitcase? Had he heard rightly? His temper began to rise. If the man had not asked me first, he thought, but told me to open my suitcase, that would have been, so to speak, all right. But seeing that he had already asked me if I had anything to declare and I had said that I had not, he ought to have believed me. Now he's accusing me of being dishonest.

The student lowered his eyes. He bit his lip. Then he caught sight of the policeman's heavy holster.

He dismounted and went to the back of his motorcycle. Ridiculous, he thought; I'm a student: I haven't anything of value; the man must be able to see that. He began unlashing his rucksack with a dull feeling of irritation. Everything was so beautifully packed and fastened; the way he had built it all up on the carrier was a work of art; and now he was having to undo it all, his suitcase, of course, being at the bottom! There were strings and straps, straps and cords, all knotted and tied with care and calculation. It had taken him a quarter of an hour that morning at Hirtshals. . . . And where was the key?

When the lid of his suitcase finally jerked up, the student lifted up a couple of rolled pairs of stockings that lay on top to show that he had nothing but innocent things. But that did not satisfy the policeman. He got to work. His great fingers rummaged in the contents, kneading them, heaping them up, and the student went cold at the sight of such vandalism. If there was one thing he loathed, it was people who made his things untidy, people who had no feel for things and their place. He stretched out a beseeching, threatening hand, but the policeman did not see it.

"Ah—books!" the policeman exclaimed, suddenly interested, as if he had made a find. He shot a triumphant look at the student. Then he picked up some of the books.

"Französische Bücher?" He looked at the books, took one, opened it, licked his long finger, turned a page.

"Yes," said the student and craned his neck to see what book the man had. Could books be contraband? Good God, he had never thought of that! There were lots of books on the index in Germany. Goebbels had made a bonfire of books. Nothing roused the Nazis more than books! Imagine him being so idiotic as to take books, and French books at that, with him through Germany! They were mostly reference books, it is true, but there was the policeman intently reading—which one?—Anatole France's *Crainquebille*; the man cocked his head to one side and censored a page, licked his finger, turned the page, looked at the print, pursed his lips, wrinkled his nose, raised his eyebrows. Then he let the book fall with a smack and dug out another, a novel, Claude Farrère's *Les Civilisés*, ooh! There's one bit in that about a man and a woman in a zoo, they are standing hand in hand in front of the lions' cage and they watch the lioness enticing her mate, and lustfully the woman's nails dig right into the man's hand, was that what the German was reading? Everything to do with sex was prohibited in Germany, wasn't it? *Les Civilisés* ... The student shuddered. He remembered being told that when a Nazi hears the word "culture" he unfastens the safety catch of his revolver. Intently the student watched

29

every tiny movement in the policeman's face, every movement in his hand: he stood there, one eye on the man's great
military pistol, stood waiting for the verdict.

All at once the tension inside him relaxed.

He looked away, gentle, mollified; he could breathe
again.

He was saved.

He stood stock still in order not to give his discovery
away:

The German *could not read French.*

The student had suddenly realized that from the man's
mouth, the play of his eyes and face—the German did not
understand a word of what was printed there!

The student did not know what to do with his victory.

"Gut," said the German, thoughtfully, importantly.

"Gut," the man repeated, caught his lip between his
teeth as though biting back one or two little criticisms of
French literature he might have made, but which magnani-
mously he was not going to mention. He let the book fall
back into the suitcase and unctuously laid his hands on it.
For a moment he stood there, looking straight ahead of
him, hands resting on the pile of books, as though lost in
literary appreciation, his gaze remote and paternal. He
acts well, the student thought. Then it was as if the policeman appeared to have reached a decision, it was as if he
had conscientiously censored the whole of French literature; he pulled the lid of the suitcase back and tried to press
it down. It would not go.

"Gut," he said, took a step back and stood there.

The student felt his eyes narrowing with hatred and for
an instant he had to look away. Create havoc and then
say that it was "gut"! Was there no law for customs
officers, nothing to say that if they unpack, they must re-
pack?

He could not arrange the things as he had had them
before and finally had to put his knee on the suitcase to
shut it. The hinges creaked. Suppose my suitcase bursts?
My things will be scattered behind me all down Europe: a

30

plimsoll here, a vest there; a whole trail of things: a pyjama jacket here, a french letter there. My trail to Paris.

The suitcase had been new for the trip. It had cost him a fortune: twelve crowns. He mopped his face and looked down at the policeman's boots.

The policeman cleared his throat.

"Also, in Frankreich wollen Sie studieren?" he said. The tone of his voice was different now. He was standing a yard away; he had hooked his thumbs into his belt, and stood there rocking lightly on his heels.

"Yes?" the student said cautiously.

The policeman detached his right hand from his belt and with one finger wiped under his nose.

"In Deutschland haben wir ja auch sehr gute Universitäten," he said. He shot the student a quick glance, but looked away again the moment the student looked at him.

The student had got his rucksack back on top of his suitcase and was tightening the last straps. The Swedish car had gone. The second customs officer was standing some distance away contemplating the toes of his boots. The yard was empty. Germany appeared deserted.

All at once he felt that he could understand the man and his question, that he could understand what it meant to be a German in uniform, with a swastika—what it meant to be a German in Germany.

There was Hitler doing everything: building motorways, holding Olympic games in Berlin and Wagner festivals in Bayreuth, making the Germans all do exercises, Kraft durch Freude, even issuing tourist marks—and then everybody goes to France!

What did France have that Germany hadn't?

"Ja," said the student. Of course there are good universities in Germany too. "Aber . . ." he added.

"Warum denn wollen Sie in Frankreich studieren?"

There was a ponderous, importunate interest in the man's voice, even though he was looking at the ground and appeared unconcerned. The student found it most embarrassing. He felt that the German was demeaning himself.

31

The man had no pride. He was like a beggar displaying the empty sleeve of his jacket, in which there had once
been an arm, and asking for alms because he was disabled. If I should lose my right arm, thought the student,
I would ask for work and would show people my good left
arm. The other's gone, I would say, pointing to the stump
of my right, but this one's first class and does enough for
two, I would say and wave my left. And if I had lost
both arms, well—I could still play football, or tramp
hay for a farmer. In France I could tread the grapes. I
could knock at people's doors with my forehead, butt it
twice, and when they came and opened up, I would take a
few dance steps and ask if they had any use for two excellent legs. . . .

Why did he want to study in France?

He remembered one of Goethe's sayings: "Dort wo du
nicht bist. . . ." He was on the point of saying it out aloud,
but stopped himself, trembling, just in time. He could
have landed himself in prison because of Goethe. "Happiness is where you are not." The policeman might have
thought the student was being impolite using "du" to him.
And he could not very well change Goethe. At the thought
of having to say "Dort wo Sie nicht sind" he almost
snorted. He shifted his feet, clenched his teeth. He thought:
Goethe would have liked that.

The student made a helpless gesture with his hand. One
can have so many reasons for taking a trip to France. A
longing for beauty can be one. Or a thirst for adventure.
Being crossed in love. Something could have happened to
one recently, not so many days ago, perhaps even in
Bergen, one could have been as dumb as a fish, unable to
get a word out; and now one might be nourishing the hope,
the impossible hope, that in France perhaps one could
acquire a little polish, learn a trick or two, a grasp, an insight, a secret formula, an open sesame that would fling
wide the door to a woman's affections. . . .

Why did he want to go to France?

"Ah," he said, "Sie wissen . . ."

32

He searched for a word, could not think of it in German, gave it up:

"Ein bisschen *savoir vivre* . . ."

"Bitte?" said the German.

"Ein bisschen—*savoir faire* . . ."

"Wie bitte?" said the German sternly.

The student rubbed his chin unhappily. He did not want to hurt the man. How could one explain in one word to a German all that France stands for? How to express the genius of France in a single word?

"Sie wissen—Paris . . . !

Hurriedly he added, in a sudden access of fluency:

"Paris—und *die Frauen*!"

The German blinked. The next moment he was beaming. Well, if that was how it was, if it had nothing to do with the standard of their universities, but was merely a question of women! Happily, the German gave his belt a hitch, his fat belly rocked; he allowed a gold tooth, two gold teeth to glint at the student:

"Ay-ay-ay, die Mädels von Paris . . . !"

The policeman whinnied, stopped abruptly, gave a little cough. He said:

"Sie können passieren."

The student opened his mouth.

"Passieren?"

"Jawohl."

The policeman was straight-backed and corpulent in his long green overcoat. He was grave, formal, mollified.

"Danke," said the student. He felt so grateful that for a moment he was on the point of holding out his hand. Instead, he bowed, quite a deep bow. He could feel his knees quaking.

He drew a deep breath, straddled his motorcycle, and got ready to start. The policeman was standing behind him. At that instant an icy wave coursed down his back.

He *had* contraband.

In his rucksack. Which the man had not looked into.

And he had forgotten it.

33

It was only a tiny bit—but was anything too small to count? In a country where a writer could go to prison for a comma, how much did it take to lock up a tourist?

He had a quarter of a pound of dairy butter in his rucksack—and a piece of smoked ham.

He had seen it in a village in Jutland, in the window of a "victuallers", having stopped because of that extraordinary word. He had seen it in the shop window. It was so small and chubby and lovely and round and shiny and brown, tied in a neat criss-cross of string that cut slightly into the skin like lace—a fabulous ham, one of the loveliest little pieces of ham he had ever seen, and he was so entranced with it that he felt he would like to steal it. But he could not afford to buy beauty for its own sake. Then it had struck him that if he bought the ham, he could just stop somewhere by the roadside, sit in the grass with a loaf and his ham and carve thin slices off it, then he would not need to eat in cafés and restaurants. That would be a purchase it would pay him to make!

The price of the ham was fourteen crowns. Fourteen crowns! Downcast, he asked if they would halve it; if so, he would take half. The man behind the counter scratched long at the back of his neck with a carving knife, but in the end began to cut it. The student shut his eyes—it was such a pity. And whoever would come afterwards and buy the other half? Seven crowns, thought the student, that is almost seven dinners; it was an expensive buy; but if I cut it really, really thin . . .

Now that fabulous little ham had become contraband —and he had denied it.

If only he had thrown the damned ham, and the piece of butter, away on the Danish side of the frontier. No, given them to that nice customs man, that was what he should have done; the good Dane's jacket had been a bit threadbare; perhaps he had both wife and children. . . .

His back to the German, he bent over the handlebars, twisted the grip, put his foot on the kick-start. Now for it! Calmly, calmly does it. It struck him that he ought to say something to the German, just to gloss over the silence, to act as a diversion.

He turned his head, looked at the man innocently and asked:

"Und, bitte, der Weg nach Hamburg?"

The moment he said that, he had to gulp. Perhaps he had been too daring. Perhaps he would be caught now. He felt the ground slipping from under his feet.

"Gerade aus," replied the German, politely, and pointed with a hand held horizontal. "Und angenehme Reise!" he added.

"Danke!" said the student. There was gooseflesh on the nape of his neck.

He prayed that the motor would start. He pressed down the starter. The miracle happened.

"Auf Wiedersehen!" called the policeman, jerking his hand to the peak of his cap and slamming his heels together.

"Auf Wiedersehen!" replied the student.

Then he accelerated. The motorcycle shot forward and up, like a rearing stallion; and the wheel struck the cement coping, but he just managed to keep the machine upright.

Hamburg, Hamburg, he thought. If I can just get to Hamburg.

Instantly he turned the accelerator back. Calmly, calmly. Don't give the policeman grounds for suspicion. Nice and calm, like a Sunday excursionist. Don't look back. The man who looks back makes himself suspect in a policeman's eyes, or so he had read in a detective story. And in the Bible there was that bit about a person being turned to a pillar of salt.

Nice and calm.

And straight ahead.

Once out on the autobahn he thought: why didn't the policeman ask about cigarettes and spirits?

The German's coarse whinny when he had mentioned the girls in Paris, wasn't there something mysterious about such mirth? A German who laughs is most suspect. And that last remark of his...Wasn't there something odd about that too? What had he meant by saying Auf Wiedersehen? It could have been ordinary politeness—but it could also have been something else! Be seeing you! Good God—where?

Now they could have him for making a false declaration. That, of course, was how they filled the prisons in Germany. First be friendly to people; lull their minds into tranquillity, then grab them the moment they think they are safe!

He did not dare turn his head. "Be seeing you!" He already felt as though they were at his heels. A whole squadron of military police on heavy, roaring motorbikes, not small Zündapps, but enormous Harley Davidsons, great beasts of things, he had seen it in films, a whole squadron of motorized police; and those fearful sirens!

No, of course! The more cunning thing would be to telephone to the first road block. That was it. They had telephoned to the first patrol post. They would take him from the front.

On the far side of the road, on the other side, lay vast billowing cornfields. But, were they cornfields? Were they wheat stalks the afternoon sun was reflected in? Had he not seen movement there? It was a glint from a bayonet he had seen! In a moment, the whole field would rise up and reveal its true self! A whole army of green soldiers; they had been lying in wait there, disguised as corn; now they were rising up, rising in waves, now they were coming; the whole field was quivering; they were storming up the slope to the road, with fixed bayonets, he could hear their shouts of "Hände hoch!" He was surrounded. Finished. This was the end.

Slowly, slowly, his fears receded; slowly, a bit at a time the gooseflesh lost its stiffness and subsided; slowly, only slowly, he was able to breathe again.

B ROAD AUTOBAHN as far as the eye could reach.
As a socialist and democrat he had made up his mind that he was not going to admire anything in Hitler's Germany. But here, on the autobahn, for a moment he weakened.

He came from Norway's narrow, bumpy dirt roads. The previous evening, on the mountain road between Stavanger and Kristiansand, on a bend, in sudden deep loose gravel, he had almost killed himself. . . .

The autobahn extended broad and firm and flat and concreted as far as his eye could reach.

It was divided into two with a strip of grass down the middle. There were two lanes in each direction. That gave one a feeling of lavish space.

The country was surprisingly flat—almost flatter than in Denmark. There was no speed limit. The only prohibition he saw on any sign was of bicycles, horsedrawn vehicles and parking. "Streng Verboten!" But, he thought, if a poor devil is unfortunate enough to have a puncture and has to stop, *has to stop*, what then? He decided he would not have a puncture.

Where there was one of the rare crossroads it was carried on a bridge across the autobahn. In that way those driving along the autobahn never had to reduce speed. He looked at the four-leafed clover design and felt furious because it was so ingenious, because Hitler had invented it.

Wait, he told himself, wait until I am in charge of the roads in Norway . . .

He had thought the traffic in Germany would be heavy: people, motorcars, hay-carts, regiments, military bands, pedestrians, prams, tanks, circus vans: after all Europe was a thickly populated part of the world. . . .

He did not see a soul. The flat countryside appeared deserted.

And the whole time he was on the autobahn he saw only two cars, perhaps three. But to make up for that they were going at a murderous speed; he shuddered as they swept past, whining, like dark shells.

He himself did not dare push his motorcycle along at more than forty-five, fifty at the most. "Fifty's the most," the salesman had said. "Fifty's your top speed."

It was second-hand; he had bought it on credit in Bergen. Purchase price: 600 crowns. 200 crowns down and the rest on a three-months bill. He had gone about for several weeks doing mental eeny-meeny over the idea; for it was an astronomical sum. Then one day he had gone in and clinched it. He would never forget counting out two red hundred-crown notes and placing them in the dealer's hand, never. First one large note that you spread out, slowly, and rubbed between your fingers to convince yourself that, well, to convince yourself; then, slowly, another large note and that too you rubbed between your fingers.

But rub as you would, there weren't any more, only the two notes, and then they were there in the dealer's hand, you looked at them, it was like taking communion.

Strangely enough he did not have the same detailed memory of the moment when he signed the bill for 400 crowns. A signature on a piece of paper, a few scribbled letters—how could that occupy as important a place in one's memory as two good, solid, tough hundred-crown notes?

Improvident, improvident!
Time will find a way.
Improvident, improvident!
Accept a bill for 400 crowns falling due in three months and which you don't know you can meet!

One day things are bound to go wrong for that young man, aren't they? Improvident, prodigal! Wasn't he earmarked for ruin and perdition? Wouldn't the obligations that he had so frivolously shoved aside come pouring back one day like a comber and catch him and break over him and crush him?

Stop.

Perhaps prodigality was a principle, a natural law. Perhaps prodigality far from being the exception, was really the rule. Perhaps all creation followed the law of improvident prodigality; perhaps the whole universe was secretly based on it. Didn't roses live on credit? Did cats have a written guarantee of the morrow? Has anyone ever seen a star's bank account? Roses, cats, stars, how thriftless they were, and should man be less trusting? After us comes the future; all by itself!

Perhaps, providence is the opposite of prodigality. Perhaps improvidence is the most serious thing there is . . .

Roses, cats, stars.

As the last car, a Mercedes, whined past him, he had caught a glimpse of its solitary occupant, a youngish, pallid man in a dark suit and grey soft hat. The man had sat crouched over the wheel, he appeared to be sitting at an angle, almost in pain. Was he being pursued, or was his back hurting?

Dusk was beginning to fall.

He had reckoned that he would reach Hamburg about nine o'clock. By half past nine he had still not seen it. Ten o'clock came. The autobahn stretched endlessly ahead of him.

He had seen signs with Hamburg on them and something about 20,000 metres, or 2,000 metres, and something about Hamburg West and something about Hamburg Ost, but when was Hamburg coming?

In the end he was riding along with his head half turned, his brow puckered, his mouth half open. He realized that he must look pretty unintelligent; he slackened speed and glanced behind him. Not only was it forbidden to stop on the autobahn, but to do so could also be dangerous. If there was a car behind you, it might well run into you.

He dismounted and hastily dragged his machine over the verge on to hard gravel and coarse grass. He drew a great deep breath and scratched the back of his head. They can't put you in prison for stopping a bit to think, he thought. It had now become quite dark. It had also grown chilly; all at once he shivered. I shall have to put my anorak on again, he thought, and perhaps my gloves. He felt that he had to have a pee. He looked round, to the left, to the right. Was peeing forbidden in Germany? Anyway, here I am, he thought. It left him with a sense of irritation; to have a pee is a good thing. You can tell that from animals, children and, though seldom, from grown-ups: you can tell it from their gaze, faraway, relishing, unconscious; but if it is to be good, the process must be complete, it must have all the time it needs, the last drop must be lovingly shaken off. The student's slight irritation was caused by the fact that the last drop had not been shaken off, but drawn in. His fear of Germany had made him break off a moment too soon and now he could feel the last drop where it should not have been, inside, on his thigh, half warm, half cold.

What had the signs meant?

In Norway, there was always somebody on the road whom you could ask. That's what roads were for! And if there was not anyone, you would soon see a church spire or come to a shop or a youth club or farm. If nothing else, there would be a barn. It would not have people living in it, but it would be evidence that people had lived there and, if need be, you could go in and burrow down into the hay —and you would probably have a very good night, warm, fragant, secure!

Here there was just the autobahn. Concrete; a flat countryside and a naked sky. No houses, no people. Not so much as a horse. Oh, a horse! His heart softened. The warm smell of horse, its muzzle, snorts, whickering. . . . He used to have a day-dream of getting himself a horse, a white horse, and riding to Paris. It had been a dream about a comrade; the white horse. . . .

Not a soul.

And no poetic little kilometre stones as in Denmark.

He stood there alone beneath the enormous evening sky; he looked at his little motorcycle. "Hm," he said and patted its chest.

Suddenly he thought: I must switch on my lights. If only they work. Suppose the battery was dead! Which knob could it be? Could it be this one? he wondered. And which way do I turn it? If I turn it the wrong way, could I cause a short? Then the lights would explode with a bang, I suppose? I could get a shock, he thought.

Suddenly he remembered, vividly, the two occasions in his childhood when he had had an electric shock. Screwdriver, electric point. . . . It was as if the world had been rent, split open, had shrieked; the most paralysing part was that it was so utterly unexpected; it came like a log springing up and hitting you on the head, only inside; it had made him go rigid and open-mouthed, as though turned to salt, or iron; his scream had been cut off short; instead, it felt as though his teeth were going to fall out and his nails drop off: that blue second in which you felt your whole body as a pounding unit, from the soles of your feet to the crown of your head, a pillar of burned cry, and your right hand held out incredulously for insane inspection.

I ought to have rubber gloves, he thought.

To be on the safe side, he stood a pace away from the machine. Slowly he stretched out his hand towards a knob. He turned it. He gave a little jump as a fierce cone of light, white and enormous, struck out into the empty darkness.

"Thank God," he whispered. He felt his teeth chattering slightly. Why hadn't he been shown how the lights worked before he left? Or had he, perhaps? And not taken it in?

There were some large insects in the cone of light now, some were fluttering in front of the headlamp, soft, dancing, like hairy bats. Others were coarser, hard, filled with hatred; they took a run in the air and flung themselves against the glass with a metallic report. They were insects of a kind he did not know; evil, foreign. He shivered. Hurriedly he mounted, wanting to get away. He trundled the machine to the road.

Carry on? Or turn back?

Having gone so far, he could go a bit further. Perhaps Hamburg lay just ahead. He drove on. What fun it was riding with the headlight on.

He rode for five minutes.

He rode for ten minutes.

He saw no sign, no cars, nobody.

He stopped.

He hauled his machine across the grass division in the middle. It gave him a queer feeling, as if he were doing something wrong. Reaching the side of the road, he was careful to look behind him, so as not to get a car running into him. Then he turned the accelerator-grip, fiercely, angrily, the back wheel scuttered on the cement—he shot away.

Back the way he had come!

What a lot of things one should have found out before setting off into the wide world! A map was another thing he ought to have bought. . . .

He had been so certain that a main road leads straight to a large town—hadn't the policeman said "Gerade aus!" and didn't that mean "straight ahead!"?

It was now half past ten. How much petrol had he used unnecessarily! If it went on like this he would soon be ruined.

Besides, when had he last filled up? It only needed

to run out of petrol now! Then he would have to spend the night... He tried to smile, but could not produce one. Ahead of him there was something with dark wings dancing in the shaft of light from his headlamp, he thought he could see a skeleton, a scythe. . . .

He came to a sign. He stopped at it. West. So presumably this was—what was it called?—an approach road. He sat there thinking. West. One of several approach roads? He had no idea what part of the city he wanted: only that he wanted the Youth Hostel. West? That smacked of England.

Nonetheless he rode on. He came to another sign. Ost. He was no better off. Ost? That smacked of Russia! But he could not stand any more. He had to choose between Russia—and spending the night in the open. He chose Russia. He turned the handlebars and swung off down the side road.

"Well," he thought, "I missed Hamburg properly!"

It was quite dark by the time he entered the city, and he asked for the Youth Hostel and found it and afterwards he was to remember nothing of the city of Hamburg.

"FAHREN SIE bis zum Hafen hinunter . . ."
     To the port?
Life affords many surprises. One of them being that when you come to a foreign city late in the evening and find your way to what you expect to be a house, you discover it to be a ship.

The student cocked his head to one side and stared.

The Youth Hostel was a superannuated training ship. A great schooner with a black hull and three or four tall masts. She was big and old and lay there heavily and squatly as though she were built to the quay, as if she had grown onto it. The first superficial impression was that the old ship lay deep in the water, content, pensioned off, as if she lay there enjoying a well-earned rest. But, having dismounted and taken a step closer, he was aware of a smell of decay, as from a raddled corpse. There were no sails. Instead, the rigging and all the masts were hung with coloured electric light bulbs that shed a garish fair-ground glow over the decks and the quay.

He did not like it. A sailing ship should either sail the proud seas or lie a wreck on the ocean bed.

He parked a bit beyond the gangway. He had joined the Youth Hostel Association in Norway, but had been told that his card really only applied to hikers and bicyclists. If you rode up on a motorcycle, you could not be certain of being admitted. He hoped they had not heard the drone of his motor. Not to be allowed to stay the night cheaply at a Youth Hostel just because of a baby motorbike of 250 cc! If you had arrived in a car, driven up in a big Cadillac, all right. "One has to draw the line somewhere." *But, has one?* Why should not a chap with a big Cadillac be allowed to sleep in a Youth Hostel if he wanted to? Was there anything wrong in driving a Cadillac? Perhaps the chap had a millionaire for a father; or perhaps his father had won a sweepstake: one day there's a brand new Cadillac outside the front door: "Whose is that?" the son asks. "Guess," says the father, and the old boy can scarcely stand still for delight-of-giving, his face is fat, inflated with happiness; "Mine?" says the son; "Umm," says the father "Try her out!" Can one say no to such a present? No. So, one is the owner of a Cadillac. But should one be barred because of it? Should one be forced for the rest of one's life to stay at Hotel Grand Royal and sleep in a mahogany bed? Even though one owns a Cadillac can it not still be amusing to go to a Youth Hostel? And could it not be fun, even quite an experience for those in a Youth Hostel to meet a real live Cadillac? Perhaps they could be taken for a drive in it!

At that moment, the young man, who was a Socialist, thought the interesting thought: what actually is Socialism?

Are there many definitions. Or just one or two? Or are there none?

None?

He blinked. He gave it up. He was too tired. Carefully he locked his motorcycle, using a chain and padlock. As he dragged his suitcase and rucksack up the gangway, there was a plank that complained. He looked down hurriedly: there was moss on the ship's side all along the water-line and from it came a sour smell.

There was a kind of reception room aboard, under the superstructure. It was quiet there. From further up the deck came a jarring sound of singing and shouting. The man behind the desk was wearing a dark suit and a black uniform cap; he was rather like a mate. He was aware of the student's scrutiny and gave him a slightly apologetic smile, as though to say that he was not there by choice. The student liked the look of him. The singing and bellowing on deck grew momentarily louder and they both turned their heads towards the sound, then again their eyes met. The man shrugged one shoulder apologetically. The student liked him even better.

The place was in semi-darkness and the man had to bend low over the passport. He opened his mouth in order to read, stopped, raised the passport up to his eyes, stopped. He tried to pronounce the student's name, scratched his ear and looked unhappily at the late arrival. The student smiled. He took the passport, half turned it towards him and with a finger pointing to each letter, read: V, in Norwegian is not pronounced f but V. Quite simply v. Like the German w.

Then the German pointed and wanted to know what sort of letter an å was. An å? It's pronounced like the German o. But, said the German, doesn't Norwegian also have the letter "o"? Yes, of course. Well, how is it pronounced? Like u.

The man blinked. What a queer world.

The young globe-trotter had a feeling inside as if his smile was slowly dying. At home, in Norway, his name had always been the cause of difficulties, always. Was it going to be the same abroad? It had proved a tongue-twister for one man in Germany already—what would it be like in France? He stood there, unable to speak.

The man pronounced the word slowly, carefully.

"Is that right?" He looked at the student, all eagerness like a pupil.

"Jawohl." Thank goodness.

"Und bleiben Sie lange hier." For a fraction of a second the man had glanced back at the passport intending to address the student by his name prefixed with Herr, as would have been correct, but abandoned the idea. The light was too bad and the name too difficult. But the student had noticed the good intention and tacitly thanked the man.

"Nur eine Nacht."

"Schön. Bitte, kommen Sie mit."

They walked off together. They had to pass through a

46

group of men with glowing, red faces, who drifted singing across the deck, so many steps forward, so many back. There was something unreal about the scene. This was partly due to the multicoloured light from the rigging, partly to the fact that the men had been drinking, but as the student made his way through this gliding, squirming, dancing flock he had the momentary impression of being in another world; as if he were watching a skating competition being held under water by artificial light. Modestly he turned aside and went round them.

There are two forms of intoxication, two categories of the inebriated. With one lot of people, wine kindles a latent wit and makes them attractive and charming: they become gods with vine-leaves in their hair and starry eyes. With the others wine turns their souls inside out and, lo! they have no souls, it is all shiny entrails and wet goblins: the wine allows them to hold a watery shiny toad up at you and they are offended if you do not love it, they become angry if you do not kiss their toad.

Some of the men—who seemed to be a package-tour and who were of all ages from fifteen to fifty—were wearing Tyrolean green leather shorts with belly flaps and leather braces. An elderly fat man, flushed and red, who was wearing such shorts, came waddling across the deck, holding a glass of beer aloft. His great pot belly strained against the flap (did it let down?), his white short-sleeved shirt had dark half-moons of sweat under his armpits, he wore stockings and had bare knees and a Tyrolean hat slightly askew on his head; he looked just like a giant child, an overfed, intoxicated giant-baby, and to crown it all he was singing something that ended in "Joch-he!" and at every "Joch-he!" he tried to stamp his heel on the deck, but he got his timing wrong.

The student looked away. Adult men should not go about with bare knees. Especially when they are fat. He had a religious conviction that when God made adult men he in-intended them to wear long trousers.

He was shown to a bunk below and said goodnight to

the mate. He was tired, but not so tired that he did not want a breath of fresh air first. After riding for more than twelve hours it was good to stand, to exchange two spinning wheels for two planted feet, just to stand and let his agitation slowly subside.

He went up on deck and stood by the rail at a safe distance from the tour. The water of the harbour was still and dark. It was a warm, soft evening. He set his elbows on the rail and rested his chin in his hands.

"You from Norway?" said a quiet voice in English from the level of his shoulder.

If God himself had spoken to him out of the cloud, the student could not have been more taken aback. His elbows skidded out to the side. He jerked himself upright. His heart was in his mouth.

"Sssh," he said and looked round cautiously. The deck was empty. He looked down quickly, for the voice had come from below, and saw the slight figure of a man of about thirty in a dark pullover, scarf and knitted cap: this fragile-looking person had dark eyes, a thin nose, slightly sunken cheeks and a brown moustache. He blinked his dark eyes like a friendly mouse. An Englishman!

The student would have liked to move away. The man must be crazy to stand there openly talking English in Germany? Hadn't he heard that in Germany you could be put in prison for listening to the B.B.C.! This might be a trap. The man could be an agent provocateur.

He was on the point of bowing to the man and going below to his bunk, but then curiosity got the better of him. He looked round the deck again, even leaned over the rail to see if there was an open, eavesdropping port-hole there. They remained standing beside each other: both rested their elbows on the rail and looked out across the water. The student turned cautiously towards the man and whispered:

"Are you from England?"

"Yes," said the man in a soft, friendly voice. "Yes, I am."

The student could not make head or tail of it. It was incredible. The little man was in mortal danger. They both were. Perhaps the little man was a refugee. The student became agitated. He wanted to know what the man was doing in Germany and began to whisper: what was the man's profession?

"Paintah," the man smiled.

"Paintah?"

"Paintah. Yes."

"Ah."

The student turned his head away, so that the other could not see him bite his lip. It is one thing to understand English in Norway, when it is spoken by Norwegians; but quite another to understand it in Germany, when it is spoken by an Englishman. When he went to college after matric he had chosen French as his language; he had chosen it because he considered that he really knew German and English: he thought that he had a particularly good command of English: in fact, that he was pretty brilliant at it. And yet the very first time he met an Englishman, he stuck. He was thankful for the darkness that hid his flaming cheeks. He was aware of a mounting, fierce bitterness, anger and shame. But perhaps the man was a Cockney. That would save his face. One is not expected to have a command of the dialects. But he did not dare ask the man if he was a Cockney: some people might be proud of being one, but others might take it as an insult.

Slowly he turned his head back and looked at the man. Making his voice easy and untroubled, he said:

"Paintah, you said?"

"Paintah, yes."

"Paintah? Is that it?"

"Yes paintah."

Then they regarded each other stiffly. Then, suddenly, the student could not stand any more. He said:

"Do you mind telling me, sir, what a paintah is?"

The Englishman pursed his lips, smiled, and the instant he held out his left hand, palm up, and made a few slight

49

drawing movements on it with his right hand, at that very instant the Norwegian understood.

"Painter!" he cried. "You are a *painter*!"

He groaned delightedly. He could have hugged the little Englishman. He wanted to dance round the deck, oh! there is no greater joy in the world than that of understanding!

He was quivering with emotion. He whispered:

"I know! You paint!"

He prodded a finger at the Englishman's chest and whispered ecstatically:

"You are a painter!"

"That's what I said," said the Englishman.

They stood for a while by the rail. The student asked if the English painter had been in Germany long. Three months, said the Englishman. What was it like for a foreigner in Germany? Oh, fine, said the man.

"A jolly good country," he added with a smile.

The Norwegian shot a quick glance at the Englishman; was there something about his hollow cheeks, his wry smile, something that... An Englishman cracking up Germany, who liked it in Germany. There was something shabby about the man, about his jacket, even about his scraggy neck. In England they were arming, working. Yet this English tramp was wandering round Germany painting pictures; he had actually made himself at home in Germany, for three whole months. Jolly good country, indeed! The student said nothing. He moved a pace away.

After a bit he said goodnight and went below.

*

The big dormitory was in the belly of the ship. He undressed slowly. Looking round to make sure that he was not being watched, he thrust his passport and pocketbook into the pillow, between the pillow and the case.

50

This was a safety device of his own invention. He was a heavy sleeper. Nothing ever woke him.

When he was twenty, he had known a woman of twenty-four, known her well, too well. He had been teaching in a God-forsaken little industrial town in the far north of Norway; he was all on his own, bitterly alone; he had nobody in the world but that waitress with the pitch-black hair and white luxuriant body. He had not wanted to know her, not well, and certainly not too well. After the first night he had tried again and again to break with her, to pretend he was not at home; he loathed the way her breath smelt of drink, and he had an inexplicable fear of something that lay at the back of her slanting dark eyes: a flicker of yellow like a flash of evil, or crime, or madness. Alone in his room, he screwed himself up to be manly and brave. He walked round and round the room, bracing himself, his tread growing heavier and heavier, the circle narrower and narrower, until he ended up beside the desk. He banged his fist on the top of the desk making the typewriter and the blotter jump, grasped the telephone. He was going to end it. Yet he could not bring himself to lift the receiver. He sank into the chair, sat there feeling bitter and looking at his hand, the ball of it chalky white from the blow, so uselessly white.

That first night he had scarcely dared look at her. The second night he had kissed one of her breasts: it was big, firm, lovely; then he had jerked his mouth away: there was no nipple. He did not know what to do—to be polite he laid his cheek against her breast and rubbed it a little. On the third night he plucked up courage and inspected her: where there should have been a nipple, there was a hole. The other breast was the same. "I'm like that," she whispered. "I always have been. . . .

He was terrified of a baby resulting. When he thought of that possibility, it felt as though the trap-door had been jerked from under his feet and he was falling shrieking through the universe. To counteract his fears and to have something to talk about in bed (and also to hide the fact that he had grown fond of her), he showed a great interest in her breasts, a scientific interest. On their fourth night he set to work—surely it must be possible to put this right? He began sucking. He sucked harder. Nothing happened. So he sucked even harder. One nipple came half-way out, popped back again. He returned to the attack. Now it was almost all out. At the root of it was a yellowish ring, a thin layer of skin-grease. It had a bitter taste. He wiped his tongue on the pillow and continued, both sucking and carefully picking it out with the reverse end of a match-stick. In the end he got the first one out: there it stood, pink, hard, newly kissed, newly born. They both stared at it. Then he tackled the other. On their fifth night, when she had undressed, she turned round for him to see her. He asked her, in bed, how on earth she could have gone all—he skipped the word "all"—those years with in-grown nipples. She put an arm round his neck and whispered. "No one's done that sort of thing to me be-fore. It was you got them out." She snuggled her face into the hollow at the base of his neck and whispered, almost inaudibly: "They're yours...." He turned pale. He thought: "That's given her a hold on me. Now she's turned herself into my creation. Almighty God!" Any doctor could have put a breast-pump on her. It would have taken two minutes and cost three crowns. But I did it, so now I'm her creator. Now she belongs to me. A good deed never goes unpunished.

They went to stay in a hut in the mountains.

He had wanted to refuse, say no to the suggestion, but had not been able to bring himself to do it. Youth, that's when you cannot say no. He felt like a dishcloth in the hand of an unknown force; he desired her body, desired to sink into her; he was will-less, spineless; he was drawn, drawn; they were sitting in a hired car being driven across a deso-late moor; she laughed her hoarse laugh in the back seat; she held his hand; her breath smelt of wine; the car drove on across the moor, it was like being flung, cuffed, pushed, hustled along. Youth, that's when God wipes the floor with you.

A strange bed in a strange hut in an unknown bit of the forest. He was drinking a bit himself then. That way he forgot some of the ignominy; it spread a protective haze over the room; perhaps he would be able to wake up the next morning and find that it had all been a dream. . . . He had read in books about men who by sheer will power, sheer strength of spirit, had been able to transform the world, make it into something other than it was. If I could only make my imagination strong enough, he had thought, I would wake up in the morning and find that I was not here: that there were no dead flies on the peeling windowsill, no clammy, sour-smelling camp-bed, no old patched sheet: I would wake up in an enchanted land of grapes, music, charm, roses. I would wake up and find myself free.

She had begun reproaching him for always being such a sleepyhead. She was in her nightdress standing bent over the bed, making it up for the night. It was a yellow nightie as wide as a tent, with a drawstring round the neck. She's making the bed, he thought—it's as though we were man and wife. He clasped his hands for a moment. It was a thin nightie and she had nothing on under it; he looked at her bare feet on the floor, saw her strong, shapely legs, her ankles. He got up heavily and went towards her, took hold of her breasts; they lay heavy and firm in his hollowed hands; he could feel the nipples through the material; her breasts were like birds, big, warm, wild birds, they throbbed, tickled, waited. He turned her round: he was tall, thin, strong.

"But promise . . . !"

"Hm?"

"Promise you won't go to sleep at once afterwards!"

"Yes."

"Saturday evening and everything!"

"Yes."

"You won't fall asleep afterwards! You promise?"
"I promise!"
"You see, it's no good if you only do it once!"
"Mmm!"
"You're sure?"
"Yes!"
"You promise?"
"Yes!"
"You won't cheat?"
"Yes."
"What?"
"No!"
"It's always best the second time!"
"Yes!"
"And no sleeping afterwards, you hear!"
"Yes!"
"Oh, that's so lovely! Keep on with that!"
"Yes! Yes!"

And he clenched his teeth in the effort to keep on with it for a long time and managed to; but then came the time when she raised herself under him, arched herself like a quivering bridge, flung herself about in ectasy; she was as strong as a mare and he had to cling to her in order not to fall off; her muscles swelled, her sinews stood like taut stays; then she gave a sudden gasp, collapsed and lay limp, as though killed, only her eyes and her belly were alive; she drew her knees up to her chin, softly, caught him by the small of his back, squeezed his waist; she lay there eyes turned up, whites rolling, gave a sudden snore and for the fraction of a second he was on the verge of convulsive laughter, but then her heels came and chafed his shoulder blades; it was like an order and he exploded into her, deep in, and instantly fear was there, come from below, like a dagger, but she held him and sucked him out with strong, jerky movements and little wails; he felt it like an inner sea of warm honey, he saw stars, he was sinking.

After that he fell asleep.

He fought against it; he had promised, and in good faith,

but it had been too violent and his promise went by the board. Drowsiness came. His cheek slipped away from hers, his head took the pillow. Why didn't she want to sleep? It's good to sleep.... He could feel his features relaxing, his muscles and body going limp, his head felt so heavy and loose on its stalk. He felt that his cheeks were rosy, felt like a baby after sucking, his lips were full and good, he licked his lips, smiled sweetly. He was aware of her indignation, raised his leaden eyelids and caught a glimpse of her kneeling over him, shaking him. He could feel her breasts on his stomach, feel her long black hair sweeping his chest like a mop; she called, but he did not hear what she said; he smiled, amiably, she tugged at his arm, it fell back like a piece of rope; he was sinking; she seized his head and pulled it up and down; he smiled and crowed; she seized him by the hair and shook him, fiercely; he smiled; she grasped his ears and, cursing, banged his head on the pillow; he smiled; she took a gramophone record and smashed it against the side of his head; he turned his head a little on the pillow; he was smiling; he was asleep.

Once asleep, nothing could wake him.

He slept like a log.

That was why he had thought of this way of hiding his passport and pocketbook, of putting them in his pillow, under the pillowcase. Because, he had thought, if a thief comes he would first have to slip his hand under the nape of my neck, then in under the pillow; then, once inside the cover, he would have to turn his hand round, slide it back, grip, turn it back again; then ... No. No thief could manage that.

It was a water-tight system. It was so good, it was too good. I can rely on it to such an extent, that tomorrow, or the day after, 300 miles from here, when I am at the French frontier, I will discover that my valuables are being safely looked after in a pillow in Hamburg!

The first thing I must do tomorrow, early, is to remember my pocketbook and passport. The first thing tomorrow, the first thing. Is. He gave a great yawn.

Artist. He could not get the little Englishman out of his mind. Art? Artist? A stick of a man like that? Those sunken cheeks, that mean little figure, so under-nourished and pallid, that wry, evasive smile—he a painter?

A painter, thought the student, is either a madman with green eyes and a shock of red hair and oblique wolfy teeth, who perhaps has lost one ear, or a tall, straight aristocrat, so wonderfully handsome that women stagger and have to have support when they see him in the street, a tall aristocrat with an aquiline nose and hair brushed back, carrying a walking stick with a slim silver handle and a black silk cape with wine-coloured lining; or just a squat, corpulent, athletic, sun-tanned man with bare torso on some beach in the south, a gladiator who sets about painting as though his brush was a cudgel and the canvas a lion. Strength. Beauty is strength.

And that old Japanese painter, what was his name—Koku—Koku something, no, Hoku, Soku? these Japanese names! Hokusai! Did not Hokusai once write that it was only when he was a hundred that he would start painting in earnest. . . .

That little Englishman . . .

And in Germany of all places! When there was danger of a great war, imminent danger of another world war between the two countries, this little man from England sat at his easel in Germany. While Göring was busy manufacturing guns, this little English painter sat right in the middle of enemy country, wearing a knitted cap, perched idyllically on a folding chair, under the open sky. Sat there humming. On a river bank. The sun was shining. Birds chirrupping. The little Englishman surveyed the scene, moistened his moustache with his tongue, scratched his ear with the end of his brush, selected a colour on his palette. A dollop of cadmium red. Two strokes of ochre. Germany's guns were piling up round him. He did not notice. He hummed to himself, dipped his brush in Chinese blue.

A cold-blooded race the English.

He called Germany a "jolly good country".

He was already more than half asleep, when his mind seemed to bump into a secret. He jerked his head up, wide awake. Lay there in the dark listening. There was no sound from the tourists on deck. Cautiously he raised his head an inch off the pillow and looked round the bowels of the ship. He listened. All he could hear was the faint lap of water against the ship's side. He lowered his head again and drew the blanket up to his eyes.

Perhaps the English were not so stupid after all; perhaps Chamberlain was not all that stupid. Perhaps that little artist did not go in for abstract art; perhaps his activities were highly concrete. Landscape painting... there are many ways of painting a landscape. You can depict it; but you can also copy it. Perhaps he sat on his camp-chair, with his knitted cap and moustache, and simply copied the landscape. There are rivers and trees—but there are also bridges, railways, power stations, factories, shelters, arsenals.

The Gestapo, of course, was always on the look-out for photographer-spies; but had Hitler, who was so crafty, also given orders for them to keep an eye open for painter-spies?

Had Hitler thought of painter-spies?

When the little Englishman left Germany, the customs men would take an interested look at his roll of canvasses; they would give him a word or two of kindly praise; "Sehr schön, mein Herr, sehr schön!"; they would feel honoured by the painter having sought his subjects in Germany; they would step back a pace or two and salute and click their heels; politely they would wish him "Angenehme Reise!"—and say "Auf Wiedersehen!"

The student's eyes were big and round under the blanket. He thought: I could not have thought it out better myself. If there is a war, England will win.

He heard the chuckle of water on the hull.
"Paintah," he thought.
"A jolly good paintah!"
He slept.
Like a log.

THE NEXT morning, rested and well content, he walked down the gangway. For the seventh time he patted the breast-pocket of his anorak. He had remembered. He was setting forth for another day of sunshine on the autobahn. He had had breakfast. The first cigarette of the day, newly lit, was between his lips. Europe and the autobahn and adventure all lay waiting for him.

He thought lovingly of his motorbike, its good handle-grips of warm ribbed rubber, its soft leather saddle; it was his bosom friend, his sweetheart. But where was it?

Where was it?

He stopped on the bottom step of the gangway.

His motorcycle had gone.

He looked to the left. He looked to the right. In a second he had scanned the whole quay. This was nearly a mile long. He saw lorries, cranes, sheds, but no motorcycle. And he knew exactly where he had put it the evening before; and he had locked it with chain and padlock.

He tried to grasp the whole extent of the catastrophe. He realized that his face was white. His trip was ruined. The summer was ruined. With his motorcycle stolen, he would have to take the train to Paris and from there to the Pyrenees; and he had not the money for that. Consequently he would have to take the train back to Norway; and he did not have the money for that either.

Everything was ruined. His whole world, his life was bound up in that motorcycle.

For two seconds he stood there on the gangway, then, dropping his suitcase, like a wounded bird he flapped in tortured bounds the whole length of the quay, behind cranes and packing cases and sheds. Suddenly he thought of his suitcase. He became desperate. Now that would have been stolen too! He gave a gasp and flapped back, stormed back, almost falling over a taut ship's hawser. The rucksack on his back was so heavy that as he stumbled, it almost sent him to his knees; but he recovered his balance, pulled himself up and ran on.

There, he could see his suitcase.

And there—

There—*was his motorcycle*!

He slowed to a walk. Stopped.

Suspiciously, slowly, he went a little nearer, stopped. He stood stock still, trembling, looking at the motorcycle. It was fifty yards from where he had parked his. Was it his?

Slowly he walked towards it, from in front. Not till he was level with it and could look at it from the side, was he able to see the number. But he had already recognized the chain through the back wheel.

It *was* his.

A profound sense of God's goodness came over him, and he would have liked to have given thanks to Him, but he was a socialist and stood there helpless. . . .

He looked at the training ship. Could she have moved during the night? She lay like a rock firmly anchored, rooted. Impossible.

He was right beside the motorcycle now. His heart was pounding. Was it undamaged? He scrutinized it bit by bit through narrowed lids.

There was something wrong with the back wheel. Two or three of the spokes were bent, one quite twisted. Had someone been wheeling it under cover of darkness, trying to steal it!

He squatted down. His hand was shaking so that he could not get the key in. Oh! The padlock was bent too. They had destroyed his padlock! Now he wouldn't be able to get the chain off! If he wanted to reach Paris, he would have to shoulder his machine and carry it!

He had found his motorcycle, only to discover that it was wrecked. . . .

He was stranded.

Stranded in Hamburg.

Now he bowed his head and closed his eyes. He tried to think. He had no thoughts. All was black.

Slowly he opened his eyes. A man was coming down the gangway from the training ship. He had a mate's cap on. It must be the warden of the Youth Hostel. The student gave a low howl and raised his hand. The man saw him and came towards him. The student opened his mouth but could not get anything out. He waved his hands, pointed to the back wheel. The man squatted down beside him.

"Kaputt!" said the student, pointing.

The man examined, saw, nodded.

"Kaputt!" the student repeated.

All at once he found his tongue again, forgot that he was in a country where it was dangerous to be frank, the word just burst from him:

"Diebe!"

The man felt the padlock, tested it. Yes, it was broken. He stood up.

Well, said the man, that sort of thing could happen anywhere in the world, especially in dock areas. He spoke calmly and quietly. Not only in Germany, he added with a slight smile. The student glanced up at him and in that momentary look was aware of a hint of solidarity in the man's face. He looked down again.

"I'll fix this, you'll see," the man told him "Just wait here. . . ." And he walked off, leaving him.

But there he was already, coming back down the gangway: he had a sort of spanner in his hand, no, it was a pair of huge pincers. The man stopped beside the back wheel. Explained calmly, carefully, that it might take a long time to fetch a locksmith; and it could be expensive too. The simplest thing would be to cut the chain. Provided the Norwegian agreed? The Norwegian did agree. He thought the German a genius. Genius consists in doing the only right thing, in the right place, at the right time—and to do it decisively. He himself would never have thought of cutting the chain; it was too near and dear to him, too precious, it was only a week old, it had been new when he bought it. . . .

The mate squatted down and set the pincers round a link. The student watched round-eyed, could not understand that it should be possible to bite through a steel chain. The man set one handle of the great pincer on his thigh, gave a sudden downward thrust with his other hand. And it was done. There was a jingle of steel links on the concrete. They got to their feet. The man looked at the student with a faint, almost imperceptible professional smile.

The student stood there holding the severed link. Stood there weighing this wreck of a safety device. At that moment that spoilt chain seemed to him to symbolize the transience of all security. It was heavy in his hand: together with the twisted, useless padlock it weighed over two pounds.

He walked toward the edge of the quay.

He was a poor young man; he felt as though he were at a funeral. From ten feet up he let the chain and padlock slip with a plop into Hamburg Harbour. He stood and watched them sink glinting into the depths. He gulped.

There went five crowns.

He walked back to the mate who was kneeling and straightening the spokes. The man spun the back wheel: it ran smoothly and true.

All at once the student thrust his hand into his hip pocket, searching: could he? He had never done it before. . . .

The man was on his feet.

"Alles in Ordnung!" he smiled.

The student shook his hand, a firm clasp. The next moment he held out a mark, a whole mark. The man blushed slightly and shook his head: he did not want anything; it was an ordinary act of helpfulness; but where things for which he could not be imprisoned were concerned, the student was adamant; here he felt strong, for he had right on his side; the young barbarian felt on safe ground here; this was his first opportunity out in the great world for the courtly gesture and he intended to take it; it was a sparkling, dangerous moment; it was like a wave; he gave the man *a whole mark*, pressed the coin into the man's hand and shut his fingers round it.

The man realized that he was in earnest, in deadly earnest, and for a moment he looked down to avoid the blazing eyes in the young face in front of him. He took the coin, shook the student's hand, drew himself up, took a pace back and jerked his hand to his mate's cap in a salute, a salute worthy of a captain that made the student feel like an admiral; it was an extravagant moment.

He rode out of Hamburg, his head held high.

WHEN HE set out on his travels, he was wearing riding boots and breeches (there! for a trip to France, motorcycling to Paris, they had proved not only servicable, but, since they protected the outside of his leg from the wind and the inside from the heat of the engine, the best footgear a man could wish; he had known it when he was fishing for them in his wardrobe and, after two years spent in the dark, they all but fawned on him as he drew them out . . .) above he wore first a vest, then a red checked sports shirt, then a grey wollen pullover and on top of that an anorak of windproof material with a hood; at that time of the year, the hood was little more than decoration and hung on his back: he wore motorcycle gauntlets and a pair of huge goggles made of brown celluloid.

Perched on his head was the little blue ski-ing cap topped with a white tassel which is the permanent distinguishing mark of the Norwegian, his international visiting card, his little pennon, half sad, half gay: just a little blue cap with a white tassel. He will have made jumps on skis, will know what a turn is; he will have made many a jump and known many a turn; he may have jumped enough; he may in a moment of mortal danger have understood the vanity of all things and all jumps: hence the dark blue colour of the ski-ing cap and the secret sounding-board of melancholy in a Norwegian's soul; but he will wipe his fingers under his nose, smell the good smell of sunlight and hot sweat and tar and ski-wax, look up at the jump, whistle and: "Damn it, I'll go up again!"—hence the tassel on top of the Norwegian's ski-ing cap: small, hard, impudent, white.

The weather had been lovely when he left—and there had been so little room in his suitcase . . .

In a fit of rashness he had left his oilskin hanging in his digs. He knew that it was taking a big risk. If it started to pour during his trip, he might be forced to spend days sitting at a mouldy wicker table—and wicker tables always have a sour smell in wet weather—in some god-forsaken Youth Hostel feeling his soul becoming mildewed and gazing viciously at the legions of rainwater bubbles breaking in the puddles; sitting on creaky, wobbly, stinking chairs—there are always little nails in wicker chairs—without even a pack of cards to cheer him up; while with a fine oilskin and sou-wester he could have been astride his motorcycle, with a Red Sea wake behind him!

But he had chanced the weather being good. He had had such a strange feeling before he left: that this was going to be a lucky trip . . .

And the sun was blazing: summer had come with an enormous blue sky.

On his way down through Europe the anorak was the first to go; then his ski-ing cap, then his gauntlets, then his pullover; then his string vest; he kept his sports shirt on, but rolled the sleeves up to above his elbows, for he did not want to go through Germany with a bare top, did not want to give the Goths an opportunity to criticize a Scandinavian.

The concrete was hot; the autobahn glistened in the sun.

Looking down past the front wheel he seemed to be going incredibly fast. If he looked up at the sky, he seemed to be going incredibly slowly. The sky was like a blue scalp being peeled with infinite slowness backwards off space. Now and then he ran his fingers backwards through his hair, as though to help speed him along. He hummed. He whistled.

It sounded so strange; in fact, it did not sound at all. He had to hum loudly, practically had to bellow down his nose if he was to hear it above the sound of the engine. After a while he caught the note of the engine and held it for a while. Then he moved to its third, then the fourth, then the fifth. There he sat making a little melody with the note of the engine as the bass. It was rather like the tune of "Lille Postbud, Min Due". She's tuned in G, he said referring to his motorcycle, listening to its hum. I *guess* she's tuned in G, he corrected himself—for all I know she could just as well be tuned in A.

He had once for a couple of months conducted a small student choir, as an amateur, but he had never been sure of getting A without using a tuning fork.

He thought of his father. That man had perfect pitch.

Take Jeanette MacDonald, one of the few film-stars his father had ever praised; once when Jeanette MacDonald sang that song on the radio, as the last note was dying but still hung in the air, his father said E. Then approvingly he added: "High E. *She* can sing." Then he got up from his chair and walked quickly across to the piano, held his beautiful, strong index finger over a key, waited a moment or two till he was sure that the son was following, then struck the note.

When his father said E, it always was E. That man never missed a note.

He wondered if he would ever become like his father. Adult. Master of a craft. Efficient at something. Able to do something, no matter what, with assurance, certainty, unfailing accuracy. It was always the son looking up wide-eyed at his father: "I don't see how you manage it! . . ." And his father, with the hint of a smile: "Well . . ."

Suppose one day their roles were actually reversed! So that it was his father who looked wide-eyed at his son, and the son who imperceptibly shrugged and, with the shadow of a smile, said "Well . . ."

He was driving along the autobahn; he had dared screw her up to fifty and was listening to her with a lover's ear: she must not over-exert herself.

66

Mentally he spread out his arms to the horizon. The sun was blazing down out of a blue sky. He had eaten.

After half a dozen miles he began to blink; he sat slack and inert, feeling drowsy. The autobahn stretched ahead of him, dead straight and uniform. He felt that he needed variety. After all his motorcycle went along on its own. With a car, if you take your foot off the accelerator pedal, your speed drops, but a motorcycle's accelerator is worked by hand, if you take your hand off the accelerator-grip your speed remains the same: the accelerator is fixed in the position to which you turned it.

First he took one hand off the handlebars. That worked all right.

Then he took his other hand away. That worked too.

For a while he drove along without touching the handlebars; felt himself a boy once more, a trick rider. Then he took hold of the handlebars again. He felt slightly ashamed. You should not tempt Fate. One has only the one life. And it is darned precious. . . .

But the autobahn stretched straight ahead and the motorcycle ran on its own. The adventure had grown monotonous.

Surprised, he repeated the thought to himself; he had never thought such a thing before: that even adventure could become monotonous.

Also his bottom was getting tender. He shifted his position first to the left, then to the right, well out. In that position he propped his left elbow on the petrol tank, and that rested the small of his back. After a bit he rested his chin on his left hand. He sat like that for a long time, slewed round, riding along. Then he began to smile. His smile grew into a grin.

He thought: here I am riding through Germany with my chin in my hand . . .

Later in the day he thought:

"I ought to have got someone to make a clip for the handlebars.

"Got someone? I could invent one myself. To hold a book. So that one need not be bored on an auto-strada. The autostrada-clip. No, that's too long. The Strada-Clip, that's better. The Strada-Clip. Registered design. Patented. It could make me a millionaire.

"I could have sat here reading. Held the handlebars with my left hand and turned the pages with my right. Just looked up from the book now and again to see where in Europe I was. Ah, that was a sign flashing past. I stifle a yawn with my right hand: was it Bremen? I was on page 112, wasn't I? In the middle of the page. Let's see. There's another sign. Hanover? Hanover's right. Where was I? Oh, the wind blew the page over. Page 164? Quite an interesting book. Wonder if they get each other in the end."

THE YOUTH HOSTEL was a large old-fashioned wooden building, a big, white, two-storeyed house, slightly dilapidated, neglected, beginning to open at the seams; it looked as though it was years since people had lived in it. It lay back from the road, in a big garden with tall trees. He had a strange impression that he was the only one staying in the whole of the great house. As he stumbled after the warden the sound echoed in the gloomy corridors of brown gloss paint. She was an old woman, gruff and taciturn.

When morning came, he took his luggage and went down to the ground floor. He heard sounds in the kitchen, the door to which was half open. He gave a little cough. He knocked cautiously. The opening became suddenly filled with the warden. She was a woman of over fifty, fat, squarely built, substantial; she had a firm bearing and a firm voice, but she was not unfriendly. That she was a woman was obvious to anyone. She was wearing a white house-coat with a belt round the waist; it was a hot day and she did not appear to have anything else on. Yet there was also something strongly masculine about her as though she had a secret built-in moustache. She was in the process of washing the floor and stood there now with a scrubbing brush in her hand: she gripped it as a farm-hand would a pole. Politely, cautiously he mentioned the word breakfast. She had to throw her head back to look him in the face. No, she said in a deep firm voice: they did not serve meals at Youth Hostels. Schön, he said and bowed. He was full of admiration for this forth-right person who was able to say "no" without even blushing. There is something barefaced about refusals; he himself found it torture if he had to say no to anyone; oh, he thought, if only one day I could become as self-assured, as secure, as firm-fisted as this woman. Firm-fisted was the right word to use. He dared not glance down at his own hands; they were small; all his childhood he had secretly compared his hands with his father's.... He bowed. "Schön," he repeated.

Butter, she said and took another look at him, butter was rationed, as he knew, and he did not have butter coupons, did he?

"Butter coupons? No." he said.

And she had only ersatz-coffee in the house.

"Ersatz-coffee?" he said, he had never had that.

"Well," she said, and her gaze travelled up him again, if he would make do with that...

Oh, he was only too happy not to have to make his own breakfast: delighted not to have to go to a restaurant! He thanked her heartily and bowed.

She had asked him to go out into the garden and sit there. Asked him? She had ordered him. He liked that. No uncertainty, no awkwardness, no would he prefer to sit in the living-room, or perhaps the kitchen, or in the garden perhaps. "Go into the garden and sit there." He liked that.

In the garden, in a corner by the house wall, was a little iron table in ornate Jugend-style that once had been painted, but now was rusty and peeling. Three slender iron chairs went with it. He sat down on one, cautiously. He stretched his legs out on the grass, glanced at his riding boots, wiggled his toes inside them, put his head back and clasped his hands behind it.

It was going to be another roaster, he could feel that. But it was still quite early. In the garden, where he sat beneath tall leafy trees, the air was hot and cool at the same time. It was still. Some distance away, beyond the trees, on the other side of the fence, was the autobahn; he caught a faint glimpse of a filling station with a yellow sign and a blue lorry; he could hear the traffic, but it was remote and unreal. Where he was, was like being in a world of his own, beneath tall, green, still trees; an almost

70

imperceptible breeze passed through their foliage. He laid his hands in his lap; he sat quietly without breathing.

All at once, unheralded, a feeling of happiness came over him. He sat motionless, his eyes half raised, relaxed, his mouth half open; he could feel his heart quietly beating. Later, he did not know how long he had sat thus, whether it was one minute or three or a second; but during that time he had had a feeling of utter, perfect bliss; for however long it was he had had no cares, no memories, no griefs, no hopes, no aims; past and future had no longer existed; he was sitting on a wobbling little iron chair in Germany on a cool morning, beneath tall, green trees, sitting leaning back and looking out at a strange autobahn that ran behind a line of tree trunks and not seeing it; hearing a small bird chirping in a tree top and not listening to it.

He woke from his trance and sat up blinking, when the warden came stomping out carrying a large tray. She set it on the table, took a step back and stood there with her arms akimbo. He had always thought that people drank coffee from a cup, but she had brought him a bowl, a big white china bowl, like those that you beat eggs in; he had to hold it clasped in both hands to drink from it. She must have had milk in it, for the colour of it was light brown, almost beige. He nodded a smile to her and with a word of thanks on his lips raised the bowl. He took a gulp. She stood there fat, firm, sturdy, arms akimbo, wanted to know how it tasted. "Gut," he said through tears, looking down into the bowl. She remained where she was. He could feel her eyes on him. He looked down and to one side, saw the lower hem of her housecoat, her fat legs were bare, white, with pimples on the skin; she had blue plimsolls on her feet. He closed his eyes. Elderly women should not go about with bare legs. Especially not when they are fat and have incipient varicose veins. He had a religious conviction that when God created elderly women he intended them to wear long stockings.

"Gut," he nodded. "Sehr gut."

She stood for a moment, eyeing him from the side; then she clicked her tongue, as if to a horse, wished him guten Appetit and shuffled into the house.

I could go on the stage, he thought. He sat on, munching a piece of bread. He listened. His ears grew, became animals' ears straining to catch every sound within the house. Innocently he swivelled round on the chair; he chewed, hummed, looked up at the tree tops, glanced casually at the house. There was the door, there the kitchen window. His gaze swept across the other windows in the house with a mere tourist's interest. All was quiet. No one to be seen.

Lithe as a cat he rose from his chair, took hold of the bowl, crept noiselessly across the grass, right up to the wall of the house: there he was safe from view, and there too was a bed of aster-like flowers behind which he hurriedly emptied the bowl; it made a yellow lake, he shuddered, for apart from throwing money away there is nothing so ungodly as to throw away food; his hair stood on end in holy horror, then, with his back to the house and the bowl held out of sight on his stomach, he walked back to the table, his mind at ease, untroubled.

I must sit for five minutes, he thought, otherwise she might suspect.

He sat for five minutes. Then he went in and paid.

He drove quickly down the drive.

"I do hope she didn't see me," he thought heavily. "She was really rather kind. She meant so well. Wanted to help a wayfarer who asked for a bite of breakfast. Nice, kind old girl, and then I poured her coffee on to her flower bed. I did, indeed. Let's hope it won't kill the flowers."

Once he had put Osnabrück behind him, he breathed again. He had acquired a map at a filling station. Münster was the next town. He knew that he was heading for the Ruhr now. When the sudden dizzy realization came to him that he was now heading for the Rhine and that on the other side of the Rhine lay France, oh, France—his heart swelled, it felt as though there was nothing but air in his bones, as if he had been turned from human into bird.

He had such a curious feeling, as if he had reached the top of a hill. As if he had hitherto been pushing uphill, and that now the going was all downhill. . . . Was the earth really round? Had he now reached the top and did the earth now slope downwards? He felt suddenly gay, liberated, as if he had successfully escaped. . . .

"Am I a fugitive, then?" he asked.

"Yes," Conscience replied.

He thought this over, and then he nodded.

"Yes," he said.

There was a pause. Both gave little coughs, arming themselves for what was to come.

"You drew four hundred crowns out of the Bank," Conscience began.

"Yes," he said. "Plus two hundred for the motorcycle, making six hundred."

"For a two months' holiday in France," Conscience said.

"To study," he amended.

"You borrowed the money on a Bill of Exchange," Conscience said. "It will have to be paid back sometime."

"Yes," he said.

"What did your parents say when they heard you were going to France? On borrowed money?"

"That I was crazy!"

"And your wife and baby son? Did you borrow money from the Bank for them too? So that they could have a nice summer holiday as well?"

"That," he said, shifting in the saddle, "is another matter altogether. Private consumption. That is a maw that can never be filled. The more I had been able to give her, the more she would have demanded. One thing I learned at the School of Economics and carefully noted, is that one should never borrow money for private consumption, only for investment. My trip to France is an investment. I am investing in my future."

"A deserted wife and a fatherless child . . ." said Conscience.

"Oh, come now!" said the student. "It was I who saved her."

"I beg your pardon! said Conscience. "What did you give her?"

"A gold ring."

"Twenty crowns."

"A gold ring. I made her pregnant. I made her a mother. I made her a wife. No other man in the world . . . I'm not saying this to boast—"

"Don't be so modest."

"—but in me she met the world's greatest sucker. She saw her chance. Her historic chance. She seized it. She seized *me*."

"Genius consists in doing the right thing, at the right place, at the right time—and doing it decisively."

"Yes, It was a stroke of genius."

"A deserted woman and a fatherless little boy . . ."

"She has her parents," he said, shifting in the saddle. "And anyway she has got a job as stewardess on one of the mail boats."

"Weren't you to have met her?"

"Yes, but I funked it."

"You're a fine one?"

"Yes."

"A nice one, I must say."

"Yes."

"A pretty good cad, in fact."

"This is like listening to her."

"How is it that you don't appear bowed with guilt?"

"I find it surprising myself."

"Are you actually chortling over it?"

"Yes."

"May you drop down dead!" said Conscience.

"I'm holding the handlebars," said the student. "With both hands!"

They rode for a while in silence. The student scratched the back of his neck.

"I think the thing is this," he said.

"Yes?" said Conscience, alerted.

"I believe I'm over the counter-threshold," he said.

"What's that peculiar word . . ." muttered Conscience.

"It's *my* word," said the student pulling himself up with a characteristic little jerk of his head. "You see, all the way down, right as far as Bremen, it felt as though I had something round my neck, a rubber fetter . . ."

"That was me," nodded Conscience.

"A voice kept telling me that I ought to turn back."

"That was me," said Conscience.

"But I wouldn't pay attention," said the student.

"That's true," muttered Conscience.

"But today," said the student, rubbing his hands, "today I'm over the counter-threshold!"

"What a word . . ."

"Right as far as Bremen I could hear my father and my mother and my wife scolding, threatening: Turn back, you crazy fool!—turn back, you good-for-nothing!—turn back, you wastrel! But now . . . !"

"Now what?" whispered Conscience.

The student looked behind him for cars, slowed down, stopped. He even switched off. It was utterly still on the autobahn.

"Now," said the student, "now, suppose I really did turn and go back to Norway."

Conscience began to tremble.

The student turned his head away, so that Conscience should not see his smile; one should not exult unnecessarily.

"They would change their tune then, wouldn't they!

Cannot you hear them, my mother and my father and my wife?"

Conscience stood looking down at the cement.

"What's the meaning of this!" they would say, all three of them, "turning back, when you were half-way there! That's ridiculous. That's just throwing money away! No, indeed! having got *so* far, you really ought to have *gone on*!"

There was a pause.

"Over the counter-threshold . . ." said the student.

"Those who till now have been entreating me to turn back, now beseech me to carry on. Those who hitherto have been cursing me, now give me their blessing. One stroke of the wand and everything is the other way round. Now I am followed by nothing but good wishes!"

He pondered.

"Distance changes everything. Does liberty, then, lie in distance?"

The student turned his head this way and that. He was alone on the road.

For one brief, dizzy second it seemed to him that he had been close to a great secret, to a great discovery, more sensational than squaring the circle, more far-reaching than squaring the circle, more far-reaching than the theory of relativity: that he had discovered the formula for the neutralization of conscience. He stood for a second with his mouth gaping, then he had forgotten what he had thought. He started the engine and rode on.

He listened to the engine. Would she keep going? He gave her a pat on the underside of the petrol tank, patted her flank. "Humske," he said tenderly. "Humske, good old Humske."

He had christened her in a rush of exultant pride-of-ownership the day before he left Bergen. He had stood the machine on the pavement, padded round it, devouring it with his eyes. His motorcycle! Oh, what should he call her? Irmelin Rose! Too poetic. Beatrice? Laura? Runa?

Oh, his love's name: Runa the inaccessible; *la belle dame sans merci.*

In a fit of sorrow, to avenge himself on the exalted one, he had chosen the most plebeian name of all.

"No," he had said. "You are no beauty. You're fat; worn, second-hand. But I'm fond of you. Did you hear what I say? I'm fond of you. As I am fond of my old slippers. You are good, faithful and you look as though you would understand a joke. I hereby christen you . . ." He stopped. He had forgotten the bottle of champagne, not that he could have afforded one if he hadn't; he ran in to his landlady and came out with a half bottle of Hansa lager. There he stood, at a loss because he did not want to break the front mudguard with the bottle. He dashed back inside and got hold of a bottle opener. Then he jerked the cap off and carefully poured the beer over the front wheel. He stood devoutly watching it foaming onto the pavement.

"Humske!" he said quickly, and so she had her name.

Then he drank the rest of the bottle himself.

He listened to the engine. Would she keep going? "She'll get you to France all right," the man had said. "May need a re-bore when you get to the South, but that's a bagatelle. Any garage will do it."

A re-bore?

He listened. Might she be groaning ever so slightly? He dropped down to forty-five.

Anyway, he was over the threshold now.

He knew now that he would be there in time.

H AD HE taken leave of his senses? Here he was in Germany, in June, 1939, riding along on a motorcycle feeling as giddy and gay as a schoolboy!

It may have been due to the fact that one had been a couple of days in the country; had been hearing the language and speaking it; memories had returned, scraps out of books, bits of tunes. . . .

It may have been due to the fact that one softens when one has nothing to do but sit hour after hour looking at an unchanging autobahn; even though one has taken a stand against swastikas and barbed wire, there are composers and writers; one softens and opens to the other things, for there are *other* things. . . .

Perhaps it was the roar of the motorcycle that dulled the socialist in him; perhaps the democrat in him had been slightly poisoned by ersatz-coffee; or perhaps he had had mild sunstroke from not wearing his ski-ing cap; perhaps solitude had really confused his mind a bit.

Because, right in the middle of Germany, he began to sing.

More; he began to compose!

More; he had written out the parts and handed them to his musicians!

More; he himself was conducting, was Der Herr Kapellmeister!

More: he had raised his hand from the handlebars and tapped the music stand with his baton!

More: the sixty village musicians in their gay uniforms had raised their instruments, moistened their lips!

THE 1939 OVERTURE

DER HERR KAPELLMEISTER (*raises his baton*): Seid Ihr fleissig und gehorsam?

OBOE: Zwei Seelen wohnen, ach, in meiner Brust!

DER HERR KAPELLMEISTER: Seid Ihr . . . !

TUTTI: Jawohl, wir sind alle fleissig und gehorsam!

DER HERR KAPELLMEISTER (*conducting*): Eins—zwei—drei!

TRUMPETS: Ich hab dich einmal gefragt—

CORNETS: Ich hab dich zweimal gefragt—

TROMBONE: Hier stehe ich, ich kann nicht anders—

CLARINETS: Doch erst beim dritten Mal—

FRENCH HORN: Gott helfe mir,—

CLARINETS:—hast du mir endlich ja gesagt.

TUTTI: Amen!

HELICON: Eine feste Burg ist unser Gott.

KETTLE DRUMS: Das ist die Liebe der Matrosen . . .

TROMBONES AND FLUTES: Duldet mutig, Millionen! Duldet für die bessre Welt!

BASSOON: Einen Regenbogen, der eine Viertelstunde steht, sieht man nicht mehr an.

CORNETS, TRIANGLES, DRUMS: Die Fahnen hoch, die Reihen fest geschlossen!

CLARINETS: Das gibt's nur einmal, das kommt nicht wieder—

TUBA (*solo*): Blut is ein ganz besondrer Saft.

CLARINETS, FLUTES, FRENCH HORNS:—das ist zu schön, um wahr zu sein!

DER HERR KAPELLMEISTER: Kann ich Armeen aus der Erde stampfen? Wächst ein Kornfeld in der flachen Hand?

TUTTI: Warte nur, balde, ruhest Du auch.

79

E-FLAT CLARINET: Ich bin von Kopf bis Fuss auf Liebe eingestellt . . .

FRENCH HORN: All unser Übel kommt daher, dass wir nicht allein sein können.

CLARINETS: . . . und das ist meine Welt . . .

HELICONS: Das Böse ist des Menschen beste Kraft.

CLARINETS: . . . und sonst gar nichts.

BASSOONS: Was schert mich Weib?

BASSOONS AND TROMBONES: Was schert mich Kind?

TRUMPETS: Mein Kampf.

DRUMS, TUBAS: Stöhnen ist die halbe Arbeit.

FLUTES: Bier her! Bier her!

TUTTI: Im Westen nichts Neues.

BASSOON (*solo*): Jede Erfahrung ist fast immer eine Parodie auf die Idee.

TROMBONES, CORNETS: Krambambuli, das ist der Titel!

E-FLAT CLARINET: Stets brüderlich zusammenhält.

FRENCH HORN: Mutig, unbekümmert, spöttisch, gewalttätig,—so will uns die Weisheit: sie ist ein Weib und liebt immer nur einen Kriegsmann.

TUTTI: Alle Vögel sind schon da, alle Vögel, alle!

CLARINETS: Kraft durch Freude!

TUBA (*with Flute obligato*): Dann magst du mich in Fesseln schlagen, dann will ich gern zugrunde gehn!

TROMBONES: Morgen kommt der Weihnachtsmann.

TUTTI: Und das hat mit ihrem Singen die Lorelei getan!

He was riding along.
The applause died away slowly.
A strange thought came to him:
Where were the Germans?
Suddenly he couldn't remember having seen anyone in all Germany except that fat, gruff woman with the gym shoes.
Where were the Germans? Not a motorcar, not a motorcycle, not a horse, not a soul. Strange.
Perhaps the Germans had emigrated.

Perhaps they had all quietly emigrated, while the rest of the world thought they were busy arming. The entire German people. Perhaps they had quietly emigrated to Switzerland and dug themselves caves in the Alps.

Perhaps Germany was empty.

That would mean, he thought slowly, that I own Germany. It is a rule of law that where there is nothing. . . .

In other words; Emperor of Germany.

Softly he rubbed his chin.

Mother would love that, he thought, to be able to live in the west tower of the palace in Berlin.

"My son, the Emperor," she would say and draw herself up.

He grimaced.

At one point, suddenly he came to a great sign: "Road Works in Progress. Diversion." A fat arrow pointed towards the left, to a side road.

He stopped, stroked his nose. Diversion, what does that involve. It could be five miles or it could be two hundred. His heart sank. For a moment he thought of overlooking the sign, or shoving his machine under the barrier and riding on, but one look ahead and he gave up the idea. There was nobody to be seen, only excavators and cement-mixers; and as far as the eye could reach was a wide street of road-metal, heaps of road-metal; like that, he would have to drag his machine from heap to heap; it would be like crossing the inland ice of Greenland with a fully-laden sledge but without runners and without dogs. . . .

Besides, he might be nabbed and put in prison.

He sighed, turned the handlebars and rode off down the Diversion.

He was brought out on to a country road, a firm dirt road that ran through flat, slightly broken country. It was a heath, foreign looking, desolate, almost treeless; the soil was sandy and in it grew tall clumps of coarse heather. It was a quiet, silent area. And there was no scent from the heather. Heather does not have a scent.

He had been going along for some minutes, when he became aware of an immense wooden fence running along the right hand side of the road, miles long it was and very high, more than six feet high, perhaps ten feet. It was made of unpainted, weathered, grey vertical planks that fitted close together, it was compact, opaque, more like a wall than a fence. On the inside was a line of deciduous trees that seemed to have been planted to mitigate the hard impression given by the fence. But not only were the trees all exactly alike, and planted exactly the same distance apart, sixteen feet between each, thus making the total impression even more sinister; but also through the hum of the engine he heard, or thought he heard, shouts, the tramp of feet, yells. His blood ran cold. There was something about that long, high, grey fence, as if he had seen it before in a nightmare, one of those when there is only a high wall between you and the unspeakable; and in the dream you try to whistle and walk along unconcernedly beside the wall, but your heart is pounding because you know that on the other side of it . . .

As he went along, he stood up in the saddle and craned his neck and caught a brief glimpse of something, did not know quite what, did not dare look properly. . . .

"Drive on."

"Yes."

"Drive on. Pretend you haven't noticed."

"Yes."

"You could be shot as a spy."

"Yes."

"It might be a military area."

"Yes."

"Or something worse."

"Yes."

"They do things to people in concentration camps that you could not bear to see."

"Yes."

"And you can't do anything about it."

"Yes."

"Drive on."

"Yes."

He pulled up at a crossroads. He had seen the sign which showed the way he should follow. He got his map from his rucksack, held it out in front of him, turned it this way and that, let his eyes look past it at his surroundings. The map shook slightly in his hands. Then he turned his machine and rode back slowly. He did not look to the side, but his senses told him that there were no guards on the outside of the fence. He put the gear lever into neutral and let the machine roll along noiselessly. Stopped. Got his map out again, studied it, scratched it, scratched the back of his head. If there had been eyes watching him from the fence, he would have felt them. As he studied the map, he groped for the stand, pulled it down, heaved the machine up onto it, laid the map on the saddle. Pretended to be reading it. Then slowly, he crossed the road, stopped by the verge, as if he was going to pump ship. Stood for a moment listening. Then with pounding heart he stepped down into the ditch which was about three feet deep; whilst he was in it, he looked along the ditch in either direction; he saw it in all its immeasurable length, it was empty: he jumped up onto the other side. Now he was right by the fence, next to a tree. His heart was in his mouth, at any moment he could expect a heavy hand to descend on his shoulder, a shout, a shot; his jaws were stiff with terror; his gaze searched the surface of the fence; it was massive, close-fitting. Ah, but down there he could see a space, a little crack between two of the boards. Did he dare? Did he dare? If he was going to, he would have to squat down. And if he was found in that attitude? "Was machen Sie hier?" Could he answer: "Erlauben Sie, ich pisse..." could he say that? Who had ever seen a man kneeling to piss?

He looked round, hurriedly. Again he heard shouts coming from inside; abruptly he knelt down and put his eye to the hole. He could feel his body quaking with fright. There was a cloud of swirling sand in there. They looked like young recruits. Between fifty and a hundred very young recruits were being drilled in the blazing sun; they had broad, shiny, peculiar bayonets on their shoulders; no, they were spades, polished spades. There was something desperate about their performance, a suggestion of a hospital; they were not drilling, but being driven staggering along in ranks, cursed forward, flung forward—ten men in each file and their ranks were supposed to be straight. It was rather like a circus act, when a line of liberty horses turns like the hand of a clock, the outside horse having to gallop, while the one at the other end stands still, turning round on itself. But while a circus ring is completely flat, the ground inside there was broken, the soldiers had to run up and down large grassy hummocks with loose sand between, they were pouring with sweat, it was physically impossible for them to keep in line; also there were five, if not ten lines of recruits with different centres. And, the most savage thing of all, they had to run, run without bending their knees! in formation, in fits and starts, as though for their lives. No sooner had they been given one order, than they got another: Double! Halt! Double! Halt! Shoulder spades! Order spades! Left turn! Right turn! About turn! Double! Halt! Halt! Double! They trampled the sand, kicked at the heathery slopes, trampled, panted, ran, stumbled, one fell full length and the sergeant pounced. It was obvious that the sergeant had had his eye on that particular file; it was suddenly obvious that the sergeant had had his eye on that particular youth. The Norwegian knew what was coming, he knew it; he drew a tortured breath, momentarily drew back from the hole in the fence, he wanted to get away from the spectacle, but cruel curiosity compelled him to put his eye to the crack once more. The recruits were very young. 15–16–17 years of age; they wore a sort of green uniform and half-boots; he could tell they were young from their red, unhappy, strained faces, and also from their boots: their tops came only half-

84

way up the youths' calves; they were of small sizes, had small feet, like girl's boots. ... The sergeant, a middle-aged thick-set, bull-necked man in uniform with a short stick in his hand like a riding crop, had found himself a victim. He had a rasping, angry voice, like a screeching saw, it cut right through the tramp of feet. While the others had to go on running, he called the youth to him; and no one on either side of the fence had any doubt whatever that it was the sergeant with his crazy drill who had caused the youth, the one at the end of his file, to collapse. The sergeant showered him with curses, bawling them into his face and emphasizing what he bawled by whacking his thigh with his stick. The student got a glimpse of the youth's downy face, dirt-streaked, quivering, shattered; there was something about that face, so young, so small, so fair; the student had a thirteen-year-old brother in Norway; he suddenly remembered his boyish face, he had seen his brother unhappy, perplexed, abysmally ill-at-ease, a face that so badly wanted, so badly *wanted* to do everything right, but did not always manage it and stood there in despair listening to the reprimand. But this youth also wore spectacles, which made him utterly helpless; perhaps he could not even see where he put his feet; they were extra-ordinarily cheap-looking spectacles with their thin steel rims; perhaps it was because of his spectacles that the sergeant had picked on him. The sergeant spat oaths into the youth's face: Du Dreck! Du Dreck Du! Du Schweinehund! And on the last syllable of Schweinehund his voice rose to falsetto, it sounded like the crack of a whip; and, thought the student, it's one of his own people he's treating like that!—he yelled at the recruit, this child of a soldier, that he would kick his brains out if he did not learn to march properly; and the youth was formally dancing in the sand, his outstretched girlish legs longing to obey orders, going like drumsticks, but when the sergeant shouted left, he went right, and when the sergeant shouted "Shoulder spades", he did an about turn, a salvo of shouts fetching him back, now he was to double,

double! but he stumbled, a fresh salvo of curses greeted this; the youth jerked his legs about as though he was in a trance, his face was naked, lips trembling, he was on the verge of collapse, soon his face would crumple, the other recruits continued their liberty horse run, they would have preferred to look at the ground, but had to look straight in front of them, you could tell from their shoulders that they were aware of it all, they had their heads pulled in, they doubled in formation, stopping and starting again, numbing themselves to what was going on, the sand seethed and swirled, no one dared protest against the monster, sweat poured off them, the drill-ground resounded.

The student's knees gave under him, he felt his forehead grazing against the planking. He slithered down into the ditch, got up, brushed his knees; he was trembling and his mouth was dry. The shouts pursued him.

"Schweinehund! Schwei-ne-hund!"

He walked, ran up the slope. He walked straight across the road, took time to fold up the map, pulled up the stand, turned the machine, seated himself: strangely purposeful, he let the machine roll along without a sound before he started the engine.

He drove quickly, and he did not look back.

He could feel that beneath his palms the rubber grips were wet.

Shortly after midday he entered a town—was it Coblenz?—that appeared to be inhabited, alive, human. He had told himself that if he could not crush Hitler's Germany, he could at least ignore it ... but there was no air of Nazism about this town; it was a bit of old Germany; many of its houses were low, many of them half-timbered, others all made of shining, dark brown centuries old oak, with balconies and bay windows sticking out over the pavements; the houses were both foreign and familiar, semifamiliar, as though he had seen houses like them when he was a child, in a picture book.... Here he had to drive slowly; the streets were narrow; and there were lots of people walking in them; there were women with shawls, shops in basements; suddenly the narrow paved street described a sharp curve and opened out into a broad square; at the same instant a tall, dark, enormous cathedral soared skyward like an upward landslip; to take in the full height of it, he had to stop his motorcycle and tilt his head right back. He edged the machine back a few paces.

What a mighty thing such a Gothic cathedral was!

The pyramids stayed in Egypt, they got no further; but here, in Europe, they had put out fresh roots, elongated themselves into spires; a cathedral is a pyramid in the act of springing! How it stretched up towards the sky! Stood on tiptoe! It might at any moment detach itself from the ground and fly off.

Didn't the whole stony mass of the cathedral quiver with bursting, lifting, straining, longing to reach God?

And yet it was cold and evil and deep.

Yes—deep!

A church is no erection—it is an inverted well. Cold and evil and dark and deep.

He had grown up in the shadow of a steatite cathedral,

the largest in the North. He had gone there, to Nidaros cathedral, for confirmation classes, and there he had been confirmed. There, at the altar rail, he had bowed his knees (he remembered the recruit with the steel-rimmed spectacles stumbling and falling, he remembered the sergeant); there he had received the holy sacrament and given the priest his young, solemn promise. There, at the age of fifteen, he had promised—and if he broke his promise he was to be consigned to eternal torment, was to be for ever doomed—trembling, fainting, he had promised to forswear Satan, always, and to love God, always.

That moment had killed him, left him disabled. The instant he had swallowed the little wafer, drunk the little cup of wine, felt the priest's hand on his head—it had been strangely insensitive, professional, like a hairdresser's hand—at that same cosmic moment he had known that he had said too much. Of the girls being confirmed, one had fainted, one had become hysterical and wept aloud, one had been sick. Boys are not allowed that sort of thing; they are young men and must be content with being white in the face. He had felt as though he had been burned, as if the life-nerve in him had been cauterized. When he got to his feet and walked away from the rails, back into the body of the church and his mother had smiled proudly to him, a proud and infamous smile, when the organ had thundered out and the congregation sung, there had been a taste of ashes in his mouth. He was always to remember that smell of ecclesiastical stone and of let-down, the smell of steatite walls and altar candles, the smell of the chill of masonry, of vaults, of mouldering bones, of well, of death—the smell of steatite and inconceivable deception, the smell of man's fall. . . .

Yes, the smell of the Fall. . . .

*

The Church's crime lies not in the limitless scope of the promise it exacts: a yes to God, a yes from here to eternity, a yes to the outermost wall of the universe (and what is there on the other side of the wall?). The Church's crime does not lie in the fact that on God's behalf it demands a total yes—for God is indeed entitled to this and will himself see that his claim is met, in the fullness of time. The Church's crime lies in the fact that it incites the person who promises and swears to do this, to do so at the age of fifteen!

Confirmands of that age are children—infants. They have just embarked on man's second childhood, the one that starts with puberty.... Fifteen years is a lot for a horse, which is full grown when it is three; but for a human fifteen is nothing. A boy of fifteen has become an infant for the second time, is an infant to the power of two!

He has faith; he is credulous; he has the necessary willingness and longing; never will his longing be more ardent! He has the faith to promise this, the will to promise; his promise-ability is at its maximum and he makes full use of it, and promises!

Let your yea be yea and your nay nay; but the confirmand does not understand this nay, he has faith in the grown-ups, he is an infant, he holds up his arms trustingly and promises:

Yes!

Woe unto him, to whom exaltation comes too early!

Woe unto him, who gave God his promise at the age of fifteen!

Man has seventy years to live on earth.

At the age of fifteen he has reached the summit of what he can attain: he has seen the kingdom of heaven, in a blaze of glory, and he has made God a promise.

What about the rest of his life?

Fifteen is the time of puberty. A boy is then afraid of the new bursting forces he feels in his body, afraid of what is hairy, tainted, wet, he is afraid of his urges, he begs for quarter, he reaches out towards purity, strains towards the light. He needs something to believe in, someone to believe in; a hand, a ladder, a word; he is defenceless, his heart is naked and soft. He smiles at stories about witches and beings who live underground, smiles at tales of incubi and vampires sucking people's blood by night, but he believes in them; he smiles at stories of ghosts and werewolves, yet he dare not walk alone through a graveyard after dark, he believes in them; at night he lies under the covers with a pocket torch studying his pubic hair and shuddering; he reads *The Hound of the Baskervilles* and his teeth chatter.

Fifteen is the age of ghost stories. That is the time; when fifteen-year-olds are on their own they turn out the light and tell ghost stories. There is that one about the dead person who came home from the graveyard. The lights are out. The corpse comes home, from the graveyard, and it is quite dark, and he asks. What does he ask? What does he ask? The lights are out and you all hold your breath. In a hoarse voice the corpse asks:

"Who has taken my guts?"

In the dark no one dares breathe; he asks again, louder:

"Who has taken my guts?" The lights are out and it does not even matter if everyone has heard it before, for this is the climax, the lights are out; a hard hand suddenly clutches an arm in the dark and the corpse shouts:

"*Have you taken my guts?*"

This, exactly, is where the Church seizes you. The Church does not extinguish the light; it uses noise instead; this organ down below and its bells above: an ear-shattering Judgement Day beneath its vaulted roof; the Church seizes hold of the fifteen-year-old and swings him, ghost-like, with only a hymn book to support him, up and up in a cosmic spiral. . . .

Fifteen: that is one's first suit with long trousers, the

quick glint of sunlight on a girl's golden plaits, the packet of forbidden cigarettes; fifteen, that is the hell-hound, the echo in church, the clergyman, those guts, the smell of one's first sperm, God.

The fifteen-year-old borne along on a wave of terror and piety up to the altar rails—does he believe in God? Will he promise God?—the wave curls over and breaks in radiance, breaks in eonic song and the music of the spheres, the child is in heaven, in a heaven studded with carnations and garnished with roses, he is aware of the brilliance of God's countenance and shades his eyes with his hands, he sees gold dust and white angels, he sees hosts; his hands are full of pearls; his mother's tears have been turned into the loveliest pearls; the hosts are singing clad in white garments, God beckons, is beckoning to him; under him is the threat of what is warm, slimy and hairy, of perdition; the boy takes a great run, kicks the hairy thing under him and with a stifled cry he hurls himself up towards purity, remains hanging with one hand clutching the edge of a pearly pink cloud, he is dazzled by the whiteness, he knows that whoever sees that light will die—does he believe in God?—will he promise to stay with God?—always?—will he promise God?

Yes!

Seventy years man has to live on earth.

At the age of fifteen he has reached the heights.

The rest of life is one long backward journey, backwards and down, a fall.

The confirmand is aware of this, the moment he comes out of the church.

Are those pearls under his feet? It's gravel. And there's mud on one of his shoes. He tries to be with God as he was just recently, but there's mud on his shoes. His mother asks if they should take a taxi home; they end by taking the tram. He sits looking down at the floor of the tram trying to see seraphs and seeing the wooden slats and his mother's fat ankles. He is just about to take a cough pastille, but hasn't he just forsworn Satan, his whole being and all his acts?—Home smells of roast beef, gravy and green peas. On the table he sees a jar of English mixed pickles, Heinz, that he is so fond of—that he was so fond of. He does not see his grandparents who congratulate him, does not see his uncles and aunts, does not see his younger sister and small brother. For a moment his eyes meet his father's. His father has not been able to come to the church; there is always a band parade on Sundays, but he knows that even if his father had been able to go, he would not have wanted to. In that fleeting moment he understands his father. But, equally fleetingly, he thinks that his father could have spared him the whole thing— the man could have used his big powerful hand, which otherwise was so efficient, he could have used it over this, it would have been most useful *here*, he could have set it on the table, hard and heavily, he could have *banged* it on the table—is that not what a man's hand is for?—and said: "The boy is not to be confirmed." But he had not done that. They look down. The son too, for he could have said it himself, and firmly. . . .

Stiffly, the newly confirmed youth walks through the rooms, goes into his own room, closes the door, remains standing there; all is still. On the wall hangs his violin. He has loved his violin. But now it suddenly seems so cheap and mean. He has heard the music of the spheres and that reduces the violin to caterwauling. He feels an urge to smoke. Could he steal a few puffs? After all—he has been confirmed . . . ! But, a cigarette, after Golgotha? He looks at the books on the bookshelves and smiles wryly: Jules Verne, Rocambole, the Detective Magazine. A mere week before he had been an admirer of Knut Gribb; but did Knut Gribb have a crown of thorns round his head?

The earth had been green; now it has become grey.

The only thing that could have reconciled him to this, that could have given him something to look forward to in spite of everything, the life flame, was just the very thing he has forsworn!

His gaze travels on to the chest-of-drawers. There is one drawer there—that has a secret compartment in the bottom of it. Fear of hell wells up in him, and with it, immeasurable bitterness. The french letter. His first. Unused. Now it will never be used. Yes, he thinks, I may as well burn it now. Burn it in the stove.

It is all over. I have renounced life. I promised God.

I have promised too much . . .

Crushed, scorched and crippled, the fifteen-year-old goes slowly back—to the beef and cloudberry cream.

When as you occasionally do, you read melancholy in a European's face, when you read grief on the white man's countenance, it is not because he considers himself unworthy to enter the kingdom of Heaven—it is because he has already been there. . . .

THE STUDENT sat astride his motorcycle—was it in Coblenz?—and looked at the cathedral. No, he had no great enthusiasm for Gothic cathedrals. If the truth be told, he had so little enthusiasm for the Church and all that it was and did, that if he were to be appointed sovereign of his country, his first act would be to invite all its clergy in surplice, ruff and full canonicals, for a pleasure trip on board a luxurious steamship, and then, eight miles from shore, have the seacocks opened.

Why was he sitting there looking at the cathedral? He had suddenly realized that so far the trip had been nothing but autobahn and petrol. He felt a prick of socialistic conscience. Cathedrals, after all, have a certain cultural and historical value. I'll sit here for a moment or two and enlarge my cultural horizon, he thought. Let's see. Tall towers. Ah, yes. Pointed arches. Ah, yes. Copper roof, green with verdigris. Glass windows with coloured saints.

Ah, yes. Well, we've seen it now, Humske, and that was good for one's soul. Now, let's get on.

Stop.

It's not enough that I have seen my cathedral. I must be able to prove it. He frowned. All at once he remembered. He dismounted and rummaged in his rucksack for his box-camera. *My cultural alibi,* he thought; what would we humans be without our Kodaks? He blew the dust off the lens, looked at the little red hole to make sure it was loaded, and raised the camera at an acute angle to the steeple. He was not going to get the whole thing in. He walked backwards a few paces.

A voice said:

"Nederland?"

The student had just taken his snap, had just thought: that'll be a good one. He dropped his gaze and looked at his questioner—a peering, bareheaded, drunken-looking man; the man was standing between him and the motorcycle. He felt instant revulsion, knew that he had no wish to have anything to do with this person. He stood there for a moment, turning the knob to be ready for the next picture. He wanted to put the camera back in his rucksack, but the stranger had taken up a strategic position. The student could choose between ignoring him, walking into and over him, or answering his question.

The stranger stood there smiling as he tapped a finger on the motorcycle's touring plate, on which there was a large N.

"Nederland?"

The student went round, reached his rucksack and almost had to barge the man out of the way. Perhaps he'll go, if I tell him, he thought.

"Nein," he said, "Norwegen."

"Ah," said the creature enthusiastically and laid a hand on the student's shoulder, "a Scandinavian!"

Standing there beside his motorcycle the student suddenly realized with a sinking feeling that he had committed himself.

Memories came rushing in of the nameless sensation he had had on occasion in his own country, in towns, in the evening usually, in deserted parts, on a jetty or outside a railway station, when an individual suddenly detaches himself from the darkness, discovers one, crosses over and speaks to one in an evil, possessive voice: "Hallo, I want a word with you! Hi! You...." It was as though the student had an attraction for such vermin; it was as though they could see him miles away and came straight across the street, made straight for him, without hesitation; it was always him they descended upon, like a hawk on a pigeon! They leave one the choice of turning, walking quickly, even running away and so getting the resonant voice pursuing one and feeling a mean little coward; or one can stand there, stiff, buttoned-up, ready to defend one-self, stand and wait for the man, wait to feel his breath, smelling of spirits, slowly clenching one's fist inside one's coat pocket so as to be ready to strike. . . . There is only one thing one must never do: one must never speak to them, never; do that and you are lost; then you'll have this company through many streets, a hand on your arm, unwashed, brown with nicotine, neglected fingers, nails bitten down to the quick: one thing you must never do: you must never talk to them.

"Die Skandinaven, die gehen ja mit uns!" said the man.

Fury gripped the student: he was paralysed, could not get a word out. He could have bitten off his tongue for having spoken to the man. But could he let such an assertion go unanswered? Would Scandinavia go in with Germany?

"No," he said heavily. He dropped his shoulder, so that the man's hand fell off.

"Aber doch!" said the man. For an instant he looked angry, surly, but then it came, almost indulgently:

"Das hat ja unser Führer gesagt! Die Schweden und die Norweger sind ja Germanen!"

The student shot the man a quick look. Then it was as though something inside him withered. The man was stupid. And in that same instant the student perceived that all Germany was like this man. The man was unreceptive to reason. Even if he had had a hundred years in which to do it, the student could not by arguing have driven the man into a corner. Germany—and this is a ghastly thing to know—can never be convinced or made to withdraw by argument. A feeling of terror swept over him, a feeling of utter helplessness. This was a thing he had not known before. But now he knew what was coming. What had to come.

He felt nauseated; it was as though all the strength had drained out of him, yet nevertheless he had to protest. Sweden, Norway, were they a part of Germania? He wished he could roar, spit; but all he could get out was a stifled:

"Nein."

"Aber doch!" said the man. He pondered a moment, then came a triumphant: "Ich hab' es ja im Rundfunk gehört!" The student stared at him, bewildered, desperate; a morbid desire to laugh mounted inside him. The man had heard it on the radio, had he? Had Hitler said it on the radio? And if he had? What did that prove?

The student gasped. He wanted to roar, spit; but all that he had the strength to do was to shrug.

There were spots of food on the man's jacket which was a bit too big for him; his thin bird-like neck stuck up from an unwashed, filthy, frayed collar; the man was about fifty, as thin as a vulture; his sparse black hair was combed back and it needed cutting; the skin of his scalp showed through the thin hair and was of a hectic red, unhealthy colour as though he had some skin disease. The student felt that he was the sort of person who sold dirty postcards.

He wanted to get away from this horrible individual; he moved away, but the man followed. The pavement was narrow and the student was jammed with his legs up against the motorcycle. Another fraction of an inch and he would fall over it, go sprawling full length onto the street and have the machine on top of him. There was another possibility: he could bring his arm up carefully and punch the man in the face. He swayed, felt like someone who is drowning; for all his aversion he felt a secret compassion for the man and that made his hatred all the greater: he could feel the man's forlornness, his need to cling; deep down in this hateful individual was a child in search of kindness, he thought; my God why am I burdened with the ability to understand everyone? I should have killed him, the student thought, but I'm too soft; I'm too good-natured, that's my tragedy: I shall fall into the street now, and when I am lying there, run over, they will bend over my corpse and whisper: It was considerateness killed him.

At this point he must have lost consciousness.

Because, when he came to, he was astride the saddle of his motorcycle. He was on the point of starting, but curiosity got the better of him. Now that he thought about it, he had not really had a talk with a single German the whole of the trip. What was it like living in Germany now, he asked.

"Prima," said the man. Times were prima in Germany. The Führer had given people prima times.

Perhaps it would be all right to ask what the man did?

"Beamter," said the man readily. He ran his hand down the greasy lapel of his jacket, drew himself up, smiled.

The student gaped. Then he shut his mouth, hoping the man had not noticed. Beamter? That's an official, a civil servant. And yet the man was not even wearing a tie, his filthy shirt was open at the neck; the top button was missing.

With the town council, the man added.

Beamter? thought the student, perhaps he means a clerk, a messenger. . . . He asked: What department?

The man came close up to the student, nudged him in the side with his elbow, lowered his voice.

"Die Juden," he whispered and licked a corner of his mouth.

The student's blood ran cold.

"Was?" he whispered.

"Die Juden," the man repeated, softly, knowingly, sniggeringly. He looked at the student.

"Sie wissen was ein Jude ist? Ja?"

To demonstrate his meaning he bowed his back, thrust out his chin, placed his tongue between his lower lip and teeth making it form a bulge; scratched at this bulge and looked at the student slyly.

"Ja," groaned the student, desperate, ill, he knew what a Jew was . . .

But the man went on with his imitation; he wanted to convince this ignorant foreigner, he hunched his shoulders up to his ears, held out his right hand, then his left, rubbing his fingers as if he was counting money:

"Ein Jude, ja!"

"Ja!" shouted the student, "ich weiss, ja, ja!"

98

The man then told him that he worked in the Department for the Administration of Enemy Property.

He stroked his lapel, eager, proud. Again he looked at the student:

"Sie wissen was Verwaltung ist, ja? Verwaltung. Ja?"

"Ja! Ja!" shouted the student. "Ich weiss!" How long was he to sit there listening to this ridiculous, shameful individual. He queried:

"Enemy Property?"

"First," said the man, "the Jews are thrown out of their houses, they are put in prison, or in..." he rubbed his hands, became momentarily serious. "Some of them have managed to escape." He pulled at his nose, bitter, then his face lit up again. "Well, when the Jews have been thrown out of their houses, their effects have to be administered. Sie verstehen, ja?"

"Ja!"

"Many rich properties, oh, many rich properties. Furniture, paintings, grand pianos, stocks and shares, jewellery ... it's all registered by our office, it all goes through our office!" The man stopped. Again he had to convince himself: "Register? You know what register means?"

"Yes!" yelled the student.

Again the man rubbed his fingers together. Spellbound, the student had to look at them. They were like claws. And yet, for all this the student sensed that the man was a bureaucrat, and, what is more, an honest bureaucrat; this poor, shabby man did not steal any of the effects, did not appropriate any of the diamond brooches or necklaces that went through his hands (it was the others did that, those at the top!), this man just entered up paintings and jewellery, he sat at a desk and wrote them down in a book, he dipped his pen into the inkwell and registered them—and he was proud of his job! Yes, indeed, Germany could rely on that man! For all his loathing, the student found this ridiculous, shocking. Stupid the man certainly was. But *honest* as well as stupid! The man had not even intelligence enough to steal a pearl necklace for his own benefit!

99

"Prima Zeiten," said the man. "Geld. Geld für alle. Sie verstehen, ja? Geld, ja?"

In the years to come, the memory of this harrowing scene sometimes returned to him. He was a socialist, and the idea of revolution had been dear to him. But, after this, each time he was tempted to advocate revolt and social upheaval, he had stopped. In his mind's eye he saw this shady individual with the evil, counting fingers. He remembered his bestial chin. The man who had wished to exterminate the Jews,—now he had become a Jew himself, more Jew than any Jew . . . !

Does revolution really change anything? He thought. Does not society, in the last resort, remain unchanged? Revolution?—rebellion? Isn't what happens just that the bottom comes up to the top?

Revolution, he thought, is opening the door for those who had never dared venture out into the daylight, but who then do creep out. Basement people. Revolution, it's like that summer, when I was a child: I turned over a large stone embedded in the ground; I remember the blind scrambling beetles under the stone; give insects power and they will grow as tall as people. . . .

He knew a socialist song:

"New day is dawning, brothers . . ."

After that experience in Coblenz he no longer felt so sure about any such new day.

He was not so sure that he would get on with those new brothers, either.

TOWARDS EVENING he had shaken off the unpleasantness. He was then riding up through the valley of the Mosel. The character of the country had changed: these were not mountains like those in Norway, but low hills, rounded heights, billowing contours, and how green, green, green; there was something in the air that told him that he was getting nearer the south; and was he not across the Rhine?

Far up the valley he found a Youth Hostel. He carried his things in. It was nine o'clock. His body was filled with expectation. Only this night and the next day he would *be* in . . .

Only this night. . . .

He could feel that he was in mountain air. The air was thinner, purer. But also cooler. He felt that he wanted to go out and walk about a bit before turning in; he put on his thick woollen pullover. His face and forehead were burning, he shivered slightly and thought: it's the sun . . .

He walked up a narrow, steep, paved street. It wound upwards, the round paving stones were like steps to tread on; there were walls on both sides of the narrow street, house-walls, but the houses themselves were so high that he could not see them. It had begun to get dark. The feeling of expectation became suddenly strong, almost like fear. . . . He had been thinking of France. Tomorrow. France. It was as though he was once more facing the adored one's door, looking at the bell push. Wishing, fiercely, that something would happen so that he need not face her (her face, so lovely, so fine, so gentle, so gay; her big eyes, violet-blue with a brown shadow under them, a shadow of brown like sex), that something would happen, a flower pot fall into the passage and be smashed,

smashed against his head; that the railings would collapse; a pistol shot, fire alarm, war—so that he need not press that bell! Need not talk, need not put his feelings into words!

Words....

Is it not words that keep us apart? Are not words the curse of humanity?

If only he could just have held her, put his arms round her, felt her head coming to rest against his chest. If only....

That night in the park he had wanted to take her little, strong, efficient, beautiful hand; oh, how he had stared, as though bewitched, at that little, warm hand; once—they had been sitting on a bench—her hand had been only an inch from his own, a mere inch. That spring night after the ball he had walked with her in a park, beneath green, fragrant trees, walked until the first birds of morning had begun to sing. But his courage had failed him. He had contented himself with smiling; he had smiled at his love—out of fear that that was what she might do....

At that moment he had a dull feeling that, as a love trip, his trip to France was a failure; with sudden insight he knew that she, the loved one, was not to be found in France; if she did exist, it was in the country called Norway; he knew that the goal of his journey, of all journeys, lay in the country that gave rise to his longing: that love lay behind him....

If one used force, he thought, if one used force, it must be possible to break through the wall of words. Anger welled up inside him. He stamped on the paving stones. I should have been able to use my physical strength, he thought. Am I not strong?

I'll go back, he thought.

I'll run all the way down, now, jump onto the motor-cycle and ride back, all the way without stopping. I'll drive straight up to Norway, to Bergen, to her bit of pavement; her house, I'll drive up her steps, I'll drive in through the outer door, I'll drive up the stairs, drive to the third floor, not stop to ring, drive straight at the door and smash it, ride right through the door splintering it, roar into the hall (smell of young woman, swift smell of powder), rip down the curtain before the living-room—and be there in her room.

HE (*standing on her floor, having risen from the remains of his motorcycle, stands on the wreckage clasping the loose handlebars; he stands there dripping wood splinters and bits of glass, in a cloud of exhaust; for a moment he is on the point of doffing his cap, then changes his mind and keeps it on*).

SHE (*in dressing-gown, just out of the bath with a turquoise-blue towel round her head like a turban; without high heel shoes she does not seem so exalted; she can't believe her eyes, stifles a scream; blinks, is quite overwhelmed*).

HE (*left hand on the back of her big, deep, blue arm-chair, as if he owned it*): I am a man of few words!

SHE (*gasps*).

HE: I've ridden! From the Mosel hills, I've ridden without stopping—to tell you something!

SHE (*looks at his black, scratched, smutty face, pulls her dressing-gown together under her chin, her soft lips quiver*): What?

HE (*takes a step forward, shouts*): I'm proposing!

SHE (*presses her hands to her breast, staggers; she whispers*): You are so violent! This is so sudden . . . you must give me time to think it over!

HE (*standing beside the blue arm-chair; a pool of oil and petrol seething on the floor: there's an explosion. He pushes up the left sleeve of his jacket, wipes the road dust from the glass and calmly looks at his wrist watch*): . . . of course, I'll give you fifteen seconds.

SHE (*puts her hand to her throat*).

HE: Five.

SHE (*opens her mouth, looks at him, blinks*).

HE: Ten.

103

SHE: If I don't say yes, will you kill me?

HE (*motions with the handlebars he has in his right hand, which he holds as though it were a club*).

SHE (*stares bewitched at the handlebars. She takes a step towards him, seeks his eyes, whispers*): Does this mean that you—that you love me?

HE: Fifteen.

SHE (*stands close beside him, so close that he can smell the scent of her hair, the scent of her young body; she has laid one hand on his arm; softly she touches his forehead*): You're bleeding. . . .

HE: Yes.

SHE (*a bashful blush colouring her cheeks, whispers*): Come, sit down. . . . I'll get some boracic. . . .

HE (*turns deathly pale*): Does this mean that you will marry me?

SHE: Yes!

HE: Then. . . . (*collapses into the blue arm-chair; the handlebars fall to the floor*)—There's no need to bandage me; I can die now.

Slowly he walked on up the narrow alley; it was like going up a great flight of spiral stairs. His head was filled with his own vision; he was breathing heavily, there was a reddish glow in front of his eyes and his heart was hammering; he noticed that he was walking along with his fists clenched. He thought in astonishment: deep inside me I am dangerous. Deadly dangerous. I believe, he thought, that if the miracle should happen, if I should get her, whom I love, in love, there is such force stored up in me that I would go mad, a segment of my brain would burst; if I really should be able to hold her in my arms—I would burst into tears, out of pure happiness I would put my hands round her neck and throttle her.

He looked at his hands. . . .

Besides, he thought, bitterly:

Marry her? Her? But I already *am* married. . . .

Ask the gods when I'll get a divorce. Once, I thought I was cunning, that I was crafty. I went to a lawyer, privately, before we married. I got him to draw me up a document that the marriage was being contracted in order that the unborn child might be born in wedlock and that both parties would seek legal divorce immediately after the wedding. I got her to sign this document. But then I forgot to do anything about it, or perhaps I thought it was tactless to come along with a sheaf of divorce papers after the wedding—straight after the golden ring. Besides I had to catch the mail boat. I don't know. For all I know that document was not worth anything. She was smiling when she signed it. She signed straightaway, without fuss; and she smiled as she did so. Perhaps she knew something I didn't know. I thought I was crafty; but she was craftier. Sometimes her eyes were yellow....

When he was standing on the deck of the ferry that took him from Norway to Denmark, standing in the night feeling the engines thumping under him, he had suddenly remembered a Latin saying: "A fronte praecipitium, a tergo lupus." Yes, he had whispered into the night, a precipice in front of me, a wolf behind.... And for a moment he had felt profoundly astonished that a Roman should have had that experience two thousand years before, have possessed such deep insight and put it so pertinently into words. Had life on earth always been the same? Was there really nothing new under the sun, as the Preacher of the Old Testament said? Standing there on the deck he felt that he hated the Preacher. For, if there was nothing new under the sun, why should a man live? Nothing new? All at once he felt that he had it in him to give the Preacher a kick. That Roman phrase was splendid, it summed up the whole of life; but on one point it could be improved, and made new! Heavens, he had thought, I ought to have become a philologist after all. What's the feminine of lupus? I must look it up as soon as I can. Could it be lupa? If it is, then I really have created something new under the sun; I have coined a unique sentence, which sums up an era, and it could make me world famous!

"A fronte praecipitium, a tergo *lupa*."

I dare not write to my wife about a divorce, dare not remind her of our agreement; that would only draw her attention to my existence and then she would sue for maintenance! Let sleeping dogs lie. . . .

But he thought, violently unhappy, that means I can never go to Her. . . .

Oh God, he suddenly whispered,—you who are all-mighty, give me a home. Give me a good girl, a quiet girl, with blue eyes; give me Her. Am I asking too much? A home. You know; with flowers in the window, and newly-ironed curtains with their nice smell; and, well, somewhere in the house, in a side room, Her. Yes, I know: I'm a socialist and actually I ought to think exclusively of the dictatorship of the proletariat. But nonetheless, I do think, damn it, of having a home. It can be a poor one, God. I can manage a bit of carpentry and painting. A home.

Anyway, he thought angrily: if I were to come courting on a motorcycle, ride in through her door, she would not be alone. She never is alone. Her place is always full of socialists. They use her studio as their club room, as a café! She never gets anything done. They sit around her work-table drinking her tea: there is no sugar; they drink it with jam. They gossip, lecture interminably about the millenium. If I entered, on a motorcycle, in riding boots—they would look at me coldly, look at me with Marxism in their eyes, and I would not get a word out.

They are evil, he thought, disconcerted.

The village consisted of a mere cluster of houses and he was soon up on the waste land above. Along the upper side of the track ran a stone wall; all the fields were walled in that way; there was something Chinese about the landscape. He remembered such walls from his own country; there is something solemn about them: stones wrested from the grudging ground and carted off and piled up, monuments to centuries of toil.

There was real artistry there: the stones were beautifully laid, they would hold the soil in place; no cement; yet the wall was firm and solid without it. Drystone walls, they were called; the man who built them must have had an eye for stones: out of five hundred there might only be two that fitted together, only two that would lie with each other. . . .

He came to a solitary brick house at a crossroads. There was light in its windows. He heard singing inside. On the wall was a sign: "Weinstube." He pondered: He had just been in the realm of love; he did not know if he dared betray that vision. . . . Slowly he mounted the brick steps. He opened the door a little way, peered cautiously inside. Three or four men were sitting at a table, they looked like farmers, they were sitting drinking; they had a woman with them. Behind a bar, on the other side of the room, stood a middle-aged man. Otherwise the place was empty. The student did not relish the emptiness of the space between the door and the bar; when I cross the floor to the bar, he thought, the others will turn round, they will notice me. Shyly, he went in, walked quietly across the floor, nearly stopped at the bar, but, as there his back would be exposed, he walked on and sat down by himself at a little table in a corner—and did not know where to look. He ordered a glass of beer. The others heard what he said; one of the men stood up and protested, not beer, not beer in the Mosel valley, he must drink wine! The man came across, called in the direction of the bar: "Wein! Wein für den fremden Gast!" But the student took fright, shrank into his chair, no, he said blushing, he was a student, he did not have much money, could not afford to drink wine!— but now there were two of them on their feet and they

107

hauled him across to their table; embarrassed, he bowed his lanky body and smiled weakly—wine? was wine dear? Ha! not in the Mosel valley! there wine was cheaper than beer! and anyway he was to be their guest, look, now he must taste their local wine, was it not good?—without his noticing it an extra glass of wine had appeared on the table; they looked at him eagerly and solemnly while he raised his glass; he had never seen such a big glass of wine before; it had a stem and a hemispherical top; he raised the glass with its golden wine, smelled the lovely smell of it, took a sip, then a big gulp, a smile spread across his face; the others who had been sitting tensely, leaning forward, relaxed with grunts of satisfaction: "Gut?" they said, "Gut, nicht?"; he wanted to give them pleasure and searched for an elegant word; he thought of saying "Ausgezeichnet" and perhaps would have, but then he had found an even better word, "Vorzüglich!" and they murmured over his knowledge of wine and his vocabulary. He sat holding the glass, turning the stem in his fingers; it really was excellent wine. An angel passed through the room. He gave a little cough. He asked what such a glass of wine could cost. The others wanted to know what it would cost in Norway? He thought this over. Three crowns, he said. Almost three marks. They exclaimed. Three marks! Three marks for a glass of wine! Did he know what it cost there? No? 30 Pfennig! He gave a low whistle. That was not much more than 30 øre! He always had a strange feeling of happiness when he encountered something that was *both* good *and* cheap; he had a built-in respect for quality and an equal built-in respect for money; when a thing was unusually good and at the same time unusually cheap, it filled him with awe. He felt as if he had been translated to Mount Olympus; 30 øre for a glass of nectar! He started dreaming. He began making a plan for Norway to buy the Mosel valley. No, he would annexe it himself and present it to his country; he saw himself as the saviour of the Norwegians; he would immerse his people in Mosel wine; the Norwegian people should sparkle with golden wine and wealth; he drank to them: what on earth was skål in German—"Prosit!" he said and raised his glass; he had just emptied one glass and now he had another in his hand, brimming; he liked that, liberality should not be measured to within half an inch of the rim, but should brim over: yes, life should be like that: with a head on! he he wiped his lips with the back of his hand and looked round; when he first came in, he had not quite liked their faces, they were not good faces and deep inside he still had reservations; yet, now, those men and that woman seemed to him beings from Illyria; it was a symposium he had landed into; they had a concertina, too; their voices, perhaps, were not quite in tune, but they sang, and sang with gusto. . . . Just imagine, here you could sit in a wine shop and sing, sing properly—and no waiter came and threatened to have you thrown out; on the contrary, the man behind the bar joined in too! indeed, he took a glass himself, stood there taking gulps and drinking their health and nodding gaily to his customers, and washing glasses and singing, as if it was the most natural thing in the world! The student became so enthusiastic about this atmosphere of wine and freedom and song that he almost got up onto the table and made a speech—for he came from a country where singing is forbidden, really forbidden unless you are a member of a registered choir and sing in premises approved by the police and at stipulated times and didn't start till you got a signal from an authorized conductor.

Norway, Norway . . .

Rising bluely out of the grey green sea . . .

Yes, indeed.

The loveliest country in the world.

But what has happened to your voice: When are we going to hear you sing?

He did not know when it happened, but as he sat there, he suddenly knew that the others' heavy and exacting gaiety was only a mask, a film covering what was evil, un-redeemed and poor. Now a propeller was churning and the sludge was coming up. Two of them had become tipsy; one went over backwards with his chair and had to be helped up, cursing.

One of the labourers, the man who sang loudest and waved his arms about most, nodded his head at the woman on the other side of the table.

"She's my fiancée," he said with a gloomy sidelong look at the student.

"Ist sie nicht hübsch?" he said. The student could not see it. The woman herself looked down, embarrassed; she did not appear to enjoy being there. Engaged? The man fifty and the woman thirty—and engaged? To be polite he gave a slight nod, yes, the man's fiancée was pretty. The labourer, who sat on the student's right, took this as a cue, reached a long gorilla arm across the table and took hold of the back of the woman's neck. The student had to take a hasty look at that arm: the man's shirt-cuff had come undone: the hand was tanned, almost black; but the visible part of his underarm was almost white; it was like a cut, such a glaring demarcation on the skin is a social stigma, the mark of the proletarian; the man had never taken his shirt off and got the sun on his body; he had the sun, but he did not want it. . . .

The man tried to draw his fiancée's head towards him; "Bitte!" she begged, cast a frightened look at the student and drew her head away. "Hach!" said the man angrily; his hand lay flat against the woman's cheek; suddenly he gave it a shove, sending her head sideways. He sat for a moment glowering, then he tried to sing a verse, but could not. "She's from the Sudetenland," he said to the student importantly, drawing himself up. "The Führer gave us the Sudetenland back. If it hadn't been for the Führer she and I would never have met each other. It's thanks to the Führer . . ." The woman looked away. The man looked at his fiancée, proudly; if she was not affection-ate, at any rate she was German. He picked up his glass, bent across the table, wanted her to drink. She turned her head away. "Hach!" he said again, as if she was a dog that was suddenly refusing to do its tricks; he shifted angrily and himself drained the glass; wine ran down his chin. The student ventured a momentary glance at the woman. She was flashy but dull; her breasts were firm beneath her pink jumper, but pendant; she had made up her face, but her lipstick was patchy, the line of her eyebrows uneven and at too steep an angle; the varnish on her nails was peeling and the nails themselves black; he thought she looked unhappy, as if she was bored, not just in her present company; there was something indifferent, almost dead about her face. He knew nothing about the Sudetenland, he knew it only as a newspaper headline; but he felt that she had not come to this hilly country quite of her own accord—in fact, what was she? Did she work in the vineyards too?; after all there was such a thing as deportation; and if she had ever envisaged the man she would marry, perhaps it was someone very different to this peevish, touchy, thin, poor, drunkard; her hair was fair, a deep golden colour, but he could see that it was bleached; she had a parting and there it was dark at the roots; he shuddered as he always did when he encountered the spurious; at the same time he felt pity for her; he thought: actually she looks more like a Pole; for all I know she might be a Jewess. If so, she is the notional aryan; the embodiment of the aryan idea, he thought: fair at the tip, dark at the root. . . .

He got no further. The labourer, who had momentarily been lost in his bitter thoughts, roused himself; he insisted that he was going to show them a trick. He cleared the table. The student could see that the man was angry and he felt a quick rush of understanding. One is engaged to a girl, yes? One has given her a gold ring, yes? Thus one has a certain claim to appreciation, yes? Not only in private, in one's room, but in public, too, before one's friends and foreigners, yes? What's the point of the ring and all the rest of it, if her man cannot be

111

proud of her? If she isn't the most beautiful woman in the world, she can at least be the most loyal, can't she? If she isn't a mountain of delights, she can be a sea of affection, can't she? One gets engaged in order to give the world reason to envy one, in order to add to one's own importance, in order to have something to boast about; so that, when they see how tender and good she is, everyone will exclaim: "There in truth is a rich man!", isn't that it? And here I am not even allowed to put my hand on her neck in public! She won't even drink from my glass in public! I might as well be a bachelor! Hach!

When the woman saw what the man was intending to do, she started and gave a little cry. She gripped his arm, she begged him not to, but he wrenched her hands away. She put her hands over her eyes and wept; the student began to shiver. Again she flung herself at the man to prevent him, but again he stopped her, setting his palm against her cheek and giving her head a push that made it wobble like that of a nodding doll.

"You haven't seen this before," the man said to the student. He was savage, triumphant.

"What?" the student whispered.

"I am going to eat glass," the man said. He picked up his big semi-spherical glass: it was empty.

"Eat glass?" said the student. He didn't understand.

"Jawohl," said the man.

The woman screamed, the man held her off with an elbow. Someone once said: man wants to be loved, failing that, admired; failing that, hated, even loathed. Perhaps that is the law, in one sentence.... The woman screamed and again clasped her hands to her face; this seemed to incite the labourer; he opened his mouth wide, looked rigidly at the student, bared two rows of irregular teeth; put the glass into his mouth, bit off a large piece, making it go crack, showed the student the piece lying on his tongue; then drew his tongue in and ground the glass between his back teeth looking at the student the whole time; he chewed up the great piece of glass most thoroughly, put

112

out his tongue so that the student should see the tiny pieces, bit off another piece of glass, then another, it was like watching an animal eating a flower, petal by petal, in the end there was only the stem left; his mouth was full of glass; the woman had collapsed and was lying across the chair, sobbing; the student's eyes were almost popping out of his head.

Slowly, trembling, he got to his feet. The labourer opened his mouth and exhibited his tongue which was covered with glistening particles of glass and blood. He raised his hand, waved it, for now came the denouement! He swallowed the whole lot! It went down his gullet; and then he licked his thick, bloody lips.

"Sie können sterben!" said the student, deathly pale.

"Nee," said the man with a grin, then he wiped his mouth with the back of his hand, wiped his hand on his trousers, "tut nix."

The student let go of the back of the chair he had been clutching, whispered "Verzeihen Sie," backed away across the floor, groped behind him, found the door handle, got the door open, bowed, was out on the steps, out in the night. He was walking, hurrying, finally running.

*

"This one life," he thought as he ran. "This one body..."

"Whatever I do in this life," he had reached the bottom of the alley and was standing panting, prophetic, in front of the dark Youth Hostel, "I shall respect my body..."

His lips were trembling.

"I shall never let myself get TB, never get cancer, never get syphilis, never take to drink, never volunteer to fight in a war, never let myself be crucified, never eat glass. When I die there will not be a scar on my body..."

He was alone in the dormitory. He put a chair against the door barricading it.

"Let me fall into a deep sleep," he prayed. "Let this

night go quickly, God. Let me get safely to France. Let me get out of Germany. There are only devils and mad-men here."

"And," he added, seeing the woman's face before him again, "unhappy people. . . ."

THE NEXT day he was despatched across the German frontier. There is no other way of putting it, for he himself remembered nothing whatever about it. He could not remember hearing the word "Passieren!", the actual spell—there was a great hole in his memory, a large rectangular black hole the size of a piano-case. Presumably he had been unconscious and they had lugged him and his motorcycle, despatched them like a couple of parcels, under the boom and onto Luxembourg territory. . . .

All the way down through Germany he had had a secret horrible fear lying like a stone in his belly—he had never dared to fish it up and look at it in daylight and it had grown bigger and bigger. The moment he reached the customs house on the western frontier of Germany and had to get out his carnet and passport—that same moment he knew what his fear had been. And it had become the size of a mountain; and so he must have swooned . . .

The thing was: had the customs officer in Flensburg, that green-uniformed policeman who could not read French—had he *stamped his passport*?

He could not remember the click of the stamp. On the Danish side—yes; but not on the German!

If that was so, he thought, then the Gestapo really have laid a satanic trap. They have let me ride along as a tourist for three whole days, let me have a gay old time, savour all the delights of Germany, lulled me into security—and then, just at the moment when I think I am safe, on the very frontier with Luxembourg, a hand will fall on my shoulder:

"Halt! Here's one who has tried to steal into Germany! You are under arrest!"

115

"Steal . . . ?" he could hear the clink of handcuffs.

"Jawohl! A well-worn plutocratic-communist trick. There's no stamp in your passport. The Danish triangular trichinosis stamp, jawohl, but no German stamp!"

"Under arrest?" A hand pushes forward the safety catch of an automatic pistol.

"Jawohl! Attempted illegal entry and espionage is punishable in the German Reich with ten years hard labour in a concentration camp."

"Mein Gott!"

"Marsch! Hände hoch!"

One did not see Luxembourg.

On a June day in 1939, a boiling hot day in June 1939, one just did not see Luxembourg. One dared not see it, in case it was another mirage, a fresh trap; one did not dare believe that one really was out of Germany. As one rode along one realized out of the corner of one's eyes that there was a taste of France about Luxembourg: a vine-clad hillside here, a castle there, a brief glimpse of a tower, a drawbridge, a moat, a shop sign in French; one heard an odd word or two—but when one is on one's way to a princess one does not linger with her handmaid, that would be a dangerous betrayal, it would be to deprive one's adoration of its force . . .

Then one was in France.

Quietly, without noticing the fact, one was in France.

Well, yes, there had been a customs house, of course, a sort of room and two customs officers. Or was it three? No, two customs men; and a kind of long counter, or bench. But the two, one younger and the other a bit older, stood behind the counter talking together, animatedly, angrily, absorbed; one had his foot up on a packing case and a cigarette end in the corner of his mouth. They had paid no attention to him, asked no questions. Had they even

116

looked at him? Perhaps one of them had given him a look, the one with the cigarette end, the sort of look a cockerel might give: hurried, brown, blind, distant. The two men had not interrupted their private discussion; one of them —casually, using the wrong hand, had stamped the student's passport, continuing their talk undisturbed.

It was not that they disregarded me, he thought—that would have been boorish. They simply did not see me— and that was quite different.

France.

Quietly, without anyone noticing, without noticing it oneself, one had entered France.

Do not all great things happen quietly?

Completely unnoticed?

Don't pound so, he whispered to his heart, don't pound so . . .

He was riding along a fairly broad highway, dark, asphalted. It had green deciduous trees on either side of it, and curves, thank God, there were curves. It's almost like at home, he thought.

And yet there was something new, something quite new about the air, the trees, roadside ditch, his engine had a new song: he had seen road signs, road signs in French . . .

After driving a mile, he had to stop. He sat astride his machine on the right-hand side of the road. He could hear birds twittering in the trees. Otherwise all was still. His hands trembled on the handlebars.

His mouth felt dry.

"France," he said in an undertone.

He glanced round to make sure that there were no socialists nearby, then he whispered:

"Thank you, God."

He sat there for a long time with a bowed head. I'm dreaming, he thought. It can't be true that I have got across the Rhine alive; it can't be true that I am sitting here listening to French birds twittering in the trees; it can't be true. Then he pinched his thigh, hard. It is true, he thought. He hid his face in his hands. He gulped.

It is true, he thought.

He awakened, dismounted, pulled his motorcycle up onto its stand, began hopping about the road. First he hopped on both legs, then on the right leg, then on his left. He stopped, groaned, looked up at the sun. "Soleil!" he said, beaming. He looked at the blue sky: "Ciel!" he cried. He waved to the birds, but he did not know what tweet-tweet was in French, "Oiseaux tweet-tweet!" he cried. He looked at a tree. "Arbre!" he cried, he ran across the road, like an initiate, towards the tree; "Arbre!" he cried again, stopped for a second because he had exhausted his knowledge of trees in French, but the next moment he was embracing the tree without bothering whether it was lime or ash!—he was a beginner and went baldheaded!—to him it was a tree, a French tree, groaning he flung his arms around it, it had a good, firm trunk, was like a woman: "Je vous aime!" he said and kissed the bark; his groin was pressed ecstatically to the tree, his embrace was so passionate that his pelvis began making strange movements, he stopped, bowed, said: "Pardon, madame!", the next moment he knew himself forgiven, that the tree had taken it as a compliment, that made him so deliriously happy that he had to climb it; four or five holds and he was up and had flung himself onto the first branch; and there he sat, intoxicated, wide-eyed, looking out over the countryside; he raised a hand in benediction and called out: "Egalité, fraternité ... !" He could not remember the third. Breathless, timidly-happy, he sat on the branch. He broke off a leafy twig, bit it, licked its bitter sap.

After a while, he slithered down again.

"La France," he whispered.

He brushed off the leaves and twigs. He looked at his

riding boots: they were all scratched from climbing and very dusty. I must spruce up a bit, he thought.

"Il faut . . ."

He had to think. For a Northerner to have to speak French, to switch to French, is like changing to a different gear, shunting over into quite a different track; it is a mental revolution; it is like having to take out all your brain matter and put in new.

The Northerner groans and suffers when he has to do this, his mental machinery creaks with the effort.

French is not just another language, it is a foreign language. Completely foreign.

The world's frontier runs along the Rhine.

North of the Rhine lies the home of the barbarian, the Protestants; the cyclone belt with its temperate climate, the industrial belt where people work and where they actually like to work, for they would die of cold if they did not. This nordic world, which is first and foremost a linguistic world, consists of Scandinavia, Germany, England and, by extension, America and Canada. The fact that here, when you mean summer, you say summer, is an unmistakable indication that this is a world apart.

Small variations do not affect the argument: in Swedish the word is sommar, in Norwegian sommer, on the west coast of Norway sumar—but they are all summer; in the Nordic world you are everywhere at home: summer is always summer, and even though melk is milch, it is still all milk.

But the moment you cross the Rhine, you are in the Latin world, the world of the Catholics, the old world— you are in the South. Linguistically, this has nothing in common with the Nordic world, nothing. You might just as well be on Mars.

Take milk. Take anything you like. Take summer.

In France, when people want to say summer, do they say summer or anything remotely resembling it? Not a bit of it. When people in France want to say summer, they say—it is incomprehensible and quite impossible to guess —they say été.

There you are.

Été.

You can take the word "été" turn it over, smell it, twist it this way and that, shake it, jolt it, throw it up in the air and catch it again, you can even spell it backwards, which leaves it unchanged—but it is all no good. It does not remind you of anything you have ever heard before. It is and remains unintelligible, foreign, completely foreign. Like brombelignogg. It's like hitting your head against a marble wall.

The boundary of the world runs along the Rhine.

I must spruce up a bit, he had thought.

"Il faut être beau," he said, in an undertone.

That was not bad for a beginning, but scarcely outstanding.

"Il faut que je . . ."

He noticed the approaching subjunctive and took it in his stride:

"Il faut que je sois beau," he said.

He was aware that he was talking to himself and you don't really need French for that. The decisive test comes when for the first time you have to talk on French soil with a native, a Frenchman. Or a Frenchwoman.

That last thought gave him a queer feeling in the pit of his stomach.

He turned and looked back. At that comforting distance Germany seemed a nice country, free of problems, a land of brothers, home-loving.

He thought: good, old Germany.

Alte Kameraden.

A French woman . . .

In his mind's eye he saw a picture book for people in love spring open and up jumped a fan, glittering and colourful; oh, the torment of plenty when you are stand-

120

ing on a country road and have to choose a name, a face, a silhouette—Ninon de Lenclos, Mélisande, La Récamier, La Bovary, Isolde; Agnès, Joséphine, Rosette, La Dubarry; Chimène, La Pompadour, la Dame aux Camélias . . .

But those were either literature or they were dead. He had only ever heard of one real, live one. A fabulous girl.

Young, artful, a young girl, amorous, glamorous.

Estelle.

A girl, real, of flesh and blood.

The fellow had been his own age, in the same class at Trondhjem High School; and now they were both at the Commercial College in Bergen. He had been talking with him a month before he set out on this trip. The boy was the son of a bank manager in Trondhjem. The previous summer, the boy told him, their family had had a young French girl staying with them. The daughter of one of the father's business connections in France. Paying a visit to Trondhjem. Stayed a week in their house. In Trondhjem. Not even Bergen, or Oslo, or Copenhagen, or Berlin, or Rome, where there was some likelihood of a young girl from France coming to stay. But Trondhjem! A sheer miracle.

"One night I went to her room."

"What? Just went in?"

"Yes?"

"Just walked in, straight in?"

"Yes. She hadn't locked her door. The next night she came to me."

"What? But your parents!"

"Their room's in the other wing."

Silence. Quiet. That was wonderful, that was frightful.

"She was mighty frisky."

"What? Frisky?"

"Like having a rabbit in bed."

Silence. Quiet That was wonderful. That was frightful.

"How old was she?"

"Eighteen. Seventeen, perhaps."

"Seventeen . . . What was her name?"

"Estelle. She was great fun, Estelle. Well, enjoy yourself in France. Good luck."

How on earth, God, can such a thing happen?

Why, God, am I not the son of a bank manger with connections in France? Why does no French girl—laughing, amorous, glamorous—ever come to my father's house in Trondhjem, to *my* father's house? Why didn't I grow up in a house with an extra wing, cut off from my parents at night, a house with many guest rooms? Including one for a young girl, ready furnished and equipped with a balcony, thick carpet on the floor, airy voile curtains, four-poster bed with cretonne hangings, sweet little flounces on the bedspread and a big soft pouffe covered with maidenly silk in front of the dressing table: quietness, softness, seclusion; heavy oaken door with a key in the lock. . . How can such a thing happen, O God? In Trondhjem? And why doesn't it happen to me?

What does that mean, God?

Hi!

Where do we humans get our impulses from? What determines our behaviour and the steps we take? Who directs our longings?

Do we dream? Or are we *dreamed*?

If that night, a month before, our student had not been told that story about Estelle, if he had not happened to hear the story—by sheer chance!—is it certain that he would have gone to France? Would he, at that moment, have been standing just inside the French frontier, with a pounding heart??

He did not know. He only knew that the story about that young French girl had exerted a tremendous influence on him; it had been like a stab in the heart from a sugar-coated dagger, filling him with envy and visions. A frivolous little story, an irresponsible story, a mischievous story. Exactly. Freud speaks somewhere of "Die Furcht, beim Weibe zugrunde zu gehen." Exactly. One knows that fear. Of being destroyed by the woman, the mature woman. Being dragged down. By the weight of her, the tears, the arms round your neck, the sobbing constrictor's hold, the pregnant, bulging belly, the gold ring, the milk, the fear, the shame, the maintenance order, the man with the summons, ever-lasting persecution and a ruined life.

Hi!

Estelle was fun . . .

(But there was one thing he had not understood, could not begin to understand . . . that after having such an adventure the man had let the girl go . . . had no longing, no grief, did not miss her . . . did not even *miss* her! A sudden thought came to him: there must be a punishment for that. One day God was bound to punish the man most severely.)

He had often pictured her to himself. No, not her—she was second-hand—her sister! Her twin sister!

Eighteen. Perhaps seventeen. Slender, almost thin. Dimples. A summery dress of flowered linen, with great big flowers; no sleeves; bare shoulders, a nice tan, soft skin. For some reason or other she wore spectacles. Shallow, rectangular spectacles with a black frame, horn. A gay dissembler. A little animal mouth that snapped. Smiling politely at table in the big dining-room. While talking with his parents and eating with her right hand, she quietly dropped her left hand beneath the tablecloth and undid his fly buttons, one by one. Was that a quick wink behind her glasses? No one had seen it. She conversed politely, gesticulated with her fork in her right hand and her student

123

in her left. "This *is* good!" she exclaimed. "Yes, isn't it?" said his mother. "Fameux!" she cried. "Yes, isn't it?" said his father. "Oh!" cried the student.

For one reason or another her hair was shingled, almost like a boy's, and her teeth were small and white. They had a game in bed, first a pillow fight, then without pillows. She had black pyjamas. She dived under the big eiderdown, popped her head out in an unexpected place, waved, dived under again; her head appeared by the bedhead, then at the foot of the bed. She shook her shingled hair, straightened her spectacles, her eyes twinkled. For a moment she lay still, waiting. In the morning, at eleven when his parents were both out, the housekeeper woke them, bringing them strawberries and cream in bed.

Estelle. No, her twin sister . . .

Will it ever happen to me, he wondered, that what goes on in bed becomes a game?

Amorous, glamorous, light . . .

To the glory of God.

Hi!

He took the twig and whipped the dust off his boots with it; then he spat on them and rubbed them with the leaves. He fished out his comb and combed his hair. He straightened the neck of his shirt, rolled down the sleeves and buttoned the cuffs. Then he changed his mind and rolled the sleeves up again. He looked at his hands, crooked his fingers, inspected his nails. His nail file was in his sponge-bag deep down in his rucksack. He took a match stick, split it in two with his right-hand thumb nail and manicured himself with that. He stopped and considered. Well, that would have to do. It was not in his power to do more for himself. He took his handkerchief and blew his nose.

He started his motorcycle again and drove on, sitting as straight as an altar candle. He drove three miles without breathing.

Then he was in a village.

The main road was sign-posted and had a number, so all you had to do was to follow the signs. But here he seemed suddenly to have gone wrong. He found himself in a little square with tall trees: three streets to choose from, all of them narrow; he slowed down, pulled up beside the pavement. Over a shop he saw a sign: "Epicérie."

He was filled with infinite reverence.

"Epicérie."

He supposed he would have to ask the way.

The time had come.

Now he would have to speak French.

He loved France. He would put all his love into this first question. To ask: "Paris?" was not enough; that was the way of a busy commercial traveller. He wanted to show France that here was a man, a poet, worthy of France's favours. One came from a land of Vikings, it was true, but one knew how to behave, could be courteous; was the King's Mirror any worse a handbook than the Proverbs of Solomon. He was already rolling words of French in his mouth, rolling them into a poem; he dismounted; he was trembling; two women stood talking in front of the grocer's, each with a big basket on her arm; beside a tree, with the two women yet a pace away, stood a short middle-aged man in a black suit; he had his back turned; the student chose him; this was the first time, but he felt safer with a man; his heart was pounding; to him this Frenchman was St. Peter with the keys of Heaven; he walked up to the man politely, stopped, bowed, cleared his throat, looked up at the roofs so that nothing should distract him, swallowed, then, feeling as if his heart had acquired wings and was ascending, he said:

"Pardonnez-moi, Monsieur. Je cherche la route principale à Paris." (Perhaps *vers* Paris? Or *de* Paris?) "La route principale pour Paris, s'il vous plait."

He felt a surge of warmth, then a surge of cold, as you

do after an exam. He lowered his eyes in order to receive his sentence.

He saw, but could not understand what he saw.

"Hla!" the man said through a red hole.

"Hli!" the man went on; it was like the mouth of a baby elephant.

"Hla!" said the man. An arm went out in one direction, "Hla!" he said eagerly, dribbling, effusive; an arm went out in the other direction, "Hli! Hli!" There was something inhuman about the man's mouth, about his low forehead and his bulging slanting eyes; there was something inhuman about his body and those arms that he could not control; there was something especially inhuman about his nose; he really did not have a nose, just nostrils. The little man, who could have been anything between thirty and sixty, had now become fearfully eager, appreciative; he took hold of the student's arm, shifted from one foot to the other, his lower lip became wet with spittle, his slanting eyes were running. "Hla!" said the man, with childish happiness, "Hla! Hli?"

The student stood stock still. It felt as though something inside him had been knocked to pieces. He looked at the ground.

He noticed that the two women had come up. They were standing beside him. One of them pulled the man away scolding, she gave him a slap and a shake, as if he had been a child. The other woman tried to explain: ce monsieur is quite harmless but he is not quite all right. He's a little gaga, she gave a quick smile, pointed to her head, half amused, half pained, the gentleman must excuse him, they were so sorry; ce pauvre idiot—she had been quite sure he would stand quietly beside the tree while she spoke to her friend; she was so sorry, so very sorry; now she would show him the road to Paris herself; it was that street and then straight on, she begged him a thousand pardons . . .

"Hla! Hli!" said the man in the dark Sunday suit; the

126

other woman had led him off and was holding him, but this had been a great experience for him and he stood there on the pavement, brandishing his arms; he, too, knew where Paris was, would so gladly show the way . . .

"Oui, monsieur, tout droit. Tout droit."

Quietly, tonelessly, he said:

"Merci, madame . . ."

He was out in the country. He stopped, dismounted.

He clenched his fists. He hit at the saddle. He struck at it till dust flew.

"I am accursed. Conceived in sin and born to perish! Everything I touch is destroyed. I want life—I harvest death. I am a Cain! I have his mark on my forehead! I am everlastingly accursed!"

The storm inside him began to subside.

"Why isn't life as I imagined it? Why are my proud hopes always turned into defeats? My love! . . . Has any man in the world ever loved France more ardently than I? There are forty million Frenchmen to bid me welcome as I set foot on French soil, to lay palm leaves before my feet. And of these forty million, who is it I meet? Who is it that receives me? I come with open arms, having spruced myself up for France, come with arms outstretched, longing for grace and light, and then . . ." his voice caught. "Then I meet . . ."

In a whisper:

"There are forty million sane Frenchmen—and one village idiot."

"I am one of the elect. I am one of the accursed."

There was no need for her to have scolded him, he thought, or to have stood like that and shaken the poor chap's arms. It was not his fault he was like that. He was like a child. . . .

It was 250 kilometres to Paris.

Twenty-five Norwegian miles.

He tried to work it out.

His top speed was seventy, the man had said. Suppose he went at fifty? If he kept up fifty kilometres an hour? Fifty kilometres. That was five Norwegian miles. It was a hot day, the sun was still shining out of a cloudless sky, it was boiling hot and mental arithmetic not easy. Also he had started wrestling with French numerals. Counting in French is so difficult that, during the war, when the French had someone who said he was French, but whom they suspected of being a foreign spy, they asked him to count in French. Say 14394 they said. The man could not. So they shot him.

The student was sweating. In Norwegian he said: Twenty-five divided by five: makes five." Could that be right? He worked it out again. Yes, five hours. In five hours he could be in Paris.

Being new to the place, it would be better to get there while it was still light and there were people about to help one—rather than late at night when everyone was in bed and one might perhaps have to grope one's way with one's hands from house to house, from alley to alley, to find an address. . . .

He drove on. He wanted to get to the City of Light.

La Ville Lumière.

Somewhere he saw the name Metz on a sign. Metz?

On the next sign was Verdun. "Verdun, 7 kilometres." He knew then.

He glanced round at the landscape. There was not the slightest trace of death and horror. He remembered a line from one of the American Sandburg's poems: "I am the grass. I cover everything."

He had stopped and was sitting still. A strange lifelessness had come over him. A whole epoch of which he had only read was there again: the world war; he could feel he was sitting in one of Death's fields of force.

Here, beyond those green hills, the armies had faced each other. Hundreds of thousands, millions of men, had crept, crawled, lived, slept in trenches, in mud. He could see the bandages, food tins, stretchers, hand grenades; could see the muffled, bent-backed, hurrying soldiers, in puttees, with bayonets and gas masks; he could see the barbed wire and a severed hand; he remembered the descriptions of the yellow clouds of mustard gas, how it came drifting along, he could feel a stinging in his wind-pipe. Now beyond those hills, lay an enormous graveyard, perhaps the largest in the world. Just before he had left home, he had seen a French anti-war film: the dead of Verdun had risen up from their graves in shrouds; the producer had used war-disabled for his actors, one had had his jaw shot away. . . .

Seven kilometres to Verdun. He would have to give it a miss.

There are miles and miles of lines of wooden crosses there. It was enough to be sitting by the pleasant highway, beneath shady trees, and see the name Verdun on the signpost. Let the dead bury the dead. And Sandburg was the grass. Let him cover it all. I have other things to do. I'm going to Paris.

Something suddenly made him think of the Maginot Line. The Frenchmen's new gigantic belt of fortifications, with impregnable, subterranean gun-emplacements. I have passed the Maginot Line, he thought—I have ridden over it! And I never noticed it!

He looked down at the asphalt on which he stood. He tilted his head to one side and listened. It was quite uncanny. He could feel a tingling in the soles of his feet. Perhaps at that moment he was actually standing on top of the Maginot Line. Right on top of it! Involuntarily, he teetered a few steps on tip-toe, as far as the verge.

He looked round, cautiously, searching. They must be able to see from their subterranean bunkers, he thought, they must have some kind of periscope. . . . He stood there

129

for a while and let his gaze slowly travel the landscape, looking for a periscope. He could not see anything.

He looked back towards Germany . . .

What would be the point of a war? Who would get anything out of it?

He looked at the fields he was standing beside.

They don't even spare the farms, he thought. They have no sense of the value of labour. Don't you believe they would salute a field of corn, don't you believe they would go round it respectfully; they would march straight into it, the whole regiment, with horses and tanks and gun-carriages. And if they were cold in their bivouacs at night, they would cut down even apple trees! They are given the order and no one protests! It takes fifty years to grow an apple tree—and a minute to fell it.

They cut down *apple trees*!

And yet, he thought, rubbing his hands in his agitation, people honour these soldiers!—honour them as heroes!—people *honour* these hydrocephalics, the worst in the world, whose only exploit is cutting down apple trees! People set up statues in their honour, cannot set them up high enough . . . !

There was one mother in Sparta who told her son, as he set off for the war, that she only wanted to see him again *with* his shield or *on* it. For two thousand years, he thought bitterly, the world has been terrorized by that imbecile mother. We shall never get a new world until we hear of a mother who sees her son return without his arms or his shield and who greets him:

"My son you show signs of genius. He who quits the fight, wins it. I shall prepare you a meal."

He ought to be able to reach Paris before five that afternoon. Five o'clock. . . . Were people having a siesta then,

130

or working? He thought five o'clock sounded right, a suitable time to make his first call and pay his respects.

At what time in the evening were literary salons usually held?

All at once he was in the room: at an actual salon: among a lot of immortals. Along one wall were tall black ebony columns with green palm leaves: the room was filled with a faint blue cloud of cigar smoke: Montesquieux was sitting at a spinet absently turning over some music by Rameau; their hostess—La Duchesse—was seated on a chaise-longue in gay conversation with Voltaire: he could see her profile, she had a noble head; for an instant their eyes met, almost imperceptibly she bit her lip; for one moment Voltaire had been side-tracked. Descartes had taken a heavy candelabra from the table and was holding it out courteously to Pascal who was sitting with an unlit cigar in his mouth; Pascal bowed, counted; "Nine candles—for one cigar...!" he said. Descartes smiled: "Prodigality is a highly necessary thing..." Voltaire started, sat up stiffly. Descartes noticed it, turned, pursed his lips, and, smiling, said: "Yes Monsieur, I was plagiarizing you." Voltaire gave a little cough, shut his lips tight, nodded: "I thank you, sir."

Three men holding glasses stood in a group in the tall bay-window that looked onto the street, its heavy, mustard-yellow curtains were drawn back; they were discussing one of Chamfort's sayings:

"In order to become a great man in literature, or at any rate to cause a noticeable revolution, it is as in politics—necessary to find everything prepared and to be born at the right time."

L'Abbé Prévost was tugging at his ear; Diderot was stroking his beard; Beaumarchais, who was the third, was rocking on the balls of his feet; he smacked his lips and said: "Was Chamfort perhaps unlucky?" That was all he said.

They drifted across towards another group. Cardinal Richelieu who was staring furiously at Voltaire, turned to

Count d'Haussonville, seized his shirt ruffles, hissed: "Did you hear! L'infâme, c'est moi!" The Count paled. Alexander Dumas père was standing in the middle of the floor, old, alone; the maid in white apron and cap, was holding a tray of filled glasses for him; he straightened his pince-nez, bent forward heavily; her bosom showed young and white and firm in the square neckline of her dress; there had been a time; if he had been twenty years younger; he stood lost in thought; now he had no choice; he selected a glass. The maid bobbed and walked on with her tray to Pasteur, he waved her away; Joseph Bertrand did not; nor did Balzac; nor did Alphonse Daudet.

He himself was sitting beside La Rochefoucauld, who had cocked one leg over the arm of his chair; he gazed at the silver buckles on the Frenchman's shoes.

"Well," said their hostess—and at the sound of her voice everyone politely fell silent; she turned her pretty head towards the company. "Messieurs," she said, "if one is to achieve greatness, does one have to be born at the right time?"

"The first prerequisite of greatness at any rate is that one should be born," said a dry voice from the corner; it was Rabelais.

"And the second," the Norwegian heard himself say, "that one has died."

A glint of satisfaction appeared in the Duchess's eyes; many heads turned to look at the young man.

"Précisément," said Rabelais, raising his head up over the back of the chair in which he had been sitting hidden, "I remember a very interesting corpse . . ."

"None of your hospital stories!—je vous en prie!" exclaimed the Duchess lifting up her hands. She was enchanting.

He felt that this was a challenge to him. He looked at his hostess. Again their eyes met. It was no longer any secret in Paris that two weeks before he had become this cultured woman's lover; that evening she was presenting her Nordic conquest in her salon; she gave him an almost imperceptible nod; everyone saw it; she smiled to him across Voltaire's head, encouragingly; he remembered the smell of her boudoir, of her perfume, he remembered the soft skin of her shoulders; he remembered her long tumbling hair; her hand-mirror of silver and tortoise-shell. She wants to hear my voice, he thought. Now. It was a titillating thought.

"Zola," he said.

"What about Zola?" Cardinal Richelieu asked sharply.

"How great would Zola have been," the student said, "—without Dreyfus?"

"Well said!" Montesquieux.

"Amazing!" said the cardinal and looked at the student with new interest.

"Love of one's neighbour is the last expedient of the unsuccessful," said La Rochefoucauld, removing his leg from the arm of his chair.

"Shame! You keep quiet!" said their hostess, shaking a finger at La Rochefoucauld.

"In greatness," said the Norwegian, "there is—en tout cas—a qualitative difference between art on one hand and politics and science on the other."

"Pardon?" said Joseph Bertrand, turning his head.

"A quite decisive difference," said the Norwegian. "Politics and science develop out of their own mass, their own weight. What has to come, comes. Art, on the other hand, is somewhat capricious, original, inimitable, utterly and entirely dependent on the individual, miraculous, irreplaceable..."

"Did you mention science, sir?" Bertrand said, pulling himself up heavily in his chair.

The Norwegian gulped.

"Take the incandescent lamp," he said.

"Fi donc!" exclaimed Pascal.

"Le confort anglais!" sighed Balzac.

"Taisez-vous, taisez-vous!" called their hostess, again shaking a finger at them. She was enchanting.

"This incandescent lamp," said the student, "would

133

have been invented without Edison. The French Revolution would have come about without Robespierre. Small-pox serum would—you must excuse me, sir (he bowed to Pasteur)—smallpox serum would have been discovered without you."

"But never . . ." he went on.

"But never . . . ?" said the others.

Suddenly they were all with him, all bent towards him, the atmosphere was charged, they were hanging on his words.

Smiling, the student spread out his hands, palms up and stood there silent, leaving it to that company of highly gifted people to complete the thought for themselves—which they did.

A rustling stir that grew louder and louder spread through the room, and Cardinal Richelieu made the sign of the cross as eight elderly writers filled with enthusiasm tried to heave themselves up out of their deep arm-chairs; a wonderful blush of pleasure spread across the Duchess's alabaster cheeks; this was going to be an unforgettable evening; this was history; her salon would now be immortal; fondly she jerked her fan open in the Norwegian's direction, touched its handle with her lips.

"But never . . . !" cried the eight in chorus, it was almost impossible to hear what they said, the old men stamped their feet and called out, the seat of one chair tore, wigs went flying, someone's false teeth fell to the floor:

"But never *Le Misanthrope* . . . !"

"Never *Le Cid* . . . !"

"Never *La Dame aux Camelias*, nonsense, that was my son, I mean, never the *Count of Monte Cri* . . . !"

"Never *Pantagruel* . . . !"

"Never *Tartarin de Tarascon* . . . !"

"Never the *La Comédie Humaine* . . . !"

"Never the *Marriage de Figaro* . . . !"

"Never *Candide* . . ."

They held their breaths for a second:

" . . . without me!" cried Molière.

" . . . without me!" cried Corneille.

" . . . without me!" cried Dumas père.

". . . without me!" cried Rabelais.

". . . without me!" cried Daudet.

". . . without *me*!" cried Balzac.

". . . without me and Mozart!" cried Beaumarchais.

". . without *Voltaire*!" cried Voltaire and, tears in his eyes, kissed the student on both cheeks and invited him to supper the next evening.

Their hostess had got up from her chaise-longue. She stood there with flushed cheeks, she had taken the student's hand and was pressing it in warm gratitude to her breast.

"You are a phenomenon," she said into his cheek. "Writing in France has been in the doldrums. Not what it was. Motoring. France no longer pays homage to writers. France pays homage to Citroën. But see," she said, "see how you with your enthusiasm and youth have restored our faith! Corneille is dancing!" Her eyes grew wide; enraptured, she said: "I have never seen Corneille dance before . . . !" All at once she lowered her voice and whispered into his ear: "But you have made yourself two enemies. Beware of the mathematicians, Joseph Bertrand and Count d'Haussonville!"

"Madame," he said answering her smile, "What would we be without our enemies?"

She ran one finger across his hand, he felt the nail scoring the skin.

"Tomorrow at Voltaire's, but the day after tomorrow here with me . . ."

"Your wishes are my command, Madame," he whispered.

*

He bent his head nearer the engine, roused by a sound, a foreign sound. He was like a mother with her child. Had

135

Humske coughed? Wasn't that a slight cough he had heard?

He listened.

When he raised his head again, he discovered streets; he saw a street sign; Rue du Faubourg St. Antoine.

He was in Paris.

T HE SMELL of a big city . . .
He had never smelled it before and he was never to forget it.

It was on an afternoon towards the end of June that he came riding into Paris. It had been a boiling hot day and the sun seemed to have drawn every smell, present and past, out of the walls of the houses and out of the paving stones; the smell of big city met him like a warm breath.

There was the smell of hot stone, of worn, aged hot stone, the smell of brick buildings; the smell of fried liver and leaky gas pipes; the tart, warm smell of wine, of sawdust sprinkled with wine; there was the smell of over-ripe fruit, of pears and motorcar oil, there was the heady smell of newly baked bread from a bakery; the intimi-dating smell of women's bodies and hot scent; there was the smell of factory soot, the smell of ingrained dust, and of wax polish; there was the bitter smell of beer, a waft of burned rubber, the smell of vanilla ice-cream, of acrid cigarettes; the swift wonderful smell of clean, freshly ironed clothes from a laundry; the smell of hot street, of old hot stone, the smell of brick buildings and stairs; the smell of raw meat and offal from the butchers' shops, the smell of rotten fish, the fleeting inciting smell of aromatic coffee from the pavement cafés; there was the smell of mould from a rack of old, secondhand clothes on the pavement, the smell of fresh printer's ink from the newspapers; there was the stupefying smell of rancid urine from the urinals, the smell of petrol, the smell of lily-of-the-valley.

And then there was one other smell, foreign, new, which he could not identify; it came from the people, and it was not sweat; it seemed to come from the restaurants as well; a dangerous, stirring smell; new; foreign. . . .

The moment he smelled the smell of Paris, that symphony of smells—old, hot, sated, luxuriant, rich—he felt instantly at home.

This is me, he thought, gaping; I could have lived here; I could have been born here; I have always lived here—this is *my* smell.

Despite the fact that Paris is a clean city, with streets that are washed down and well-swept pavements—in one place he saw a man in uniform come out of an hotel with a small garden syringe in his hand and water the pavement, sprinkling it with elegant swinging movements; that done, he took his brush and brushed it (ah, thought the student, I suppose he did that to bind the dust so as not to raise a cloud that might annoy pedestrians, that was cunning, I shall remember that)—despite the clean streets and green trees he got the impression that Paris was a grey city, a dirty city.

But strangely enough there was nothing unpleasant, nothing repellent about its dirt; it did not hit you in the face. It was not actual filth, not refuse, not excrement; it was dust, dust and soot. Not coal dust, which is messy and sticky, but a sort of refined grey dirt; a grey patina, deep, reserved, discreet. That grey dirt had its own age and nobility, an astounding gaiety and lightness, in fact, rather witty. It was chimney smoke and dust, the smoke and dust of centuries that had been rubbed into the walls of all Parisian houses; there is this grey patina on all cornices, on all the window-frames, on all bay-windows, all door-frames, all stairs and banisters, rubbed in, ingrained; Paris is grey, grey to the bone; the soot and smoke of the centuries is in every crack and furrow, in the walls, in the paving; and, if you could find an old man who worked outdoors; some old navvy, and asked him to let you inspect the back of his gnarled old neck, if he did and you parted one of the wrinkles there to see what it was like at the bottom, you would not find it glaringly light, a virgin pink, not a bit of it, it would be good, honest grey; Paris is grey, grey to the bone.

Parisians use water; but either they despise soap or its invention has not yet reached them. All right. For could you imagine Paris scrubbed and clean, scrubbed with soap, white-washed, white? Let Paris be grey—for ever grey, sooty, grey, silvery grey, stony grey, dove grey, pearly grey, church grey, dust grey. For is it not this enormous background of dull grey that makes the other colours stand out and become alive, doubly alive?

Is not Paris, more than any other city, a city of colour? Perhaps the colours have not appeared entirely naturally or quietly—perhaps, indeed, they have had to fight their way, fight their way up in order not to drown in a sea of grey. . . .

There, a woman with a scarf as thin as gauze round her head, fluttering slightly in the breeze, a gossamer lilac scarf; how pretty that lilac colour is against the grey! —there on a tray on a waiter's lifted hand a glass with a green liqueur!—there, on the black lapel of an academician's tail-coat, hastily glimpsed, heavy gold embroidery!

It looks so obvious, so effortless, so simple—have we not always taken it for granted that Paris was a city of dress designers and colourists and painters, did that not go without saying?—but I wonder whether behind the gauzy lilac scarf, behind the bottle-green liqueur, behind the heavy golden embroidery, there did not lie a struggle, a passionate fight not to give up, a fight against the grey?

And where in the world but in Paris with its inevitable background of grey could a people have invented the tricolor? The blue, white and red flag. . . . It was in Paris the tricolor was unfurled. It first fluttered out in grey Paris. A clenched fist of colour.

*

He received an impression of style, elegance—and he saw it first in the men. That made a profound impression upon him, for he would have called it a feminine trait, had it not been here so particularly masculine. It was an entirely new form of male activity and endeavour. He saw it first, glimpsed it, in an open butcher's shop: outside it hung hams, legs of lamb and hares, tied round with silver paper or with little white frills; the butcher himself was standing on the pavement surveying his handiwork; he stood there with his head on one side, considering from a distance of four paces a whole ox he had hung up and decorated with flowers; he was looking at the carcass as if it were a work of art—and it was! In this country, the student thought, touched, even a butcher is an artist. . . . And the next moment: why not? Why should not all trades be artistic?

When I get home to Norway, I shall give lectures for butchers. . . .

He saw another man, on the pavement in front of a fruitshop; he had a broom and had just swept together a little heap of paper, rotten grapes and cabbage leaves; he made a neat, well-shaped little heap of it and carefully pushed it along to a lamp standard; he straightened the little heap with his broom, smoothed its conical sides, surveyed his work; the student half expected him to tie a rosette round the top of it—a cockade—or perhaps a silk bow, so that when the dustmen came, it would be like a present for them. . . .

TELL ME THE KIND OF ANIMAL....

The STUDENT felt that he had passed a boundary; not just between North and South; not just between cold and warmth; he had passed the boundary between approximation and perfection of form; he had a sudden strange feeling of having crossed the boundary between two animal kingdoms....

The dog is a creature with a wet, cold nose perpetually in search of food, no matter of what kind, putridness no objection; if a dog is not in the kitchen begging, it is at garbage heaps or has its head in a dustbin; it is an eater of carrion: brother to the fox, half-brother of the wolf, and cousin to the hyena; the dog is a creature that came from the air in prehistoric times, a fallen bird; if it had not fallen, not been thrust down, why should it be so restless, so nervous, so shamefaced, so fluttery, so unsatisfied with the earth? Its tail is a refashioned bird's tail, a tail that has acquired fur; its flapping ears are the shrunken remnants of the wings it once had; the dog takes after the vulture, the raven, the carrion crow; if the dog had not come from the air, why should it always—and for nothing—bark at swallows and howl at the moon?

Has anyone ever seen a useful, sensible dog, a dog that does something, a functionalistic dog? A being at which one can nod approvingly? If so, it must have been in the forest, or on the hillside or in the polar regions—places where ptarmigan hunters still live, reindeer-herdsmen or eskimos—and where dogs, when not being used, are kept properly tied up in teams, in isolation, well apart from people, outdoors, segrated, in a ghetto.

But at some time in history there was a man, drunk perhaps, at any rate less than averagely gifted, a clinging, soft man, a sobber, who opened his door to his dog, which did not need asking twice!—opened his door and took it in.

The term "domestic animal" is widely used, but is a cow a domestic animal? Not a bit of it, it is a byre-animal. The horse is a stable-animal. No one—no one!—has ever walked into a house and found a horse stretched out on the sofa or a cow curled up in an arm-chair.

But one has often found a dog like that.

A man called Spengler wrote a learned, very gloomy book *Untergang des Abendlandes*, strangely enough without mentioning the word dog once. The Occident, the West, the civilization of the conscious that began in ancient Hellas, under Pericles,—if the West is faced with downfall, is it not because the fate of thought, of human *thought*, was sealed the moment the dog was made a domestic animal?

In fact, an animal-companion!

The essence of all higher civilizations in history has been the free, unconstrained, playful, gay, undisturbed exchange of well-fashioned thoughts between enlightened, adult men. It has not been an assembly of soldiers deciding on the building of new warships and the imposition of taxes; not merchants gathering together to agree on joint warehousing of corn or to plan circumvention of tolls; not priests assembled in convention to pass an increase in tithes or issue a fresh manifesto about the sanctity of marriage—culture has no practical aim (which makes it the most practical of all); culture is not cathedrals, not stock exchanges; the sinews of culture are the improvised and seemingly aimless association of free and adult men.

One has eaten, one has listened to the flute players, one has drunk with one's meal (and afterwards some will drink more; one or two even too much); talk can begin,

142

but it does not need to; there is repose and quiet, a charged quiet; one is at a banquet for adult men; at a feast; at a symposium; one is associating.

The definition of a social, gregarious animal is an animal that makes association impossible.

At that immortal banquet in Agathon's house, when the flute players had been dismissed and Socrates, pressed by Alcibiades and Aristophanes, had stroked his beard before saying his immortal words about love (what else is interesting?—what else is serious?—what other subject befits adult men?)—when Socrates took a mouthful of wine from his beaker and opened his mouth to speak, was there a *dog* in the room?

It has been said that the Northern peoples—the Teutons, the Anglo-Saxons, the Scandinavians—have never produced a Socrates.

Well?

One evening you are in a philosophic mood; you are feeling sociable; you have even put on good clothes and a freshly ironed shirt, you have shaved, you are in a festive mood, you have a bottle of wine tucked under your left arm and in your right-hand pocket are your notes for an essay on falling in love;—not on love; it has struck you that for all these centuries humanity may have been on the wrong track; for what is love as defined by its consequence?—is it not a colourless, protracted state?—characterized by endurance, duty, frugality, courtesy, monotony, forced smiles, repetition, double-bed?—eternally the same courteous double-bed as on earth so in heaven?—no, you have been thinking about falling in love, profound thoughts, beautiful thoughts; *falling in love* seems to you to be a new philosophic principle; an unprecedented and dangerous principle; the superman?—is not the superman just the man who has fallen in love? No one seems to have dealt with falling in love before; did Socrates speak about falling in love? is it described in Plato's Republic? Did Jesus ever say that the kingdom of God was falling in love? You want to seek the company of others with your new vision; in your quivering heart a new world is dawning; so you have gone in search of a friend.

You are fantastically lucky: your friend's sitting-room is unoccupied: it is not full of his wife and her friends; his children are not in there, nor their playmates; the room is free. . . . From the door you walk towards the arm-chair, you smile to your friend, joyfully and gratefully you note that no one is hammering or carpentering in the adjacent room; no one is playing scales on the piano, the telephone is not ringing, the radio isn't switched on; there is no football match, no weather report, no evening news. This isn't luck, you whisper to yourself, this is an act of grace. There is such quiet and restfulness that you raise your face to heaven in thanks, you believe you are saved, you sit down in the arm-chair; you are holding the bottle of wine in your left hand; you open your mouth in order to share your thoughts about falling-in-love with your friend.

And?

From the floor in front of the stove comes a deep, rumbling growl. A creature the size of a calf, but it is not a calf, heaves itself up, cross and half asleep, and, with bared teeth, staggers across the floor and places its nose against your left ankle. But there is sock there and the animal requires bare flesh; it bores its nose in to where your sock ends and trouser leg begins. You are speechless; you could not get a word out to save your life. You keep quite still, sit there motionless, as though frozen rigid; the slightest movement and you know that you will have lost your left calf for ever.

"He won't bite," you hear your friend say, and his voice is tender.

Ardently, with your whole heart you wish you could believe your friend; you glance down cautiously; a ridge of dark hackle stands quivering, like an adder, along the brute's back.

The brute, disappointed by your ankle, now lifts up a paw weighing a hundredweight and lays it on your thigh; its claws scratch the material of your newly pressed summer trousers.

"He's so playful," your friend says tenderly.

The brute curls its paw round your thigh and seems to talk. The dog speaks and it says:

"I am nice, you man, aren't I."

It's not a question, it's a statement; you can't speak.

The animal curves its paw tighter round your thigh and says:

"I am frolicsome, man, aren't I?"

You cannot speak.

The brute now puts both its fore-paws on you; it feels as if your thigh will break.

"You have something nice for me, man, haven't you."

You cannot speak.

You can smell its animal smell, you think of fleas, bacilli, distemper, haemorrhoids, tape-worms. It rises up to its full height and lies across you. It says:

"You, man, what have you got in that bottle?"

You sit there in the chair, the bottle raised aloft as though you were drowning; your only hope is to let it smell the bottle—and don't let your hand shake; disappointed, the beast drops down, but the next moment it has clasped your knee between its front paws; perhaps your knee will serve as a source of pleasure, perhaps your knee can serve as a bitch.

It arches its back over your knee and says:

"You do like me, man, don't you?"

You close your eyes.

When you open them again, the beast has turned its

145

head so that its cheek is lying against your knee. It has got your knee in its mouth, your kneecap between its jaws. It is a large dog. If it is not a sheepdog, it is a Great Dane; if it is not an Alsatian, it is a St. Bernard; for all you know it may have its virtues: one of its ancestors may have found a robber in the forest, or a child in the snow; you do not know. All you know is that its teeth are huge, sharp, yellow at the base, with bits of dried fish in between them; the brute's lips hang like thick, pleated flaps of membrane ranging in colour from muddy brown to corpse pink. Out of the corner of its mouth flows a pool of foam and slobber that spreads across the thigh of your light coloured summer trousers.

"Pat him," your friend says.

Something in your expression must have told him that you cannot; wondering and uncomprehending he gets up and comes across to invite the animal to leave you; it won't; politely, tenderly and exerting all his strength, he manages to lift the brute off you and away; apologetically he takes the brute by its chain collar and drags it across the floor; at the door he whispers something into its ear; it does not understand; he opens the door with his foot; now begins a struggle that is a cross between all-in wrestling and a gladiatorial contest; he manages to get the brute out, puts his shoulder to the door and succeeds in shutting it. He stands by it, panting; somewhat distracted, he says to you.

"You were saying?"

Germania, Angelsaxia, the North has never produced a Socrates.

Well?

Despite the mortal fear that is still chilling you through and through, you could yet have a chance, for the room is now empty; you have the chance to collect your thoughts and immortalize yourself. But, in order to be a Socrates, old or new, it is not enough that you are Socrates; a Socrates in isolation is pointless; to be a Socrates you must have someone listening to you. And that is just what your friend is not doing. His face is anxious, unhappy, tormented, as if he had just let a friend down; indeed, as if he had betrayed man's best friend; his ears strain towards the hall, from which you can hear little wails, whines and soft barks coming; then man's best friend begins scratching on the door.

You wanted to talk about a new vision.

You wanted to talk about falling in love.

"Poor fellow," says your friend, "he's all alone."

Remorse and self-reproach came into the world along with the dog. And where there is bad conscience, culture cannot be. In that house there was a choice. A choice between dog and Atlantis. The new Socrates got quickly to his feet. He should never have been born in the North. Out on the street he tore his essay on falling in love into tiny pieces and strewed them on the wind; he opened the bottle of wine and drained it there on the pavement, by himself.

When people from the North journey to France, they do so in order to gain respite from dogs. They are not aware of this themselves. Nor had the student realized it before. He had left home in order to meet other people, to win insight and to train for his private duel; be that as it may, he stopped for a moment, surprised, when in Paris he encountered an atmosphere of cat and contours that were feline.

The initial impression perhaps came from his seeing a real cat, a black cat. It was lying on the sill of a concierge's window basking in the sun. It glanced at him with half an eye, then shut its eye again.

The sight surprised and moved him. After all he was

entering a great city: a foreigner expects to see strange overpowering things: circuses, balloons ascending, gigantic orchids, processions of Bayards, military parades, camels, elephants; but what he saw was a cat, a perfectly ordinary cat. A domestic puss. A granny's cat. . . .

But it was not the actual cat that set him thinking, and let no one think that Paris is a city that consists solely of cats, that swarms with cats, a city whose streets seethe with cats, where cats throng the trees as tightly as thrushes, and new-born mewing kittens rain into your hair—it's nothing like that.

Paris is intellectual; it is not dominated by the cat as such; but there the feline principle is the accepted one; Paris, you are aware, has used the *formula of the cat.*

The cat is a sagacious creature with a dry nose; like a stone, it is utterly and entirely in repose. The cat is enough unto itself; is there greater wisdom than that? Had the cat required more wisdom than it has, it would have jumped (which it doesn't)—it would have jumped lightly up into Socrates' lap; and—this is of historical importance— if he had had a cat on his lap it is not at all certain that Socrates would have been side-tracked. On the contrary, if he had had to pause to search for a phrase, the touch on his fingers of black, soft, electric, clean fur might have provided just the subtle word he sought, the exact word.

As a cat itself has insight into what is correct, so it can inspire the exquisite.

The cat is an unfathomable being, come in prehistoric times out of the waters, from the deep. It was not hunted or belched up; it swam up of its own accord and took up residence on land, as if it found it easier from there to see through life and plumb its secrets. If it had not come to us of its own free will, how could it be so placid, so assured, so utterly satisfied with the earth? The cat is the only creature that, as we know, hums over life; it purrs. Far back and deep down, the cat is related to the shark and the electric ray; it is a second cousin of the black lobster, first cousin of the dolphin, and sister of the silvery salmon. If it did not come out of the deep sea and had relations there, why does one so often come across cats sitting on jetties, or on a stone beside a stream, thoughtfully gazing down into the water? Even indoors, a cat will take up position on the kitchen table and from there with the deepest interest watch the swirls made in the water of the wash-ing-up bowl by the housewife's mop; sometimes it can be induced cautiously to lower a paw towards the surface of the water to try and snatch a swirl; you will hear then that French is the language of the cat, for it will say ah! It is cautious about its pleasures, never goes too far, it pulls its paw away and does not repeat the experiment; it has learned its lesson; it shakes a drop of water off its paw, flicks it off, then it just sits and looks; it is content to look; it is wise.

And the dog talks to itself, it talks and says:

"Why does the cat never make a boob," asks the dog. "Why does it never fall into a mud-puddle and then run indoors and onto the carpet as we others do. Why does it never knock glasses or flower pots over? It always steps in the right place. Why does it never upset a vase of flowers and smash it, which is such a pleasure."

"Why is it so prim when it has to go?" the dog asks darkly. "Why does it dig those elegant little holes; why does it cover it up so neatly afterwards. It buries. I dig up. And that is such a pleasure. Daffodils, tulips, bulbs. Why doesn't it deposit its turds on the road, openly, in the middle of the pavement; that's what we've been taught; and while we are about it people stand holding our leads and watch us admiringly. Why doesn't it want to be admired by people?

"Why has the cat such good manners when it eats,"

growls the dog. "Why doesn't it gobble its food, like the rest of us. It takes its time; it actually relishes it. It plays with mice. Is it good manners to play with your food? It thinks it witty, I suppose. Afterwards it wipes its mouth."

"Why does it not pay any attention to me," growls the dog. "People say that dog and cat are enemies. That is not true. It is not my enemy; it is only that I am its enemy. Why doesn't it hate, like the rest of us, which is such a pleasure."

"Why is the cat so superior, so exalted," growls the dog, feeling a taste for blood mounting. "Why doesn't it mix like the rest of us. Why does it keep itself to itself. All should be equal. When I see a cat, I feel as if I were sinking and falling. What did the aristocrat, André Chénier, say. In the tumbril on his way to the scaffold, he pointed to his head and called to the crowd: 'J'avais pourtant quelque chose là!' He had something there. But what. It's enough to drive one mad. I've got a taste for blood. I'll attack. If only I can get it from the side, I'll be able to break its back. It's worse from in front. It's quick then, quick as— oh, this everlasting *thought*; before I know what's happening it has stuck a paw out and got out one of my eyes. Plucked it out. If it even ate it, like the rest of us would. But it just wipes it off on the grass. Would not even have my eye. I can't stand it. I'm going to attack. I must."

"Why do I never manage to get at it from the side," groans the dog. "Always just from behind. And why can it climb, when I can't. Why won't it fight on the ground, like the rest of us. Up in a tree; it isn't fair. Having just escaped death it sits up there on a branch and licks its chest. What does it mean by that? It's devastating. I'm going to bark it down. Perseverance, that's the thing. I'll bark it down. Of course, it's sitting, while I have to stand on my hind legs. That can be a strain. It's sitting, as if it had chosen the better part."

THE STUDENT had been sitting on his motorcycle at a crossing, while the other stream of traffic was being directed by a policeman with a passionate whistle and white baton—he had been dreaming of a noble existence, high above the baying of the world.

He had been half-thinking of approaching the Lord Mayor of Paris, or to the President of the Republic. There was a ship in the city's coat of arms, was there not? But what connection was there between Paris and shipping? None. It was an age-old misconception. Now, however, he had discovered the real symbol of the city's soul, the secret formula of Paris. They would perhaps offer him a million or two for the idea, but he would not accept it; it would be a real pleasure, an honour—of course, if they liked to bestow some trifling token of appreciation: make him a count or a member of the Academy, or perhaps give him some old chateau that was standing empty and not being used.

The policeman had begun behaving most peculiarly. He had his whistle between his teeth and was blowing piercing, apoplectic, furious blasts, and was pointing his baton in the direction of the student; the policeman in fact was leaping up and down. The student woke and looked hurriedly round: behind him was a queue of thirty cars. All their drivers were leaning out of their driving seats and they too were pointing: thirty drivers were shaking their fists and shouting at the same time as blowing their horns. Who in all the world could be holding up the traffic, the student wondered. What clot . . .

He started, he gave a wan smile and rode on quickly, but not quickly enough. They all leaned out of their seats as they drove past him, leaned half out of their windows and shook their fists at him and blasted him with their horns and shouted. They have a word in Paris. It is the city's

151

welcome. It's a three-syllable word. Thirty drivers hung out of their windows and shouted it at him.

He had planned to reach Paris at five o'clock. But he had not stopped to think what it would mean.

After a quarter of an hour's riding towards the centre—he sincerely hoped it was towards the centre—he felt like a Theseus who in the labyrinth suddenly discovers that he has lost Ariadne's ball of thread. He had a map, it was true, an enormous map about a yard square; and it is true too that all streets in Paris have name-plates, excellent name-plates, white letters on a dark blue ground, placed on each corner building, up on the flat, light cornice that everywhere acts as the division between first and second storey; these name-plates are readily visible, the letters on them unusually distinct; Paris is probably the best signed city in the world—but what help was that to him?

As he rode along, he dared not shift his gaze to look up at the cornices; that would have meant instant death. And when he came to a crossroad and had a bit of a breathing space, the moment he had spread out his map and was trying with a finger damp with perspiration to discover where he was, at that very moment the policeman blew his whistle and swung his white baton—he did not even have time to fold up his map, but had to start up and ride on with the map in his teeth like a pirate.

You drive on the right in France. Consequently, a new-comer expects that if a car overtakes him from behind, it will pass him on his left. The student was so frightened he got hiccoughs the first time a taxi drove up like a shadow and passed him on his *right*. ... The traffic in Paris is a kind of slalom on the flat, without posts or rules; you take any space that is vacant and you take it swiftly; the rest is up to God. In his twining, twisting progress he expected any moment to hear a terrible crash: when would it come?

*

There were bicycles, motorcycles, private cars, taxis, the latter more often than not six abreast. He had also begun to see lorries—and what lorries! They were enclosed transporter-wagons with huge superstructures; later he learned that they were called camions. They are about forty-five feet long and sixteen feet high; they are as heavy as locomotives and as tall as houses; they carry enormous loads from the Mediterranean to the English Channel; they transport furniture, tomatoes, obelisques, electrical power stations, bombers; they weigh two hundred tons and drive along at over fifty miles an hour even in Paris; there's nothing in the world can stop them except a policeman. One result of this was that the student acquired a new, hitherto unknown interest in the traffic police; the police became his one hope of continued existence; he developed an eagle eye for policemen, for the black, chubby uniform cap with white edging, the white bandolier and white baton; he could see a policeman half a mile away and made straight for him; there lay salvation, there were mother's skirts, a rock in the sea; at crossings where there was a pleasant looking policeman, he would ride as close up to the man's little platform as he could and snatch a mouthful or two of air; as long as he kept close to a policeman nothing ghastly could happen.

At one crossing where the policeman looked bad-tempered, he had to sit on his cycle and wait at the pedestrian crossing. Something made him turn his head to the left. He was looking straight into the hub of the front wheel of a camion. He had to crane his head right back to see the top of it. The next moment he was aware of something on his right. A new wall had come up alongside him, another camion.

The sun was no longer shining; he was in a narrow gorge of darkness, a deep shaft, a catacomb. And while he sat there, in the dark, with hammering heart, he suddenly realized that if, when the policeman blew his whistle and they all moved on, the two enormous trucks and he in between on his tiny motorcycle—if the mountain on his

153

left moved in a couple of inches and the mountain on his right turned in a couple of inches, for perhaps they had not seen him from their windows up there, perhaps they thought there was an empty space between them, perhaps they did not know of his existence!—if they did that, he would be squeezed to death, crushed to a mush of metal and blood; his death would be so constricted there would not even be room for a shriek; his mortal remains would be smeared over the paint on the sides of the two huge trucks and the next day he would have vanished without trace down the drains of their respective garages; one smear washed off in Le Havre, the other in Bordeaux; a death so dreadful and incomprehensible that not even the theory of relativity included it.

"If I could manage to be first off the mark," he thought, "I'd have a chance."

He held his elbows out as if to force the two mountains apart; the sinews in his neck were taut as back-stays, the policeman blew his whistle; the carriageway quivered beneath the thundering camions; he *heaved* himself forward.

But that was his undoing.

Once at the head of the queue he had to stay there or be crushed. He was hounded through Paris like a haunted beast, whipped, whistled at, shouted at, blared at; he had the pack at his heels, a great baying barking wall behind him, he could smell the gaping jaws of predators, a tidal wave caught him up and bore him along, prodded him through the whole of Paris. Later, he thought he must have criss-crossed the city from north to south and from east to west, to have been hunted from Place de la Bastille to Place de l'Etoile, from Place de la Concorde to Place de la Republique and back again. Somewhere he glimpsed the name Garibaldi and almost swooned, thinking he had got as far as Italy!

Somewhere else he came to a vast roundabout.

It seems simple enough when you steer into a roundabout; you just have to drive round half of it and then dive into the street that is the continuation of the one you have left. But twelve streets radiated from this Place and suddenly all streets seemed alike and how do you know when you have gone half a circle? Before, he had been able to stop for a few seconds at every crossing and get his breath and look up at the name-plates; it was never the right one he saw; he was going to a street called Rue de Vau something or other, but at least there had been name-plates. This enormous roundabout was surrounded by a belt of tall trees and street name-plates are not hung on trees—and anyway he could not stop. He had escaped the tidal wave only to land in the maelstrom. The concentric traffic was an uninterrupted, seething mass, churning round and round and round. Years later he saw a picture postcard of Place de l'Etoile and the Arc de Triomphe and it reminded him of the structure that for a full half hour in 1939 he had been forced to keep on his left as he desperately looked for an opening on his right into which he could escape! Everything was going round in front of his eyes; the world seemed to be a turning, glowing merry-go-round; his only concern was to keep upright, not get under the wheels of any of the other vehicles, fourteen abreast, rushing along at forty miles an hour; never again, he told himself, never again shall I ride a motorcycle in Paris; never again shall I come to Paris before I am rich enough to take taxis; never again . . .

It may have been centrifugal force that saved him, that finally drew him out of the depths and spewed him out on land.

Ten minutes after that he was in a quieter neighbourhood and felt that he dare pull up alongside the pavement. He just sat, stupefied; for a while he could not even raise his head.

In front of him, on a corner of the pavement, was a round transformer-housing plastered with gay posters.

He saw the word BYRRH. He had seen it before, but did not know what it meant.

He looked up at the name-plate on the corner building; his eyes dead. Already he had seen a thousand such and he no longer cared; he looked round for a man, a kind Parisian, who might perhaps help him to find his way. The street was almost empty. He pulled the map from under his belt, where he had had to tuck it, but stopped: On the name-plate was: Rue de Vaugirard. A queer open-mouthed feeling came over him. He dug into his pocket for the envelope on which the man had written his address. He unfolded the envelope. There it was: Rue de Vaugirard.

He looked with pounding heart at the number of the house. it was No. 350.

He looked at the envelope.

There was No. 344.

He began to shiver.

If I just turn slightly, he thought, if I just turn my head at right angles to the right, I will see that I am sitting right outside, exactly outside the house I want.

For a moment he was seized with a fear (or, oddly enough a hope?) that the house might have been pulled down; that there had been an explosion after that letter had been posted; that there was no No. 344 left, only an enormous crater with a pool of water at the bottom and netting fencing it off in front. When you know that you have stopped outside No. 344 your mouth goes dry and you have to swallow; you feel that you want to turn back or accelerate hard and drive past.

For when you have arrived, when you have switched off and pulled the motorcycle up on to the pavement; when you are sitting in the saddle getting your breath after such a ride; when your body is still quivering with the effort and your forehead sticky with sunlight and sweat and you run your fingers through your hair; when you are there and slowly turn to face the house which of course is there, undamaged; when you see the house that, though you have not thought of it as such, has been your goal through the

156

whole of Europe; the house it has taken you a week and two thousand kilometres to reach—a sudden stillness descends upon you; you are in a cloche of stillness.

Perhaps the people who do things, complete long, dangerous expeditions, cross Greenland on skis or penetrate the jungle of New Guinea, feel something of the same kind. They must have felt this stillness, when they reached the sea. They must have had a feeling of weakness, of emptiness, a taste of ashes in their mouths; and perhaps the same thing happens with the artist when he has finished something that has needed a long period of concentrated work; behind them lies a mountain landscape they have conquered and created; now they are there, they have arrived. The will that kept them going no longer has a goal to focus on. Do they stand there on the beach, in the stillness, and ask themselves: for what?

Yet those men at least have the secret knowledge that they have conquered, done something. In their heart of hearts they feel that. They may fall exhausted to their knees, sink to the ground, vomit, gasp, lie without being able to move—nonetheless in the very heart of their consciousness they know that they have moved a frontier and created something, where before there was nothing.

How different, utterly different, when you are young, a casual traveller, a student. . . .

In the stillness, the bitter, helpless stillness of youth, you realize at that moment that you are a fraud; worse: a fool; worst of all: a pitiable, ridiculous person.

There you stand on the pavement looking at a four-storeyed grey building, an office building.

Firm's name-plates: vehicle entrance; you glimpse an open yard inside.

A grey brick building. It reminds you of, is almost identical with, is in fact like any brick building in Bergen.

You have come two thousand kilometres, exposed yourself to mortal peril, imprisonment and perdition, been pursued by the Gestapo and hunted by camions as huge as prehistoric monsters.

Instead of all that, you could just as well have stayed in Bergen, in your digs; you could have donned your hat and gone out, just crossed the street and attained what you have attained here: seen what a brick building looks like when it is grey.

Then you could have turned and gone back to your room and studied economics. You could have spent the summer doing that. You would then have had the satisfaction of having done something useful, laid the foundation for a good pass the following year, worked wisely and sensibly and intelligently for your future.

You could have walked across the street in Bergen to a grey brick building and back to your digs and it would not have cost you an øre. While, here in Paris, what has it not cost you to be standing here staring at this brick building... Rue de Vaugirard, is that any better than Vetterlidsalmenningen? You have spent a fortune, 200, 300, 400 crowns, you are ruined. You have defrauded your wife and child; but forget about that; the really bitter thing is that you have defrauded your love. It was not Paris you wanted to go to, but to Her; and you did not require a motorcycle to get to her house; you would certainly not have needed to spurt up her stairs and smash her door; you could have gone on foot; it would have taken you three minutes; you could perfectly well have rung her bell, without a motorcycle. You are here in Paris, standing in front of a grey brick building because you are a fool, ridiculous and craven; because you did not dare go on foot to a young woman in Bergen and say, well, what novels make people say.

And what have you come to just *this* house for?

Why were you so weak as to write to your father and ask him for the name and address of one of his old schoolmates, a relative who had a business in Paris? And why did you then write to this man and ask him to get you a cheap room in an hotel for a week and otherwise help you in Paris? Why? Why couldn't you have managed on your own?

You could have gone straight to a youth hostel in Paris and been your own master. It was so hot you could even have spent the night on a bench in a park, been a grand seigneur beneath the stars of France! You would have landed right in the midst of the most exotic company, you would at once have been conversing wittily in French —with Sacha Guitry, and Michèle Morgan (who is a bit like Her... or the other way round), and Léon Blum, and Joséphine Baker (who also is nice, terribly nice)—on that park bench you could have owned all France and been your own Roi Soleil!

Instead, you have to go in here, into a grey business building and say how-do-you-do to a business man—not to go in and see him would be impolite, it would offend your father and his family—you have to go in and say how-do-you-do to a Norwegian. A Sunnmøring! The man might even talk New-Norwegian.

THE TALE OF THE DRAUGS

or

Longe fugit quisquis suos fugit.

Y OU HAVE to fly far to escape your own people. That is
a hard truth. But if it was hard for an ancient Roman,
it is *doubly* hard for a young Norwegian. . . .

The student was born and brought up in Trondhjem.
Trondhjem was the first and oldest capital of Norway. It
is so no longer; but it is still the geographical centre of the
country, the intersection between north and south, west and
east, the heart of Norway.

His mother, who was a Trondhjemmer, and thoroughly
urban, ate with her fork; his father who came from Sunnmøre and was a "foreigner", ate with his knife.

That is not to say that his father handled his knife in-
elegantly; on the contrary, he used his knife with the same
style and precision as he did a morticing chisel at his
workbench. First, a piece of cod on the knife, then the
knife into his mouth; then a piece of carrot on the knife,
and the knife into his mouth; then a piece of potato onto
his knife, and the knife into his mouth. He never, ever
dropped a bit onto his plate. And when he had finished,
he used his knife to scrape the plate, his son would watch
his knife bend, elegantly, noiselessly, to follow the china
bottom; the plate was always as clean as a whistle. When
the man noticed that his son was watching him, he would
say: "You must always eat up properly." Finally, last of
all, his father licked his knife; he never ever cut his tongue.

It may well be a matter of indifference how you convey
food to your mouth. Some people use a spoon, others their
fingers; there are supposed to be whole nations who use
chopsticks. But it mattered to his mother.

"Please," she would say to her husband across the dinner-table, "please, when the children can see you . . ."

A wry little smile might then appear on his father's face, a hard smile, or a smile of melancholy. He would not say anything, just went on eating with his knife; year out, year in; stubborn, imperturbable.

(Secretly, the boy sided with his mother; he thought his father might have eaten like other people. But at times he sensed that his mother ate with a fork in order to make their father look small in his children's eyes, and then he sided with his father.)

Those two gods. . . .

Such warfare at the dinner table left you with a feud in your mind, a feud between your right hand and your left. After such a childhood you preferred to keep you hands in your trousers pockets, deep, out of sight, each by itself; it could be many years before you dared to take them out and use them, freely, unconstrainedly, purposefully. . . .

There was once a philatelist in America who found himself with a number of Norwegian stamps. Suddenly, his attention was attracted to one of them. He had seen something that wasn't right. Being an experienced collector he knew that in Norwegian Norway was Norge. This must be a printer's error! He picked the stamp up in his tweezers and held it under the light; there was no doubt: the two final letters had been transposed making Noreg! He put down the tweezers and his magnifying glass and got to his feet, trembling, convinced that he had made a real philatelist's coup.

Alas—the poor philatelist did not make his fortune.

It was not a printer's error.

Foreigners find it difficult to understand, and Norwegians do not understand it themselves, but it is a fact, an incontrovertible fact, that Norway has two official written languages, Standard or King's Norwegian and New Norwegian. In King's Norwegian the country is Norge, in New Norwegian it is Noreg.

All Norwegians understand each other's dialects perfectly well. There is no greater difference between the two languages than between English and Scottish. There is no greater difference between hjem and heim, than between home and hame, and they all mean the same. But has anyone ever heard of Scottish being made a language for the whole country on an equal footing with English, and that it should be especially meritorious and especially British to write Scottish? which was now being called New English. Or that there should be something suspect, imported, foreign, even Continental about a word like church—for which the only good, old genuinely English word was of course kirk?

One has never read of that in Britain's history; never.

But that is exactly what one reads in the history of Norway.

Norway has two enemies.

Sweden is one—although in 1905 enmity with Sweden was declared at an end. Norway had become an independent state of its own. To show that the two countries were separate a strip 100 feet wide was cut through the forest along the entire frontier between them. This road through the forest which is 100 feet wide, is also 534,000 feet long; and it is to be kept open for ever.

Love thy neighbour, but leave the fence standing.

The country's relations with Sweden after that were polite, correct, even downright friendly.

Fortunately—for what would we be without our enemies? —If we did not have one would we not feel a trifle denuded?—fortunately, there on the west coast of Norway, on the outside of the chain of tall mountains called Lang-fjellene, there lies a small peculiar district containing one-sixtieth of the population of Norway.

Sunnmøre.

At all times the people of Sunnmøre have had a strange ability to induce terror and bad conscience in the Norwegians. They are one of the smallest tribes in the country, yet they have been able to keep the rest of the population in a state of perpetual terror.

Sunnmøre lies right out by the sea, alone, poor, isolated. Once it may have been a centre, but, if so, that must have been in the days when all traffic and transport went by sea.

A short distance from Aalesund, capital of Sunnmøre, is a place called Giske, which is said to have been a seat of sea kings in the days of the Vikings. This is not unlikely, for if you held Giske, you were well placed, indeed. All Norwegian traffic, you could almost say the whole world's traffic, passed there, right in front of your boat-house door. If a ship came from the south, the sea king rowed out and nabbed it. If a ship came from the north, out he rowed again. If he did not always nab the ship, at least he pocketed a good ransom. Dues you could call it, too. Or toll.

But then came Christianity, and the Black Death, and the Middle Ages, and Danish dominion and the ban on piracy. World traffic found itself other routes, not least into the Baltic; and there, by the strategic Øresund lay Copenhagen, which became exceedingly prosperous by pocketing exactly the same sort of compensation as Giske used to exact. If there is an express antagonism between Denmark and Sunnmøre, expressed by the people of Sunnmøre, there is a very definite reason for it.

Then came the modern era with its roads and railways, but that all passed Sunnmøre by. . . .

It may be dreadful to be seen through, but it is worse to be overlooked. . . .

There are two parts to Sunnmøre.

The inner part, on the mainland, consists of fjords, valleys, mountain walls, glaciers.

The outer part is a string of bare, windswept islands little suited to human habitation and, indeed, a surprising number of them bear animal names: Goose Island, Hare Island, Ox Island, Pig Island. . . . They are almost treeless with just a few stems of wild honeysuckle creeping close to the cracks in the rocks, and an occasional currant bush hiding behind a stone wall. The people who had to live on these outer islands must have needed a peculiar obstinacy and tenacity in order not to be swept into the sea, when the winds were raging.

When the student's father cut his nails, as he did regularly once a week, he did not use scissors, they were no good to him. He cut his nails over a piece of newspaper with a freshly-sharpened sheath knife. He cut with precision, like a surgeon, and a little heap of slender, horn coloured half-moons formed on the newspaper, sending a shiver down his son's back.

The people of Sunnmøre are divided into two tribes: the outer-tribe and the inner-tribe.

The outer-tribe lives on the islands, is light-complexioned, often depicted wearing red tasselled caps, and supports life energetically by fishing. The look in these people's eyes can be gay and open, possibly because they have never read a book. If you show such an object to one of the outer-tribe, he will purse his lips and whistle. Then he will dart like a squirrel up the rigging of his boat: he has something he wants to show *you*. There, in the crow's nest, he takes up fiddle and bow and plays a roundel for you. All the outer-tribe are born musicians. If someone does not have a fiddle, he will have an accordion. And if he does not have an accordion, he will sit up in his crow's nest thirty feet above deck swaying gently with the boat from side to side. He looks innocent, but you know what he's doing: he is sitting up there counting his money.

The inner-tribe is more dour, shyer. They live in the valleys leading down to the fjords, beneath the glaciers, in the shadow of the tall mountains. Some of them have black hair and look like gypsies; others have red hair and freckles and look like murderers. (There is too a strange legend according to which the people of the inner-tribe have daughters of dazzling beauty, whom they hide in caves in the ground, girls so lovely that a man may be enchanted by them and lose his soul . . .) No one knows what the people of the inner-tribe live by. Fiddle and accordion are forbidden them. But travellers have heard the sound of a domestic organ. They sing behind locked doors—cold, quavering cries; they might be singing a funeral hymn over the body of New Norway.

There is one thing the people of the inner-tribe know: they know what a *book* is. Put a book into the hands of one of the inner-tribe and he will weigh it, smell the cover. You will see a glint deep in one bloodshot eye, and he will ask:

"Is it in *Danish*?"

If you were a Norwegian—and had lived through the poverty and darkness of the Middle Ages, through the Black Death and the Danish dominion—till the 19th century came and at last you glimpsed the light, the light and a new life, where would you hunger to go? To the towns, wouldn't you? Abroad, wouldn't you? Out into the wide world, wouldn't you?

When, in the 19th century, Norway was gathering her strength to take the step into a new era, Sunnmøre was gathering its dark powers in order to hang on to the old. The people there dropped the grapnel, took firm hold of the seaweed on the bottom; would not budge.

Shyness could be the explanation, nakedness, poverty.

While the climate in the eastern part of the country is so dry that two Viking ships have been dug up, almost whole and undamaged, a thousand years old, and yet made of wood, with the loveliest dragon's heads and carvings—that of Sunnmøre is raw and damp. If ever there have been antiquities and works of art there, they have mouldered and rotted. From the entire Viking age there is not one boat in Sunnmøre, not an oar, not a high-seat post, not a cart, not a chest, not a spinning wheel, not so much as a stool.

Sunnmøre, right out by the sea, is now treeless, whether this is due to some change of climate or to the trees having all been cut down. There used to be woods there, even on the outer islands, as the inhabitants can see when they cut peat for fuel. Right out on a moor they can come across a tree root. But—and here one must admit the people of Sunnmøre are right—it is not easy to cut much of a figure before the world with an old fir root under your arm.

Take Trondjhem, take Bergen. In the early Middle Ages these two towns were in turn the capital of Norway and they still bear that stamp.

Not only have Trondhjem and Bergen railways, symphony orchestras, trains, libraries, theatres, cinemas, bookshops, dance-restaurants, skating rinks, museums and stuffed animals, colleges with professors and brass bands that play in the streets—both towns reek of ancient history and rattle with picturesque past: they have paved streets, ruins, castles, bishop's palaces, royal palaces, fortresses, Trondhjem even has the most famous canonized king in the North, at least, his coffin, at least the cathedral in which his coffin used to be.

Sunnmøre has nothing.

When you are asked where you were born and you say Trondhjem, you can to a certain degree—not too far, but to a certain degree—lean back and feel that you have Kristiansten fortress behind you. You have had a free christening present. The same thing goes for Bergen. As a Bergener you can to a certain degree, but not too far, lean back and feel that you have Haakonshallen behind you.

If you say that you are from Sunnmøre and lean back you fall straight into the sea.

As a Sunnmøring you have nothing.

And yet . . .

When Alexander, the provincial, left Macedonia, and when Napoleon, the provincial, left Corsica, was either richer or better equipped with culture than a man of Sunnmøre?

Conquer . . .

How land in Norway?

How conquer Norway?

Once, when Henrik Ibsen applied for a state writer's grant, he wrote:

"I want to teach my people to be great in their thoughts."

Is not to conquer to offer a better milieu? a richer milieu?

The strange thing is that for all their benightedness and obduracy, their lack of intellectual outlook and constructive imagination, the people of Sunnmøre possess other qualities which a conqueror must also have. They are rugged, persevering, tough, they seem to have an innate immunity to weakness. Part of Napoleon's genius consisted in his ability to stand up to blazing desert sun or lashing snowstorm in the tundra and not be bothered by either— one day he was in Egypt, the next before the gates of Moscow. It is just like reading about a Sunnmøring.

Add to this their practical sense, their ability to use their hands. When motor-boats took the place of sailing-boats on the Norwegian coast, it was a Sunnmøring who was the first to buy one. He had never seen a motor before. He surveyed the mechanism for ten minutes, after which he

167

understood it. They are the quickest to learn of anyone in Norway. Give a Sunnmøring a grass-cutter, an alarm clock, a tram—and in five minutes he will be able to take it to pieces and put it together again correctly. And if anything breaks, he will not be like other Norwegians and sit waiting sedately for a couple of months while a spare part is got from abroad. The Sunnmøring never sits sedately. He will repair the thing on the spot, himself, with nails or wire. It will not perhaps be as good as new, but he will make it work.

Practical versatility, independence.

In his heart of hearts the Sunnmøring despises the world of mechanization and specialization of the factory; he despises the factory worker, the office worker, fixed rates, he despises the assembly line, he despises a working day that does not consist of more than eight hours; in a factory he would break all output rates; the Sunnmøring is the terror of the trade unions.

The land has never been a sufficient outlet for their enterprise; they have never been able to settle permanently on the land.

Thus, for centuries, the sea has been the field of their activities.

The sea is big.

The Sunnmørings must have lain in salt water for many centuries, pulling on ropes, pulling on lines, up to their waists in icy water—how have they managed to survive?

Gradually, they became the best in that element, always farthest out, always bringing home the largest catch.

Oh, other Norwegians are good fishermen too! Take those in the North. When it comes to occasional sport, or a rowing race over a short distance, the men of the north can even beat the Sunnmørings, but for that there have to be women to cheer them on. The Northerner will not even smile if there is not a woman to see him.

The Northerner is Norway's dreamer and fantast, the

one who cuts a dash. I wonder whether the Northerner is not in many ways the incarnation of the soul of Norway?

When a Sunnmøring comes home after a trip to the fishing grounds having earned 400 crowns, he puts 400 in the bank. When a Northerner comes home from a fishing trip having earned 400 crowns, he spends twenty on a silk scarf for his sweetheart and the rest on pastries. His private motto is: "One must have a little enjoyment in life..."

In the same way, when he goes out on a long trip, the Northerner fills his chest, the whole boat in fact, with delicacies, clotted cream, roast reindeer, cranberry jelly and there is almost no room in the hold for the fish he is going to catch.

"Fush," he says contemptuously; he has no intention of eating that.

But when the Sunnmøring sets sail on a long trip, he takes no provisions with him at all. He not only wants and is going to catch fish, he simply has to. This gives him an awe-inspiring strength. He stakes everything on the one card.

The Sunnmøring lives by what he can catch. If he gets pollock, he eats pollock; if he gets cod, he eats cod; if he gets haddock, he eats haddock.

If the trip lasts forty days, he will eat cod for forty days: boiled cod for breakfast, boiled cod for dinner, boiled cod for supper. And he will think fish the finest food there is.

"Feesh," he says reverently, clasping his hands.

In emergencies he will keep going by licking rain water off the deck.

They have a saying in Trøndelag which the student heard when he was a boy:

"You can nail a Sunnmøring to the byre-wall—and he'll live and grow fat!"

They have never penetrated inland into Norway. The Langfjellene became the Sunnmørings' wailing wall.

It is an odd thing, but the Sunnmøring's way of speaking

excites and provokes the Norwegians quite excessively. It is a singing chant, a drawl, and is spoken through the down-turned corners of the mouth; it has a hint of someone having been whipped, of fawning, whimpering, a note of wailing and aggrievedness, of toothache and fretfulness and poverty, as if Sunnmøre bore Norway's cross. As if they of all Norwegians have it worst. As if they have the Nor-wegian monopoly of suffering!

They are detestable, all the more so as they possess all the virtues. They have never produced or conceived any-thing great; they have never produced a writer, a statesman, a demagogue, a scientist, a composer, an explorer, an in-ventor, not even a skating champion; they have never pro-duced an admiral, nor a general, nor a captain, not even a private to fight the Swedes, indeed, not so much as a foot-baller for the team against Sweden—for one reason or another they have not discovered Sweden, perhaps because there is the whole of Norway between them and it; they insist that it is the *Danes* who are the enemy, though there has not been a Dane to be seen on Norwegian soil since 1814; the Sunnmørings are, historically, tilting at windmills; they are fighting backwards—this army of Nor-wegian Don Quixotes, has never performed any doughty deed, but they have all the virtues. They are frugal, thrifty, bold; they are honest, reliable, men of their word, god-fearing; they are great family people; they stick together like the Jews, like a flock of rooks; their whole lives are based on their parents; or, failing that, on their relations; they are Norway's dark klan. One has never heard of a Sunnmøring embezzling, drinking spirits, dancing with a girl, swearing, climbing a lamp-post or bathing naked from a beach.

They are unimpeachable.

They are the best hated people in Norway.

They have never penetrated inland into Norway . . .
A small flock of them roamed along the coast, from fish-

170

ing-station to fishing-station. Modest hawkers of gill-nets, buyers of bait, salesmen of motor-oil and ready-made suits, secretaries of co-operatives selling herrings and raw fish, preaching against alcohol and for the Kingdom of God. Have none penetrated into Norway? None. Apart from the odd one who may have started a fruit shop in a town (but he must not get on too well; must not prove too clever; if he did, the other shopkeepers in the street would be roused, their hackles would rise; it would be as if they felt the presence of some underground threat; apart from the odd one who became a musician; who thought that if one was not allowed to speak, one could at least blow a horn . . .

There are many descriptions of them in books. If an Englishman ever had such a relative, he would have referred to him with bated breath as the skeleton in the family's cupboard. Ibsen, in Peer Gynt, has called them Huhu. But the best description of the Sunnmørings and their nature is by an anonymous Northerner.

You will find it in a folk-tale called the *Goblins of Sandflesa*:

"When it came closer, he heard splashing and horrible howls and cold, quivering shrieks, and he smelled the foul smell of low water. Terrified, he ran up into the shanty, and there he saw the draugs come ashore. They were short and squat like cocks of hay, wore ugly leather clothes, leather skirts and sea boots, and big mufflers that hung nearly to the ground. In place of heads and hair they had tangles of seaweed. As they crawled up onto the beach, they left a light behind them as from burning birch bark, and when they shook themselves, sparks flew."

The student remembered how in his childhood in Trondhjem there could come a sudden ring at the street door, for some strange reason, always when his father was out.

Into the hall then stepped a heavy, great creature, like a man, in oilskins and sea boots, who said he was one of the family, come from fishing up at the Lofotens, and that he

171

brought greetings from home. His r's were like rolling stones, there was the sound of surf in his voice. The boy's heart would be in his mouth; he could not think of anything to do but to take the man into the sitting-room and settle him in an arm-chair: the man's wet sea boots would leave a dark trail across the floor.

Then he went to the kitchen. His mother who had seen it all, would be standing there white in the face, supporting herself against the dresser. "Oh God," she would whisper, "not another?"

*

Sunnmøre lies by itself, separate. It is a piece of Norway that has been divided off, or—if you like—a piece of Iceland that has been left behind. Often and often you will find an expression of bitterness and homelessness in a Sunnmøring's face, as if he were thinking: that time, a thousand years ago, when the *ancients* refused to pay taxes to the King of Norway and sailed off across the sea, and settled and founded a republic in Iceland, why didn't I go with them?

In Iceland I could have been president today.

No Sunnmøring has ever become president in Norway. A man from Bergen, Trondhjem, Odø, or anywhere else, but never a man from Sunnmøre.

In Norway I am a relic, a half-caste, a pariah, an object of ridicule, a by-word for my people. . . .

But, won't people say—this is dreadful? This is insupportable? One must do something for these poor people or whatever they are? Are there no warm hearts in Norway? Surely one must let them in? They can't be left outside for all eternity, in the cold and dark, like a Norwegian version of the Little Match Seller?

Quite right. And many good Norwegians have thought exactly that. Poor people, they have thought. But, they have thought too—for the Norwegians take a practical view of things—where shall we put them? We cannot put them into industry or trade, they'd sweep the board there; nor can we put them into research or diplomacy, they'd cause scandals there; but there's a thing called the school system; proletarian children have to have certain essential knowledge stuffed into them: a bit of arithmetic, a little Bible knowledge, a little grammar; *crambe repetita*, as the Romans said; and it is, indeed, an uninviting task to sit up on a dais year after year stuffing school children with everlastingly the same old dish; a marathon of a job; but the people of Sunnmøring seem to have a certain bent for it, as well as a certain interest for—what is it they call it?—their mother's tongue: there's a chap in Sunnmøre—what's he called now?—the chap with the mother's tongue and landsmaal complex?—Aasen, that's it, Ivar Aasen, he's supposed to have written a grammar for local dialects in the west, a dictionary presumably; strange chap, a sort of Sunnmøre Moses; he says Noreg instead of Norge, and glow-kite instead of rocket; it's true; ah well, those are local trifles; a Sunnmøring can at least wield a cane. Suppose we tried offering them jobs as elementary school teachers? Wonder if they would be content with jobs as schoolmasters?

The meek shall inherit the earth. . . .

The Sunnmørings did not need to be asked twice.

And suddenly (after all we know that a good deed never goes unpunished)—all at once, quietly without anyone noticing it, overnight, the Sunnmørings had captured Norway.

What Denmark never attempted and what Sweden would have failed to do, if she had tried, Sunnmøre achieved.

The people of Sunnmøre did not burst in. They did not stride across the Langfjellene; they did not even dig their way under; the nation had become porous and they just filtered in.

When the history of it comes to be written, their coup will be described as osmotic.

They began with the schoolrooms, went on to the masters' common-rooms; one after the other they subjugated all the primary schools in the country, all the normal schools, all the middle schools, all the high schools, all the colleges; they rose up from schoolmaster to housemaster; to headmaster; they rose from school-inspector to head of the department of education; they rose from Norge to Noreg. . . .

To conquer . . .

When Alexander, the provincial, came from Macedonia, did he require that the Greeks should discard Greek as the language of Hellas and introduce Macedonian?

When Napoleon, the provincial, came from Corsica, did he require that the French discard French as the language of France and introduce Corsican?

When Lenin, the provincial, came from Ulyansk, did he require that the Russians should discard Russian as the language of Russia and introduce Ulyanskian?

Alexander would have been impaled, Napoleon guillotined, Lenin liquidated by a firing squad—the world would never have heard their names.

The Sunnmøring is the strangest being the world has seen: *he is a conqueror in reverse.*

Far from teaching people to think great thoughts, far from lending wings to Norway, he has forced the Norwegians down into a confined, dark, damp, poor, milieu that lacks culture; he has forced Norway down into something that is the exact copy of a bow-net, where people waste their strength fighting a civil war over the spelling of words; a net at the bottom of which the Norwegians crawl about in the dark nipping each other like crabs.

The student was reading politics and economics; he was a socialist. And all at once, standing there on a street in Paris, one day in June 1939, he had a vision.

174

Of course, a Sunnmøring could never be made a member of the cabinet.

(The only way would be for the whole of Norway (Norge) to be re-named Noreg. ... In a country that called itself Noreg, who would be the obvious leader? An interesting thought; a daring thought, daring enough to make you giddy; has anyone ever thought it?)

Of course, a Sunnmøring could never be made a member of the cabinet.

But, on closer inspection, is the position of cabinet minister so greatly to be desired? Is not such a job really that of a visiting artiste, an opera job, a circus job—is not a cabinet minister just a gilded figure head? (I must tell that to my comrades in the Socialist Students Society when I get back. How often haven't we talked about capturing the power in society.... Why did nobody mention the draugs!) The one really secure point in the state, the point that matters, the shipowner's point, the point of the pen, the point of the ink, the point of the chalk, God's point, the organ's point, the fixed point, the unchanging, the point from which one can have one's hand on the entire people and keep it there for generations—is somewhere else.... It is in the Department of Ecclesiastical Affairs.

And conveniently, almost as if it were fortuitous in Norway this Department also includes the Department for Education. This Department controls not only every word spoken *from* the country's pulpits and radio, but also every word directed *at* the country's schoolchildren from primary school to university. The control is watertight; the dictatorship absolute. "Approved by the Department for Ecclesiastical Affairs and Education for instructional use." "Directed by the Department for Ecclesiastical Affairs and Education to be learned by heart, verses 1, 2, 4, 6, 7."

Governments come, governments go.

But heading the Department for Ecclesiastical Affairs in Norway, seated in its holy of holies, uninterruptedly for over a hundred years, there has been a draug.

175

What *is* a draug? A philologist perhaps would derive the word from draw, draw under.... In Norwegian mythology the draug is a spectre which gives warning of death; its special characteristic as shown in all pictures of it, is that it sails in *half a boat* ...

Has the draug felt expatriated all these hundreds of years? Is he now going to get his revenge by making the whole of Norway homeless? By gradually setting the ground quaking under the nation's feet? By slowly making the people feel insecure and homeless; slowly undermining their self-respect and sense of fellowship? Had not the self-confidence of the Norwegians already been so pulverized that some of them would even listen to Quisling's call for national consolidation? Norge, Noreg.

*

My dear fellow, people will say, can the transposition of just two letters, be so important? My *dear* fellow, can that really make me homeless?

That's just the question a Sunnmøring would ask; and he would smile innocently and benignly as he did so, with a hint of reproach in his voice. He can almost get you to feel ashamed of attaching such importance to two miserable letters, when you are so rich and have so many. You hesitate. And in that moment of confusion and shame and pity, in that half second of pity, he quietly moves his foot forward.

Anyway, perhaps, he's right. Norge, Noreg—that should not be anything to get wrought up about. The name of a country, how often is one confronted with that? A curiosity for philatelists....

Such a dual form should not make a Norwegian more

disrupted and insecure, than if an American as well as coming from U.S.A. was also a citizen of A.S.U.—Anited States of Umerica. No more desperate and homeless than if an Englishman who thought he came from England, when abroad was asked:

"Sir, are you from Gneland?"

Homelessness goes deeper than that.

Was it mentioned that the student was born and brought up in Trondhjem? He was. But, one day in the year 1930—that was the year he was fifteen and had his first suit with long trousers, and was confirmed and made his promise to God—the first day in that year, year of the heart, he woke up and found himself the inhabitant of an entirely different city. So did 50,000 other such citizens of Trondhjem.

Thanks to one stroke of the pen of the Minister for Ecclesiastical Affairs, who five years previously, had succeeded in re-naming Christiana Oslo, which had whetted his appetite, he woke up and discovered that he was living in a city with the unheard-of name of Nidaros.

That was like a Londoner waking up one day to discover that a Scottish cabinet minister had changed the city's name to Mouth o' Thames on the flimsy grounds that the last syllable of the ancient name was un-English, of Spanish origin; don.

That really started things.

The name of one's town is a thing you come across every day: it encompasses one, enfolds one; it is, indeed, one's *home*.

One has a lot to say if one is deprived of one's home. Londoners would, so did the Trondhjemers. Civil war was the result. The people of Trondhjem are normally good-natured, quiet, sober, people. One time, down at Brattøra, a man was unlucky enough to fall into the water. The people

177

on the quay at once threw things down to save him: margarine boxes, orange boxes, bits of plank, logs, showered down over him. A boy was sitting on the edge of the quay watching. He leaned forward a bit and said to the drowning man: "If you want to save your life, you'd better duck . . ."

But in 1930, the people of Trondhjem lost their quietness, their good nature, their sense of humour and style. Style? Once King Haakon and Crown Prince Olav came to Trondhjem. There was a banquet in the Harmoni. The Crown Prince, who was twelve or thirteen, was seated beside his father. When the dessert had been removed and it was time for coffee and liqueurs, an old, venerable waiter appeared with a tray of cigars and cigarettes. He held the tray for the King, on the opposite side to that where the Crown Prince sat; cautiously the old man prodded the King's arm, bent his head a little closer to the King's ear and said in a low discreet voice: "What about it, does the lad smoke?" The King looked straight in front of him, he was originally Danish, but he understood that language, understood the tradition, the delicacy and the tact, yes, the man-to-man-ness in the old waiter's approach; for where except in Norway would a man speak thus to his King?— almost imperceptibly the King shook his head; like one father to another; the old waiter walked on with his tray, missing out the Crown Prince.

But in 1930 the people of Trondhjem lost it all: they could not even be articulate. "Mærh!" they cried. That was all they could get out, "Mærh"; cobbles flew about the streets, window panes rattled; the only quiet place was a dinner table, a nodal point where the father was Sunnmøring and the mother Trondhjemmer, and there silence reigned; you could hear knife and fork scraping on the bottom of the plates; the elder son kept his eyes on the floor.

This state of affairs lasted just over a year.

Then in 1931, the Minister for Ecclesiastical Affairs in Oslo had to withdraw the name Nidaros.

What excitement, what jubilation, what relief!
Trondhjem had got its name back!

With just one tiny change in the last syllable; almost invisible to the naked eyes.

You will not find Trondhjem on the map today; it is Trondheim.

This corresponds to the people of London after having been forced to live for a year in hated Mouth o' Thames, waking up to find themselves citizens of a city called Lonnod.

We do not know what the people of London would have done in such a case, though we have an idea; but the student never forgot what the people of Trondhjem did; Norway will never forget it: they bent the knee, they *accepted* the name, Trondheim!

Perhaps they were exhausted by the struggle and excitement: brought to a standstill, turned into jelly; perhaps one or two of them wanted to spare some Sunnmøring or other loss of face—they adopted a compromise... and there's nothing in the whole world more fateful, more demoralizing than a compromise; in a compromise both parties lose. The Trondheim on the map does not signify victory for anyone; it is evidence only of Sunnmøre having lost Nidaros and Norge having lost Trondhjem.

And for a moment the student despised the Norwegians, the people of Trondhjem, as intensely as he loathed the draugs; at that moment he did not know which was worse: the person who perpetrates the injustice or the one who sits down under it. . . .

From then on you have two names for your town. Trondhjem you must not use; Trondheim you cannot use. So you have no city. It's like having a coat which, when you put it on, you find one sleeve cut off at the shoulder, the other sewn up at the cuff.

Norway's heart, that broke in 1931. . . .

You'll perhaps find one or another who can write and *say* Trondheim.

But you cannot *sing* it.

It is officialese, a wooden word, a rod in your throat. As impossible as singing a Lonnodderry Air—as completely impossible as singing "Trondheim, Trondheim, att æ resit ifra dæ. . . ."

And a city where there can be no song is a dead city.

"I believe we have a corpse in the hold," Ibsen wrote.

"Yes," whispers the student, "the corpse of Trondhjem."

He shut his eyes.

It felt like being under water.

When he surfaced again, opened his eyes once more, he saw in front of him a poster and on it in large gaily coloured letters the word BYRRH.

Suddenly he felt a smile coming.

It's not only a loss, he thought, it is also a challenge. If Olav Trygvason managed to walk outboard along his ship's twenty oars, surely I can manage to hold the balance between two cities? Perhaps I'm actually rich. . . .

And not quite bereft of hope for the future, certainly not without hope, in reality quite light-hearted and in full possession of his powers, Student Valemon Gristvåg from Trondhjem/Trondheim—half-draug, half human— pulled his motorcycle up onto the pavement in front of No. 344 Rue de Vaugirard.

Steal a little sunshine to take on your journey. . . .

He was in Paris.

THE NAME of the firm he was looking for was not immediately visible. Then he saw another cluster of name-plates under the heading "Dans La Cour"; that was the first thing he read in French and because he understood it, he was never to forget it.

He glanced at his wrist watch: a quarter past six. If only the man was still there.

Hurriedly he wheeled his motorcycle through the entrance and into the yard. He halted and looked around him. He raised his eyes and looked at the buildings. Their architecture was foreign, stand-offish: what made it so? Then he saw why: where a Norwegian brick building would have had windows, and perhaps curtains, there were shutters in front of the windows. Horizontally ribbed wooden shutters. They are to keep out the sun, he thought; the air can get in, but not the sun.

It was quiet in that big yard. A gay stillness. When he listened he could hear coming through the shutters the remote sound of voices, excited voices, the muffled clatter of typewriters, ringing of telephone bells.

He had seen the name-plate now. Over there, on the ground floor, above a glass door standing ajar.

"Instruments de Musique."

And under it the name:

"N. Røsok et Cie."

The family name . . .

For a while he stood rigid.

Man cannot live without other men. A person in isolation is a biological impossibility. And yet—is there anything in the whole world as odious as relatives?

The student had himself acquired a wife and child; he kept his forced marriage a profound secret and did not wear a ring. He was one of those with a tender conscience. He could not endure the thought of an unmarried mother and a fatherless child; as a child he had read Dickens's *Oliver Twist* and Hans Andersen's *Tale of a Mother;* a child in the world, naked, without covering, without name —no, for him, that was the hardest thought of all. And, as people always follow the rule that you take the line of least resistance—or is it greatest?—and jump the fence where it is lowest—or is it where it is highest?—he had married her. He had got her to sign a paper first; and then he had married her. It was a small town. (Anyway, he had thought, what do I want my matrimonial freedom for? I shan't need it for many years. If I throw my name to the she-wolf, perhaps she will let *me* go.) It was a brief marriage. The town was a small one and had no magistrate of its own, so they went with their certificates to the lensman. "Will you take this woman who stands beside you," the lensman read. There was no answer. The man looked up from his book, over the top of his spectacles, looked at the student, looked at the woman, she was five months gone. "Will you," said the lensman. The student felt the woman's hand come and lay itself reassuringly over his below the edge of the table— they were standing side by side in front of the lensman's table—he glanced at her; she gave him an almost imperceptible smile and an encouraging, reassuring nod. At that moment she seemed so upright, so calm, so dignified, so enormous, so strong, so healthy, her cheeks were like red apples, a mountain of maternal health. "In good times and evil, until death shall part you," said the lensman. The student closed his eyes. "Yes," he said. He felt a sharp pain at being compelled to lie. "Then," said the lensman, "I pronounce you man and wife." The student felt as if his eyes were going to drop out; he had to use his left hand to guide his right when he had to sign his name. He went with the woman from the lensman's office to her home; there he drank a whisky and soda with the bride's father; he looked at the rising bubbles in the tumbler; he looked at the floor; he looked at the clock; after half an hour, he stood up, said good-bye, shook her hand; outside, in the corridor, she put up her face to be kissed; he shook his head; he saw her face in the door as he was standing outside on the steps; he saw a smile at the back of her eyes: a narrow smile. When he got out onto the street, he began to run; he had to catch the mail-boat; never had he run so fast.

That marriage had lasted exactly half an hour. He had thought that that was all there was to it.

It was only a month later, when he had still not been sent divorce papers as agreed, that he realized that just by writing his name on a piece of paper he had acquired a family and relations!

And less than two years later, when she wanted to come and see him at the college, where he had thought he was safe, when she had demanded to see him to discuss the future, money, the child. When in her letter she wrote: "After all I am your wife . . ." he had gasped in terror and impotent fury.

What right does being a man's wife give a woman to go and see him!

There is affinity of the flesh.

And there is affinity of the mind. . . .

The next thing will be, he had thought, that one day a *man* will come and ring at my door.

183

"Unfortunately," I'll say "I'm busy."

Isn't there something familiar, half familiar, about the man?

"Come now," he says, his head on one side, "You're surely not *so* busy. . . ."

"I am," I say.

"Come now," he says with a fawning smile.

"I am," I say. "I'm working."

"Come now," he says, "Surely you haven't all *that much* work . . ."

"I have," I say.

"But," he says, almost reproachfully. ". . . you and I are related . . ."

I stare at the man speechless.

"I'm your father-in-law," he says.

The man is right inside now. He put his arm round my shoulders.

Schiller sang.

"Seid umschlungen, Millionen!"

Every time the student was reminded, as he was now, of those words: "Be embraced, ye millions!" he thought it the most terrifying line of poetry in the world.

Doubly terrifying because it came from a poem entitled:

"To Joy."

Humanity: an enormous, massive, entangled, embraced mound of flesh. A gigantic lump of flesh.

Joy?

World lump!

He had thought: I could have two bell-buttons on the door.

One that said: "Relatives in spirit press here."

And one that said: "Relatives in the flesh, press here."

184

It would be a secret what would happen when anyone pressed the latter button.

I'll patent that invention, he thought.

And get a Nobel peace prize.

H E WALKED across to the glass door. There was no step, the floor was on the same level as the courtyard. He peered in through the opening. He knocked on the jamb. There was no response; but it had not been much of a knock either, the door jamb was of brick. He pushed the door a little way open. Cautiously, feeling his way, he set a foot inside. There was semi-darkness in there.

He did not know what he had been expecting. A shop? This was more like a garage, or a warehouse: a large room with unpainted cement walls. The large floor, also of cement, was covered with wooden packing cases, opened or half-opened with wood-wool peeping out; it could have been the back room of a fruit shop. Had he come to the wrong place?

He knocked again, this time on a pane of glass on the inside of the door and it was a good knock.

Well into the room was a dividing wall of brick with a sliding window in it; perhaps that was the office. A door he had not noticed suddenly opened and a man came out. He was middle-aged, short, bald, with a ring of grizzled red hair round his pate. He had an ugly walk, with his toes turned in. The man who had a slight stoop, looked like an elderly warehouseman, rather tired, rather off-putting. The sleeves of his shirt were rolled up and he had a pencil behind his ear. Had the man noticed him? Had the man looked at him?

The student did not know what he should do. He bowed, stepped over a packing case and almost stumbled.

Should he speak French or Norwegian? He swallowed.

"Bonjour," he said; after all the man might be a Frenchman.

At that same instant he saw that the man had hair in his nostrils and ears, lots of bushy grizzled red hair; he could

186

only be a Sunnmøring. He took the risk: drawing a deep breath, he said:

God dag, er det . . ."

The man gave a quick smile, a shy and slightly twisted smile, and then in impeccable Norwegian said:

"Yes."

The student heaved a great sigh of relief; he almost groaned.

"Ah!" he said.

He shook the man's hand. The man's grasp was firm enough, but hurried. The next instant the man had taken the pencil from behind his ear and was standing there holding an invoice.

He had expected the man to say "Welcome to Paris," but he did not. Didn't he seem a bit surly, if not actually resentful? Had he, Valemon, done something wrong? Had there been something wrong in the letter he had written from Bergen? Hm. How could one know? How ought one to behave? The man had disappeared back through the door into the office. Hm.

Paris.

When the man reappeared from the office, Valemon ventured to ask if he had managed to get him a room. Yes. Where? Just round the corner. Cheap, he hoped it was cheap? Yes, both cheap and good. Over the years, quite a lot of Norwegians had stayed there.

"Ah," said Valemon, "that's good. And thanks awfully for all your trouble!" He bowed.

"That's all right," Røsok said.

He seemed to have a number of things to do. A busy man. He slouched in and out of the office door, with the pencil now behind his ear, now in his hand. He asked Valemon to take a seat on a packing case; he would not be long.

Valemon sat down.

Paris.

187

"I expect you would be glad of a meal?" said the man, from the depths of the room.

"Yes," Valemon said and suddenly he realized that he was hungry. He had been about to say "Yes, thank you," but he did not know if that had been an invitation. He did not know whether Røsok intended to ask him home, to his wife, or whether they were going to eat out.

"Well, we'll be going soon," Røsok said.

"Thanks," said Valemon.

He shot a quick glance at the man who was pottering about at the back of the store. He could not see any family resemblance to his father; perhaps he was just an acquaintance. All he knew was that the two had been at the NCO's school, but had parted company after that. His father had become a member of the Divisional Band, while this Røsok had gone to Paris and started a music business. Valemon had thought this rather romantic; adventure and breaking out on your own. And he had married in France, too.

Imagine being married to a French lady . . . Talking French together every day; at the breakfast table; and at the dinner table; and in bed. That was life! He threw a covert look at the man who was standing about morosely, the pencil behind his ear. It did not seem to fit properly. No, he thought, nothing did. . . .

To give himself something to do, he got up and looked into the packing cases. Music shop—he had imagined it meant selling sheet music, pianos, guitars, violins, violin strings. But this was wind instruments. At the back he had seen something that resembled a small tuba; there were two clarinets lying on a shelf; and in the packing case in front of him, down among the wood-wool was a glint of yellow metal. For the sake of saying something, he asked:

"Do you sell wholesale or retail?"

"Only wholesale," the man said. "To bands."

"In Paris? Or all over France?"

"All over France," the man replied. He spoke with reluctance, without interest, looking to one side. Hm, thought Valemon, that could mean that he sold a cornet to Cherbourg last year and a big drum to Marseilles this. Perhaps his business is not all that flourishing.

But it's dreadful having to sit twiddling your thumbs. He had to say something. He asked if the instruments were made in France? Yes, the man replied, but he imported as well. From Germany, from Austria, from Czechoslovakia.

"That's wonderful!" Valemon said; it gave him pleasure to have got the man to raise his head momentarily. But at the same time he had had a vision . . .

Instruments from France, from Germany, from Austria, from Czechoslovakia.

Here you had Europe . . .

Europe, which Dostoevsky called a graveyard; the loveliest in the world, of course, but all the same a graveyard! Was Dostoevsky always right? The flames were crackling again under Europe's pots and pans, crackle of burning thorns; again Europe's pots were bubbling with pent-up evil and unredeemed hatred. Revanche. . . . And then suddenly, here in this warehouse filled with cases of musical instruments, he had felt close to a secret, he was suddenly in a laboratory of the future . . .

Why had no politician, no statesman, no philosopher, thought of music? For a moment, a wonderful moment, he saw a vision of Europe and far from being a graveyard— it was a Europe that marched and played. He saw rifles and bayonets replaced by bassoons and drums; all over Europe he saw military bands marching and dancing. . . . Hatred and evil are only dissolved in music; in music and only in music, will that real miracle, the impossible, happen, when liberty is combined with discipline; he had never thought of that before, but at that moment he sent Marx a thought: true socialism is only to be found in music!—it is only when you are in a band, playing, marching, that loneliness and poverty are abolished!—war does not create anything new, war is nothing but an alternation between thesis and antithesis, war is marking time, nobody wins!—the world

189

may go a step up, up into synthesis, up into music! Hitherto music has been an appendage of the military, of regiments; hitherto, Dostoevsky, we have talked of regimental bands; one day we shall talk of regiments of bands!

"Oh," he groaned, "that's magnificent!"

"What," came from the man at the back of the store.

Valemon was back on earth again. He was thinking: when am I going to meet a man, a person, who is on my wavelength? On a level with my visions? I carry it all inside me. It never gets out. "What," said Røsok. My father always snubbed me too. "Nonsense," he used to say. There is a wall in the world. A wall of peevishness, despondency, narrow-mindedness, of modesty. That's it, a wall of modesty! How long is man to be kept in check? When are we going to rid ourselves of our strait jackets? And blossom out? When are we going to stand up triumphant, and without modesty, all over the world?

Be frank!—he thought suddenly.

And shuddered.

One day, he thought. One day.

He got up and bent over a packing case that had been opened. An instrument made of some yellow metal lay half hidden in the wood-wool. He put his hand in and touched the instrument. It was a trumpet.

"Can I take a look at this one?" he said to the man.

Røsok gave a little nod.

Valemon blew the dust and wood-wool off it, pressed the valves. They were a bit sticky. There was no mouthpiece on it, but even so he put it to his lips, heard his breath travelling through it. It was a strange, captivating, dangerous sound; empty, but full of possibilities. . . . You were on the brink of a note. On the brink of form. What beauty couldn't you achieve, if you only knew how!

To blow emptily through a trumpet, without a mouthpiece, is like being God, the night before the first day.

"Do you play?" Røsok asked all at once, looking up from a stock list.

190

"No," said Valemon, putting the trumpet carefully back into the packing case. He thought back. He had wanted to join a boy's band, but his father had said no. Suddenly he was speaking his thoughts to Røsok. "I suppose he was afraid I would become a bandsman," he said. "'Find yourself a better profession,'" father said. "'*Notes just vanish into thin air*,'" he said. "'*There's nothing to leave behind you*.'"

"Hm," said Røsok.

"I was never allowed to try his bugle either," Valemon went on "'Nobody's to touch that,' he would say. 'That's the family's source of income.' he would say. But one day when he was out and I was the only one at home, I did try it. Hm. I believe I was twelve. His bugle lay on a high shelf in the hall, over the door. I had to stand on a chair to reach. It was in a cover made of some thick canvas material, it was much heavier than I had imagined . . ."

"Tenor bugle, in b."

"What? Yes. Tenor bugle in b. I've never been so afraid. But all the same I could not stop myself. I took it out of its case. The mouthpiece was on it."

"Did you manage anything?"

"No. A couple of notes. Didn't know how the keys worked. So I put it back in its cover. (Couldn't get it back properly. My hands had begun to tremble. It wasn't a stiff cover; it was soft; but I had forgotten which way round it went. It had been easy to undo the buttons, but doing them up! Suppose I ruined it! In the end I just put it up on the shelf, shoved it in its place and hoped it was all right. I was wet with sweat. For a day and a night I was beside myself with fear. But he didn't discover it. For a long time afterwards I could taste the mouthpiece, salt, metal, verdigris; the taste of my father's lips.) That was my one and only encounter with bugle playing . . ."

"I see," said Røsok. And he added:

"It's not everybody can play like Rasmus Gristvåg."

Valemon glanced at the man—hadn't he sighed?

191

He bit his lip.

Suddenly in his mind's eye he saw his father. Band-lieutenant Rasmus Gristvåg.

As he grew up and became taller than his father, watching his father's hands became an obsession with him. He was taller in the body than his father, but those hands ...

There were times when he had to shut his eyes to prevent the man seeing what he was feeling. He wanted to break his father. He wanted to pick the man up and smash him on the floor (but could he manage it?), stretch him out on the floor with one blow and get a knee on his chest. "Your will is in my trouser-pocket," his father had always said. Force him to the floor, set his knee on his chest, hold him. But always the vision shattered before he got as far. In imagination he had seen his father's face, as it would have looked. Privately, he knew that his father was not so very strong. Privately, he knew that his father's hardness was a shell. He knew that if he knocked his father down, he would see the most dreadful thing of all: an adult man who had lost face ... the great father whose eyes have filled with tears. He could not stand that vision. And because he could never lay hands on his father, in imagination he turned his weakness into victory. The knowledge that he had never broken his father, once or twice gave him an odd sense of triumph. He safeguarded his father's image—divine image. . . . It was like protecting a little child. . . .

Let him believe, he thought, that my will lies in his trouser-pocket. He does not know that the fate of his image lies in mine!

*

In the midst of his hating he felt a swift puff, a little ripple of pride in his father. He pretended unconcern, looked out through the glass door, out onto the courtyard where his motorcycle was parked and said lightly:

192

"Have *you* ever heard him play?"

"Yes, you bet I have," Røsok said suddenly. There was a new note in the man's voice.

The student looked at him. He remembered that his father had been in Paris in 1937, two years previously. There had been a festival for military bands from all sorts of countries held in conjunction with the World Exhibition, and the Oslo Band had taken part. They had needed two or three extra men from the provinces to bring it up to full strength, it was like getting a national team together; and so his father had been taken from Trondhjem as first bassoonist.

"At the World Exhibition?" Valemon asked. All at once he remembered that *she* had been in Paris in 1937. She had studied in Paris for a whole year. Just imagine!—She, and his father, had *both* been in Paris in 1937! Suppose . . .

No, the man said, it was when they were young and at the NCO's school. They were both in the music class.

"Your father . . ." the man said.

"Yes?" said the student.

"He had never touched a horn before he came to Trondhjem."

"Yes?" Valemon said, aware of quickening interest; he had never heard a thing about his father's youth before.

"There are some who can and some who can't."

"Yes?"

"He had never touched a bugle before. He was able to play it straight away."

Valemon felt a shudder down his back. There was silence in the room for a while.

"We others," he heard Røsok say, "we practised five hours a day. For three years. We blew scales till blood spurted from our lips. But we never became good . . ."

Valemon did not dare look at him.

"We never became good," the man repeated, quietly, as if to himself. "But Rasmus . . ."

"You know," he said suddenly and looked at the

student "You know, though I was at the school with him for three years, I never heard him practise. He never practised."

Valemon shuddered again. When he thought about it, he had never heard his father practise either. He had lived in the same house as his father for twenty years, but when his father took the bugle down from that shelf in the hall, it was only to clean it; he held it on his lap, poured a drop of Blue Star onto it and rubbed it with newspaper until the metal shone; occasionally he dripped a drop of oil on the valves. "Play something, Father!" the boy might ask. But his father would shake his head. And inside himself the boy knew that his father was right; a bugle is not for a room; a bugle is for the wide open. . . . Then his father would put the bugle back on the shelf.

"He was born to it," Røsok said. There was a sort of vexation, a heaviness, in his voice. But his bitterness gave way momentarily and he said:

"Tone. That's what your father had. He became first bassoonist when he was only twenty-five. At rehearsals. . . . Do you remember the conductor, fat old Captain Fromann?"

"Yes."

"Sometimes he motioned to us others to stop, he had a way of flicking his right hand. Then we knew what was coming. It was your father going to play solo. And there old Fromann stood, his eyes closed. And we others, we too wished we could put our instruments down and just listen to Rasmus Gristvåg."

It was quite still in the store.

At that moment Valemon loved his father. So strange. . . . From being at home he had almost become accustomed to regard his father as a mere private: a hard, obstinate, silent failure of a man who had never risen to be more than a bandsman; a man with a poor salary; a man who did not share his wife's ambition for him to take the musical instructor's examination and become a conductor; a man who at table ate with his knife instead of with his fork . . .

194

"When I heard Rasmus," the man said, "I knew that *I* could never be a musician."

The man twisted his mouth into a wry little smile; went on working, slouching round with his lists and his pencil. The conversation seemed to be at an end. There was silence.

Valemon felt that in a hurried glance he had seen the web of life; the threads of human destiny; the forces that push and those that pull.... This Røsok could not become a practising musician himself; but he had attended the NCO's school for three years; and if he had not learned to play an instrument; he had learnt *about* instruments. It would seem rash, adventurous to go to Paris, into the unknown, instead of taking a steady job in Trondhjem. But nonetheless that was preferable to living in the shadow of another man's superiority....

Valemon thought: everyone makes for his own sun.

"There," Røsok said. He had finished. Now they could go and eat.

The man rolled his shirtsleeves down, slouched off into the office, locked drawers, locked boxes, it was quite a little performance. Valemon could see him through the sliding window. He came out and now he had put on a dark jacket. Valemon took a cautious look at him as they went out through the glass door. The man's shirt was open at the neck and not quite clean; the edge of the cuffs of his jacket were threadbare; the turn-ups of his trousers frayed, the ends of the threads hung over his shoes like a small mop. The man looked exactly like a tramp. He had to think of his father, who was always trim and neat; his uniform was always well brushed, his trousers always well pressed. Once, when he himself was seventeen and had frayed a place on the inside of his turn-ups which his mother had darned, his father had given him a rule: "You should always keep your feet slightly apart when you walk. Not much. Just an inch or so. Then that won't happen." Later, Valemon had followed that rule. Where

195

did his father get all his amazing practical knowledge from?

This Røsok, he thought, has a wife, a French wife into the bargain, but she does not look after his clothes. You can tell a lot from a man's clothes. Not that it was necessarily the wife's fault. A man can look after his own clothes, if he cares to take the trouble. . . . Even the heels of his shoes were worn down. At any rate you could not blame the wife for that.

I heard a farmer say: "A cat that grooms itself is a healthy cat."

He watched the man lock the outer door. He thought: perhaps his business isn't doing so well. . . .

But, he thought on, what actually does it mean that a man's business isn't doing too well? Musn't a business always do well, if a man puts his heart into it? There you have it! It is always a question of heart! Crises, lack of credit, tight discount markets, slumps, foreign competition —I believe it is all nonsense! An obstacle here, a bar there, that can only be an encouragement?

Yes, even if there was a war! Even if the whole business was bombed to pieces!

Ho, he thought, a real businessman would reveal his talent even in wartime. Yes, even more in wartime. If I should ever really fall in love, I know that I would possess a super-developed awareness, an alertness, that I would sense all dangers in advance, be able to protect my beloved. . . . Like a lover, the true business man should have all his senses on the alert. Should be ready, prepared. War never comes really out of the blue, like lightning out of a clear sky. The sign of a real businessman is that he simply does not have his business where bombs fall. If bombs are falling in Paris, he and his business are in New York.

I must remember to tell my professor in Bergen that, he thought.

The best manager is the one who is in love with his business!

It was still boiling hot outside: Paris smelled like an over-blown rose.

First they must take the motorcycle to the hotel; then they would have dinner at a nearby restaurant. It was now seven o'clock. "Are you going to ring home?" Valemon asked. "What for?" Røsok said. "To say that—you won't be back for dinner." "No," said Røsok. Valemon regretted having asked; the harshness of that "no" made him feel uncomfortable, distressed. Where on earth, he thought, am I ever going to come across a marriage where there is no hatred? A marriage where husband and wife are good friends? Is there such a thing?

When they were out in the street, he firmly refused to ride his machine. He told Røsok about the traffic, about his being pursued by prehistoric monsters; and a slight smile appeared on the other's face.

So, they pushed the machine along the pavement: he in front holding the handlebars; the man behind steadying the rucksack.

Paris, Valemon thought.

They passed an entrance to the Métro. He would go on that one day.... Deep down below he heard a distant rumble and he had felt what might have been a waft from hell. Out of the chasm had come a hot, suffocating gust, sweat, cigarettes—and the unknown. What *was* that terrible, hot, muggy smell that had welled up from the chasm of the Métro and which seemed to dwell in the human spirit?

For quite a while he did not dare breathe through his nose. Nor did he dare ask his guide. Because, if the man

197

had replied that Paris had recently been attacked by tonsil-
litis, that the entire population of France had got adenoids,
it would mean that his trip was a failure, the adventure
destroyed, the palace swathed in black. . . . I really don't
dare ask about that terrible smell. I'll imagine that it
doesn't exist.

Why has the Lord burdened me with such an over-
sensitive sense of smell?

Before he knew what was happening, Røsok had hauled
him up a steep flight of steps and they were standing in a
small, dark dusty vestibule. His eyes were not immediately
able to adjust themselves after the light outside. He blinked.
He was embarrassed, and elated; he had never stayed in an
hotel before. He received a hurried, confused impression
of plush, mirrors and chandeliers. Røsok was over at the
reception desk, he nodded, said a word to the woman behind it; they both looked at the student. The woman
behind the desk was middle-aged; she had a twisted mouth
and a tooth in her upper jaw that protruded slightly; she
reminded him of a bird. Valemon went to the desk in his
turn, bowed: "Bonjour," he said and heard at once that
that was not enough; he bowed again and said: "Bonjour,
madame." The woman opened her eyes and stepped back
slightly. Had he seen fear in her eyes? Why? She was
standing one pace behind the desk, as though at a safe
distance; with one hand she pushed a visitor's book across
to him, he was to write his name in it. She stood there,
open-mouthed, tense, watching while he wrote. Is there
anything wrong with me, Valemon thought? He took a
short step back, treading on Røsok's foot, wanted to beg
Røsok's pardon, but did not know whether to do so in
Norwegian or French. He felt himself starting to sweat.
Fortunately, the woman said that the hotel would see to
his motorcycle and his baggage. He bowed and thanked
her.

"Merci," he said. "Merci, Madame."

He stood still for a moment. His head was suddenly swimming with emotion. He had reached Paris, happily, safely. He had survived. He had a roof over his head. He was staying at an hotel in Paris. There hanging on the board, which the woman had shown him, was his key No. 32. Numéro trente-deux. When he came in later that evening, he could just go up to the desk and say, as if it was the most natural thing in the world: "Ma clef, s'il vous plait."

My key, please.

And now they were going to go out and have dinner.

Dine in Paris.

He felt a cry swelling inside him, a cry of joy, an animal cry.... He opened his mouth. He caught sight of Røsok; the man was standing by the door; he looked cross and impatient.

Valemon thought: I'll have to keep that cry for another time.

He could see the restaurant a long way off. It was a hundred yards down a side street. Its front was lit up, and on each side of the steps up to the door was a tall cardboard, or perhaps canvas, poster fixed to the wall like a big illuminated sign. It had red lettering and the letters were arranged vertically:

<table>
<tr><td>P</td><td>P</td></tr>
<tr><td>R</td><td>R</td></tr>
<tr><td>I</td><td>I</td></tr>
<tr><td>X</td><td>X</td></tr>
<tr><td></td><td></td></tr>
<tr><td>F</td><td>F</td></tr>
<tr><td>I</td><td>I</td></tr>
<tr><td>X</td><td>X</td></tr>
<tr><td>E</td><td>E</td></tr>
</table>

He stopped half-way between the hotel and the restaurant, and looked back.

"What is it?" Røsok asked.

"I'm taking a cross-bearing," Valemon said.

"Cross-bearing?"

"I'm bad at geography. I never know where north and south are. I'll get myself lost if I don't take a cross-bearing."

"Cross-bearing?"

"Don't you know what that is?" Valemon said. "I learned that, actually, in Sunnmøre. When you are out fishing, in a rowing boat, on a fjord. You have to know where the fishing ground is. And so you take a bearing on two points. Two mountain tops for example. I learned that from my uncle, when I was a boy. 'What are you looking for, Uncle', I said. 'I'm taking a cross-bearing', he said."

Røsok had already reached the restaurant; he was standing looking at the menu hung up outside. Valemon looked at it too, but did not understand a word. He just noticed the price. Prix Fixe, it said, and that means fixed price; a good, an excellent thing; you know exactly where you are. And it said: 7⁵⁰ Francs. He tried to convert that into Norwegian money: 1 franc is 11 øre; he calculated and calculated. He made it 83 øre, but it was so hot and he was so dazed, that he did not know if he had worked it out right. It could never be 8 crowns 30? No, 83 øre. 83 øre? For dinner? That was cheap. In Bergen he had to pay Crowns 1.50.

He felt immensely relieved. Part of the guilt that he secretly carried, loosened and dropped off. Guilt because of all the obligations he had not fulfilled; guilt because he had set forth on an adventure, on credit. But look at this: this is adventure that is really worthwhile! Even his deserted wife would be able to see the advantage of his coming to Paris! He was not earning money for her, it was true, but he was spending less on himself! He was saving the difference between Crowns 1.50 in Bergen and 0.83 in Paris; she could work the rest out for herself!

It was a popular restaurant; big and half full. It was summer and very hot. All the big windows were open. A slight breeze rippled the curtains. The table-cloths, of some cheap, checked material, were fixed to the edges of the tables by clips. Later, he seemed to remember that the ceiling of this big restaurant had been a canopy, an awning.

They found a table in the corner.

Already there was a waitress at their table. Already she had thrust menus into their hands. Already, she had brushed the table-cloth with a napkin. She was so amazingly efficient that Valemon had to look at her. Her movements were swift, a shade rough and unlovely, but right. She never picked anything up wrong, never took a step too many, never wasted a second. She was young, but not very young, getting on for thirty, short, slightly built, with a light blue apron round her front like a sort of uniform. Already, she had fetched plates, knives, forks, spoons, napkins; already she had asked what the gentlemen wished to drink with their meal, beer or wine; appalled, Valemon looked at Røsok: wine must be expensive, wasn't it? But the man reassured him: it was included in the price. Valemon's mouth fell open: did you get dinner *and* wine for 83 øre?—well, if that was the case, he would have wine. Already she had placed two wine glasses on the table. Already she had fetched a cruet with pepper, salt, oil, vinegar and set it on the table. At the same time in some mysterious way she had filled a basket with long pieces of bread. Already there had been the sound of two little bumps, and there was a half-bottle of wine standing in front of Valemon's plate and another in front of Røsok's.

"Bravo!" Valemon said. He did not know whether he had exclaimed aloud or just said it to himself; he would have liked to have clapped; he had never seen anything like it; he loved perfection; he loved anyone who could put heart and soul into his work.

There was no doubt that she liked it.... She had finished laying the table and was already standing four paces away; exactly far enough for her to be able to keep an eye on the rest of the room while discreetly waiting for the order from their table. She had the ability to divide her attention. Look at her standing there, not in the least tired, late though it was and she might have served five hundred people before them, not tired at all, she stood there rocking slightly on the balls of her feet, small, strong, content, narrow-waisted, firm-fleshed, coolly satisfied with herself and the world, ready instantly to catch a wave or gesture. She was standing looking straight ahead of her, as if she had no need to let her gaze keep travelling round; it was as if she was listening with her cheeks. She reminded him of something he had read in a book about Red Indians. When an Indian was sent out hunting and wanted to spot an animal on the move, he must keep his eyes still, fixed on some stationary point ahead of him. However, if he was trying to spot an animal that was lying on the fringe of the trees, hiding by making itself one with its surroundings, he must let his gaze travel evenly from right to left and back again. The stationary gaze picks up movement; the travelling gaze picks up shape.

This woman was using both methods. She was looking straight ahead of her, standing rocking on her toes, small, lively, ready for action; she stood with her hands in the pockets of her apron; now and then she gave them a slight hitch; playing with them as if she had money in the pockets, or a bottle opener, or a pencil. To amuse herself while waiting, she also once thrust her tongue into her left cheek, but removed it quickly. Only once did her gaze travel calmly across the table. Valemon tried to catch it, but he did not, it travelled on—and he was glad. If her gaze had stopped on him, she would have been woman; while the fact that it travelled on—impersonal, professional—made her an artist.

Yes, he thought, this woman is an artist. Not forcing herself, absorbed in herself, resting while doing her duty. That cool look that saw, yet did not see; that did not see and yet saw. She did not see me, the man; but she would

202

have seen me, the customer, immediately. The way she looked at me, the customer, must have been the way Napoleon looked at his soldiers and Jesus at his audience at the foot of the Mount. Intent on what they had to do, insensitive, filled with hidden force, utterly indifferent to the personal ("Woman, what have I to do with thee?"); that cool gaze; the gaze of a cockerel; of a Red Indian; of a military commander; or an artist.

He was completely absorbed by that little woman and her charged state of rest.

"Votre très humble serviteur."

Within her profession that woman was a Mozart, a Shakespeare.... Didn't Shakespeare write a play called "As You Like It"?

That is a fantastic title. There's a secret lying hidden there. Look at that female Shakespeare over there. A waitress. Did she look tired? Worn out? Was her attitude that of a slave, of one who is broken, exploited, a serf? Was she weeping because she could not be one of the customers? Was she weeping at not being able to sit down herself and be waited on? Indeed, she radiated an inner elation, was shifting her feet in suppressed eagerness, her face was transfigured, she stood there like a queen, radiant.

What was her secret? That she did not think of herself?

"As *you* like it."

He sat with the menu in his hand trying to read it. He had to turn it slightly towards Røsok and ask for help, there were so many courses, four or five. The first was soup and hors d'oeuvre, no, soup or hors d'oeuvre, you could choose. He plucked up courage and asked what hors d'oeuvre was. Well, said Røsok, actually it means something like "outside the work"; try it, he said, it's good. Valemon took a deep breath, made his decision, nodded; he had never had hors d'oeuvre before.

The woman must have been capable of telepathy. He could never remember hearing Røsok speak to her, yet there she was already by their table with two plates, dished-up ready—where had she got them from?—which she placed on the table. "Messieurs," she said, "Voilà." She put the two plates on top of those in front of them. Then already she had withdrawn again and was standing four paces away, rocking, quiet, correct, remote, alert; standing like a wagtail, like a deer....

Valemon looked down at his plate. There lay four radishes of a shape he had not seen before; they were not round, they were oblong, slim, reddish-pink, with white tips: the green top had been cut off, but not the whole of it, a little tuft had been left to hold it by. Beside the radishes lay two sardines in oil, they were fatter and larger than those he was accustomed to, and they had scales. Norwegian sardines are slim and remind you of dolphins, but these were fat and reminded you of whales. He questioned Røsok, who told him they were Portuguese sardines. That gave Valemon a shock. He had been so sure that there were only Norwegian sardines, that sardines were really a Norwegian invention. Had Portugal stolen the patent? He glanced at the Sunnmøring, but he was eating hurriedly, hungrily, bolting it down quite unconcerned by the treachery of the Portuguese. He's been so long in France, I suppose, that he's forgotten his own country, Valemon thought.

But there was more yet on his plate. There was a slice of tomato and two rounds of sausage. The sausage was reddish-brown, cut thin, and like a Frankfurter. He took up one of the bits of sausage, sniffed it; it smelled dangerous and nice: had he not caught another waft of that strange, frightening smell? He held his breath....

He had still not eaten any of his hors d'oeuvre. He just sat admiring the way it was all arranged on the plate.

"Aren't you going to eat?" Røsok said looking up.

The student was there to learn. Secretly he watched how the other ate. He saw that he had put some salt on his plate, a little heap of salt, and that he dipped his radishes into this. Valemon did the same. Cautiously he dipped a radish into the salt, then he held it up to his mouth. For a second he shuddered, as when you are faced with a spoon full of bitter medicine, then he bit. His teeth severed the radish, there was a crunch of white tuberous flesh; his throat burned. He had to hang his tongue out for a moment to cool it.

He had tears in his eyes.

Paris.

Røsok had taken one of the long pieces of bread, torn a bit off it and put it in his mouth. Valemon thought his manners rather bad; the man was munching.

He looked round cautiously at the tables nearby. Nobody seemed to be cutting their bread. They were all tearing bits off and stuffing them into their mouths.

He leaned forward and whispered:

"Don't we get any butter?"

The man's way of eating was unusually ugly; he was almost lying across the table, chewing. What, butter? he stopped, butter isn't used in France—just occasionally for breakfast.

Valemon was surprised. This really was a different civilization. No butter. It was as if half his world had collapsed; for a second he felt homeless, amputated. He looked round at the French people sitting at the other tables. They did not know what butter was. . . .

Then, he thought, they don't know what I am either! I shall never speak the same language as they. . . .

Deprive a Norwegian of his golden butter and you deprive him of half his history, half his being, half his soul. Deprive a Norwegian of the historical memory, the historical consciousness of golden butter and you deprive him of his individuality, his pride, his yearning—you turn him historically into a cripple.

All right: we had St. Olaf who is said to have introduced

Christianity into Norway, who is said to have given us the holy ghost. All right. But does he inspire, this saintly king? Does he move our hearts? Ask any Norwegian and, if he is honest, he will answer no. St. Olaf has become submerged in the grey herd of politicians and intrigues; his beard and his nails continued to grow after he was dead; but no miracle can help him: he is and will remain a plainsman. Whether Norway is heathen or Christian, Catholic or Protestant, is a question of secondary importance; one can be as good, or bad, as the other.

Who then is the great figure in Norwegian history? Norway's genius, alluring, strengthening, uplifting, through the whole dark Middle Ages?

It is not a man. It is a woman.

When Norway became free of Denmark in 1814, when, after that long night, Norway woke to life again, when Norway found her tongue once more and sang: in poetry, romance, drama, painting, folklore, music, Norway also had to have her first opera. Two Norwegians wrote it in 1820. Was it about King Olaf the Saint, his life? Not a bit of it. With astounding instinct for the national essence Bjerregaard and Thrane wrote a musical play called *A Mountain Tale*.

Did we say: Norway's first opera?

It is Norway's only opera.

The strange thing is that while composers of operas in other countries have flitted from subject to subject, from Lohengrin to the Meistersinger, from Rigoletto to La Traviata, without ever finding the right one, without ever being done, these two Norwegians hit the bull straight off, at the first shot; at one blow all possibilities were exhausted.

Norway has had no other opera since.

Since then there has been nothing to write an opera about.

"To the shieling! To the shieling!"

There are two official Norwegian national anthems. There is Bjørnson's in a major key "Ja, vi elsker dette landet," a lovely song; there is Aasen's "Millom bakkar og berg utmed havet" in a minor key, also a lovely song; but Norway's true national anthem, mysterious, promising, is not aimed at the countryside, nor at the sea; it aims upwards: at the hills, at the mountains where the air is like wine, and where if you just stand on tiptoe you reach the sky....

To the shieling! To the shieling!

Other countries with the same sure instinct have sited their deities and holy places on high mountains. Hellas had its Olympus; Japan has its Fuji. But whereas there were only imaginary gods on the top of Olympus and at the top of Fuji is nothing but an enormous crater, at the top of the mountains, in Norway you find the deity incarnate, the sanctuary made real. There if we are lucky, and respectful and doff our caps, we can meet her in person, as a woman of flesh and blood, mistress of the mountain, guardian of the cattle and life's protectress, history's sublime and gentle mother; her mission is eternal, eternal because it is necessary; for that reason she is enthroned high above the petty skirmishing of the day; kingdoms can come, kingdoms can go, religions can come, religions can go: she remains; there down below the others are engaged in killing; up there she protects life.

The girl from the shieling.

This is what she, Aagot, sang in *A Mountain Tale:*

> Now the sun is almost setting
> Long and black the shadows getting
> Time for night to close its shutter
> And in its arms myself to hold.
> The cows are gathered in the fold
> Time for me to churn the butter.

Ask a Norwegian, ask any Norwegian, ask if the thought of St. Olaf stirs him in any way; and he will reply, if he is honest, that it does not. Ask him, then, if the thought of the girl from the shieling stirs him and he will, if he is honest, and if his emotion allows him to speak, tell you that it does.

> My work is almost done and over
> Time now to stop and get some rest
> Sleep so sound beneath the cover
> Till the sun once more tops the crest
> Soon pillowed head asleep will be
> And in my dreams my boy I'll see.

The girl from the shieling . . .

On the rare occasion, when she has to have a name, she can be Prillarguri blowing a birch-bark horn from the mountain top to give warning of the enemy's approach. But she does not need a name; we prefer to see her without her battle-horn; she has no need to play Joan of Arc to flutter our hearts.

Heather, mountain wind, high sky, lowing of cows. Inside the hut, the smell of newly scrubbed wooden floor strewn with freshly chopped juniper; smell of sour cream-pans and newly baked flat-bread; blue heavens, red cheeks, white milk—Norway.

Once, when he was small, Valemon stole a gill of fresh cream from his mother's kitchen; he wanted to challenge the powers, he wanted to try to make butter. He stirred with the handle of a whisk; he stirred for an hour. He fared as he had, when he had tried to light a fire in the Red Indian way by rubbing two sticks together. He had to chuck the sticks away; now he drank the cream.

Once, one summer, in his youth, he had been up at a shieling. He was allowed to stand beside the woman while she churned.

He was allowed to take the lid off the churn and look in. He would never forget it. The process had begun: the mystery was at work. It smelled both sweet and sour. On the inside of the tall wooden cylinder, on its walls, were the yellow drops of the ambrosia of the North: the sacred spirit of Norway had crystallized into golden tears, shining, glistening. Slowly those golden tears increased in number and size; before his wondering gaze they turned to golden nuts, golden grapes, golden eggs, golden apples. He shut his eyes.

When he opened them again, she had placed the fresh mountain butter in a low wooden tub on the table. She smoothed the surface with a spoon. Last of all she took a piece of wood and drew a lovely criss-cross pattern on it.

If it be so that God let his son be born in Palestine, of all places—he let his daughter come to earth in Norway. And, of all places: in a shieling.

He and she. The two poles.

He: "Man does not live by bread alone. . . ."

She: "No, he needs a little butter too."

They look at each other.

He came tumbling back to earth from the heights (from one of them!) and, behold! he was sitting in a Prix-Fixe restaurant in Paris, sitting with a piece of French bread in his hand, and he thought: if the French don't have butter on their bread, the bread must be good indeed. . . .

He broke off a trial piece. The crust was golden brown, hard, crisp. Inside the crumb was white, soft and had big pores. He put his nose to it. It smelled very good. He took a bite. It tasted unusually good. It was the best bread he had ever tasted. He told Røsok so.

"Ah," the latter said, chewing.

The man had long since taken his bottle of wine and filled his glass. He splashed the wine into the glass, and he did not wipe the bottle. A dark stain spread over the table-cloth. Valemon picked up his own bottle. He held his breath. Wine, so early in the evening! And wine—with your meal! He had never had that before. It was red wine. He filled his glass, slowly. He twisted the bottle round to dislodge the drop from the rim. He glanced round the restaurant. There were fifty or a hundred people there. They were all drinking wine. They all appeared to be enjoying life and the food; the restaurant hummed with the even, satisfied, warm buzz of voices. All were drinking wine. Norway had made him afraid of alcohol, he was afraid of drunken people, in the same way as he loathed the world of the dog with its sudden, coarse, evil, dangerous baying. Here he was safe; yes, how right he had been that afternoon when he was philosophizing over the world of the cat; yes, he could hear it: the whole restaurant was buzzing with well-being—it was purring!

Perhaps it wasn't very strong wine, he thought.

He raised his glass of red wine, it glowed, he smelled it.

"Skål!" he said suddenly. He had to.

"Ah," Røsok said, taking a gulp.

Strange man, Valemon thought. No, no, he thought, that's his affair; I'm quite happy to drink to myself. . . .

Then the waitress had whipped their plates away and with a sort of sleight-of-hand set on the table a dish from which came a heavenly smell, and already she was back in her place four paces away, gently rocking on her feet, calm, quiet, remote, near. . . .

Valemon gulped.

On the dish lay two slices of roast meat, one for Valemon, the other for Røsok. Round them lay some light brown delicious-looking objects, what could they be?

"Help yourself," said Røsok.

"No," said Valemon. "After you."

"No," said Røsok, "After you."

"No, said Valemon. "After you."

Let's see if he takes the smaller piece, Valemon thought. If he is polite, he will.

The man was about to take the smaller piece, changed his mind and took the larger.

Next time he tells me to help myself first... thought Valemon. Anyway, it wouldn't help. I am so polite, I would have to take the smallest piece.

Bifteck, explained the man, and pommes frites are the Parisians' daily fare, the national dish; they have it every day.

Bifteck. The student had never heard the word before. Could it be English? Biffstek: Beefsteak? But why had the French discarded the s? And why did they have an English name for a national dish? He did not ask this. But he did ask about the other objects on his plate.

"Roast apples?" he queried, cautiously.

But not cautiously enough.

"No," said Røsok, stopping chewing. "Potatoes, Pommes de terre...."

Valemon felt himself blushing. Of course! They were called "ground apples" in some places in Norway too.

He looked down at his plate.

He took a piece of potato on his fork, swallowed. The moment he did so, his bitterness vanished. Could these be potatoes! Ordinary potatoes! He took another. And another. Not a bad word about home varieties. Boiled potatoes are good; roast potatoes are good; mashed potatoes are good. But pommes frites, fried in oil, golden, fragrant, crisp outside and soft within—pommes frites beat the lot. Oh, he would tell them about this at home! Perhaps he could start a restaurant in Norway! He took a mouthful of wine, drinking to himself.

He looked at the glass from which he had just drunk. The edge was chipped. He looked down at his plate. It

211

had bits out of it too. Then he looked at the table-cloth; it was badly stained, had not been washed for ages. He looked around him, at the floor. It was a *very* cheap place he had come to!

For a moment he sat thinking this over. Then, all at once, he smiled. He liked this. Poor places, but good food. Poor places, but friendly people.

He remembered—was it only yesterday? It seemed an eternity ago—another place, in the Moselle valley; he remembered a woman weeping convulsively, a man's gaping jaws, lips with blood on them.

He clasped his hands in gratitude beneath the table, gratitude for having crossed the Rhine safely, for being in Paris.

Very devoutly, he picked up his knife and fork again.

"What is it? " Røsok asked, looking at him.

The student tried to speak, but he could not. He could only point.

He had let his knife and fork drop. He was sitting leaning back in disgust, he could only point with a rigid first finger. From where he had cut into the beef a trail ran to a red pool on the plate.

"Oh," said Røsok, "is that all; beef is always like that in France; it's nice and juicy then."

Valemon shut his eyes; he felt cold sweat break out on his forehead. The room began to go round. He could not endure the sight of blood, he did not know why, to him it meant sickness, murder, perdition, death, dentists, operating theatres, castration, menstruation, all that was cruellest in life, blood.

Why, he thought, did no one tell me before I left that in France they serve beef bloody and in no other way! If they had, I should have stayed at home!

Hurriedly he ate a piece of bread and then took a gulp of wine. He stared fixedly at a point far away on one of the walls, kept his eyes firmly on it. He was furious, tortured, ashamed, in a trap. This is my Rubicon, he thought. Either I get up quickly from this table, if I don't pass out that is, and go straight back home to Norway. Or I eat it and stay. Grow up. Become a man of the world.

He sat; he prayed.

If I take potato with it, he thought. Lots of potato. He took two pommes frites and put them in his mouth, half chewed them, then he opened his mouth and counted:

"One, two, three!"

He popped the piece of beef in. He stared like a lunatic out into space; he could hear himself screaming; he was chewing. He was swallowing it.

He had swallowed it.

He sat expecting that he would vomit it up again. Waited. He could feel it at the back of his eyeballs. But it did not come.

Then he drew a deep breath. He gulped, wiped the sweat from his forehead with his napkin.

After a while he was sitting eating rare beef as if he had never done anything else. Finally, because he had seen Røsok doing this, he even took a piece of bread, and pressed it down on the plate, let it suck up its fill of juices and blood, then ate it. Cleaning one's plate with a piece of bread.

He sat there surveying his clean plate.

He had done away with the antithesis between fork and knife.

All at once, without knowing it, he had solved one of the world's great problems: how to eat up everything without it looking gross.

With a piece of French bread.

Then came salad.

Green lettuce salad.

Not as a trimming, not on a piece of bread and butter, but as a dish on its own. . . .

213

I'm having one adventure after the other, he thought.

He watched closely what the other did. First, he took the little bottle of oil, eased up the glass stopper and let a few drops fall. Then the same with the bottle of vinegar. Then he stirred it all round his plate with his knife and fork, so that the lettuce leaves became dabbled with the mixture.

All at once the student heard himself say:

"Pour faire de la bonne salade . . ."

"Oui? " Røsok said interrogatively.

Valemon switched from French and said:

"*Now* I understand. . . ."

Røsok wanted to know what.

"It's a phrase I learned at school. It was given as an example of the use of the partitive article. I learned it off by heart. I didn't then understand what lay behind it, that it really was salad it meant. *Real* salad."

And, almost to himself, he went on:

" . . . il faut de l'huile, du vinaigre, et du sel."

Ah, should you use salt as well?

He asked that. Røsok told him you could do as you liked about it.

After that, Valemon supposed the meal was finished.

But no: a plate of cheese followed. Cheese for dinner? Yes, said Røsok, you always had cheese.

The inside of the cheese was a yellow mass, soft and mushy; it looked as if it was in a state of semi-disintegration. The outside was a white, floury skin—didn't it look like mould? The cheese smelt faintly of lavatory. Could one eat a thing like that? He glanced secretly at the other to see whether he cut off the mouldly skin; but the man cut right through it, put a piece on bread and ate it.

"One, two, three. . . ."

Incomprehensible, he thought, how good everything in this country tastes.

He cocked his head on one side, pondering, chewing. And, he thought, how remarkably *right* it all tastes.

*

After *that*, Valemon supposed the meal was finished.

But no. Yet another plate appeared.

On it lay four red cherries, morello cherries. And also a large yellowish, unknown fruit. In a cautious whisper he asked what it was.

Peach, Røsok said.

He picked it up carefully. Fresh peach. He had only tasted tinned peaches before. He had thought peach a thing you only got tinned; but he did not say so then. . . . Fresh peach. Real peach. Carefully he felt its skin. He smelled it. Swooned. He almost put it against his cheek.

He ate the cherries. Røsok asked if he didn't want the peach.

"The waitress won't mind, will she, if I take it with me?

The man looked at him, uncomprehendingly.

"No."

Valemon was not wearing a jacket. He couldn't very well put the peach in his trousers pocket, and he did not want to have it in his hand; it looked so fragile, as if it could melt. All at once he noticed that there was a breast pocket on the left-hand side of his red-checked sports shirt; he had never used it before, and he rendered silent thanks to the factory in Norway. He put the peach into this pocket and held it there with his right hand; it lay like a little bird. All at once he felt himself becoming randy.

Was it the peach; the well-being, the wine; the good food? Suddenly there he was with a hot little rod under his trousers; all at once he was sitting there with an enormous stand hidden by the table. He tried jerking his legs. He tried pulling out his trousers to ease it upwards and back against his belly, so that it would not stick out so horribly.

"What is it?" Røsok asked.

"Nothing!" he cried.

"Well, shall we get the bill?" Røsok said.

"Yes!" cried Valemon. He made a great effort to think of something depressing; there must be some sorrow in the world, death, a corpse, wasps, was not Hitler soon to start a war?

The man asked if they shouldn't perhaps each pay for themselves?

"Yes!" Valemon cried.

Røsok looked at him searchingly for a moment, his head on one side; then he turned towards the waitress. Instantly, she was standing there at the table. Swift as lightning, Valemon seized up his napkin and laid it over his groin, then he leaned forward so that his top half was against the edge of the table. My God, my God, get me through this, he prayed. He noticed that the waitress too was now regarding him with greater interest than before.

"L'addition?" she enquired softly.

"Oui," said Røsok.

For all his embarrassment, Valemon made a note of the word: l'addition. The bill. A useful word to know.

He tilted sideways on his chair as he fished for his purse in his trouser-pocket. He opened it with his right hand. He found a ten franc note, laid it on the table. The woman took it and put down two and a half francs change. He took the coins and popped them into his purse. How am I going to get out of here, he thought? I shall have to walk, be upright; I can't go on all fours. . . .

"You mustn't forget the tip," he heard Røsok say.

"Tip?"

"Yes," said Røsok.

"But . . ." said Valemon, feeling a great leaden weight on him, "but it said . . . Why then is it called Prix Fixe?"

"The price is fixed," Røsok said and gave the waitress a hurried, apologetic smile, "but in France you always give a tip."

Valemon too glanced up at the waitress; she must have thought it strange having two men sitting there talking a language she did not understand; but at all events she understood that the older man had rebuked the younger, reprimanded him. Valemon felt it so. Slowly his face flushed. At the same time he felt betrayed, cheated. He had based all his calculations on 7.50 francs, had even worked out the difference between a dinner in Bergen and one in Paris; he had been feeling so rich, and now he felt bankrupt.

He turned his head away, so as to be alone with his blushes and his grief.

"Monsieur est peut-être étranger," he heard the waitress say to Røsok. "Oui," the latter replied, "il vient de Norvège." "Tiens," she replied sweetly, "un Norvegien. ..." Her voice was gentle, calm, with a hint of a smile, certainly not offended. Bless her, he thought. And at that moment he noticed that he no longer had an erection. It's an ill wind, he thought. After all, I did ask God to get rid of it. God's ways are inscrutable. He granted my prayer. But, thought Valemon—he exacted quite a price!

"How much?" he said to the other, in a thick voice.

"Fifteen per cent or thereabouts."

"*Fifteen per cent!*"

"Yes, that's the usual."

He tried to work it out, but his head was whirling. He did not know why, but he thought it atrocious. It reminded him briefly of the time when, as a boy, he used to spend the summer travelling the country districts of Trøndelag with his grandfather. His grandfather was a margarine traveller and sometimes let his grandson accompany him; it was like a summer holiday, the trips often lasted up to a fortnight. There would be three of them in the car: in the back seat grandfather, tall, fat, heavy, regal, with a silvery goatee; in the front seat grandfather's smooth-shaven chauffeur, his private chauffeur, who otherwise was a clerk in the office of the margarine factory in Trondhjem; beside the chauffeur Valemon. It was the gates.

217

When they came to one—and there was a cattle gate every mile or so—Valemon was never able to jump down and be helpful, for out of the grass beside each gate popped a farm boy, who opened it for them, and shut it behind them, and then stood cap in hand with the other hand outstretched: for a five-øre piece. Valemon's grandfather was used to this and just smiled; every morning he filled his coat pocket with five-øre pieces, enough for the day's drive, and with an elegant gesture tossed one of those coppery-red coins through the window, so that it glowed in the sun. Valemon never got used to this. He thought it was embarrassing, he thought it was shaming, he thought it was begging. Yes, begging. The farm boy had sat there in the grass, perhaps all day, waiting for a car to come along.... And they were not only boys. Often they were girls. He would never forget their evil, hungry eyes; their avid little hands, like claws; when the copper coin fell in the road, they flung themselves over it in the dust like wild cats. At one place there was even a woman who sat beside the gate, she sat on the grass knitting stockings; and when a car came, she dropped her knitting and became all arms and legs like a mad thing. Valemon felt sure that she lost many stitches, ruined half a stocking—in order to earn five øre.

People should not demean themselves, Valemon had thought. Being a person meant... He did not know what. He just knew that it did *not* mean standing beside a gate begging and thanking.

Tips for opening gates, tips for serving food.

He took out another franc. But perhaps that was not enough? He could not work it out. He picked out another small coin: it was fifty centimes. That surely would be enough? He threw a hurried, wary glance up at the waitress. Thank goodness, she was not embarrassed by the situation. She seemed to find it quite natural.

"Merci, Monsieur," she said and bowed her head; easily and unconcernedly she swept up the coins and put them in the pocket of her apron. Then she turned to

Røsok. Here, too, she took the coins and swept them elegantly into her pocket.

"Merci, Monsieur," she said again, bowing her head.

They pushed back their chairs, stood up.

Neither of them had hat or coat.

"Au revoir, Messieurs," she said to them, now with a slight bow from the waist, she might almost have been curtseying.

"Au revoir," Røsok said.

"Au revoir, Mademoiselle," Valemon said, bowing in his turn, but not deeply; he had that peach in his pocket.

For a brief moment he stood there. He had intended, when the meal was over, to say a few words of appreciation to their nice waitress, had looked forward to thanking her. But he could scarcely do so now. She had seen him at a loss; she had seen him blushing and humbled. Not now, he thought. Only the perfect customer can thank the perfect waitress. Another time, he thought—but not now. He looked at her hands. God, how he wanted to take her hand and kiss it! Kiss the hand of this female Shakespeare!

He gulped.

"Au revoir, Mademoiselle," he whispered, and walked out. He held his right hand over the peach; it now felt like a little breast, a girl's breast. . . .

Outside dusk had already fallen. And while they stood on the pavement, it became dark. The sky above them acquired a strange, deep-blue indigo colour. But at the same time the electric lights blossomed out from street standards, from advertisements. The city had been alive before, but now it was doubly so, it almost vibrated with light. Again he was aware of the great, mature, shaggy warm smell of big city, a smell of sin and sweetness.

The man suggested that the student might like the rest of the evening for himself?

"Yes!" slipped out of Valemon.

219

In the restaurant, Røsok, in answer to a cautious question from Valemon, had told him that he had a son. What was his name? Pierre. How old was he? Eighteen. Did he speak French? Yes, only French. Not Norwegian? No; he had never been out of France. (Røsok grimaced and looked down; was the man embarrassed over his own son? Valemon too looked down; he himself had a baby son. Hm. Its mother had christened it Viggo. Hm.) If Valemon would like, he and Pierre could meet one day; they could perhaps see a bit of Paris together? Yes, be glad to. What about the day after tomorrow, at two o'clock in the shop? Yes, be glad to.

They were standing on the pavement. Valemon shook the other's hand and thanked him for his company and help.

"Ah," said the man and gave a slight cough.

Valemon bit his lip. Blinked his eyes. This was rather ticklish. Die Mädels von Paris. Ha ha. He shuddered. He had not really thought of anything else the whole evening. But where were they? How did one set about it? He opened his mouth; he happened to catch sight of the man's face: it was a Sunnmørian face: groaning, he said:

"What is Byrrh?"

The man took a short step back.

"Byrrh?"

"Yes," said Valemon, "I've seen it on posters. . . ."

"Ah," said the man, taking a breath, "it's a kind of apéritif. . . ."

"Is it nice?"

"Ah."

"Is it e-ex-expensive?"

"Not too bad."

Such was their parting. The man had to go back to the shop, he had work that had to be done; the student was going to his hotel.

Paris.

*

A short way along the street he stopped. He drew a deep breath of relief: free; he felt his skin tingling; for a moment he was on the point of dancing. Then he narrowed his eyes, wondering. Hadn't it seemed that the man too was rather relieved? At being rid of the student?

Valemon smiled.

"Frændr eru frændum verstir," (Kinsmen are worse to each other), he whispered in old Norse. Icelandic. Then he walked on.

But, having mounted the steps to the hotel, having pushed the door open and entered the narrow, dusty vestibule, having caught the smell of old plush and seen the lights glinting in the stained mirrors, he smiled no longer.

The moment he was standing in front of the desk bowing to the woman with the queer tooth, the game had begun in earnest. From then on, he was alone.

He was never to remember what he said to her, or what he had intended to say, for again she had shrunk back wide-eyed, as if edging away from someone dangerous; her hand trembled as she took his key from the board and handed it to him. What on earth had come over her? he wondered. He glanced down to see if perhaps his flies were open; no, done up.

His suitcase and rucksack were standing by the stairs. On his way to them he passed a narrow, tall mirror; it reached from floor to ceiling. It was covered with fly-spot, but even so he caught a glimpse of himself in it. He shrank back and stood as if paralysed. That ghastly face there—was it his? He blinked; his eyes seemed suddenly terrifyingly blue. He had not seen himself in a mirror for a week. When he left Bergen, he had been a member of the white race. But now . . .! Never, not even on an Easter trip in Norway, had he been so sun-burned. He was dark-brown! A week before he had been a white man—now he was a negro!

But not evenly negro, not negro all over; for in the midst

221

of the chocolate brown shone his nose, white, sickly, like a lantern. The skin had peeled right off it—and he had never noticed!—it had just dropped off the ridge of his nose, like a shell. But the tip was even worse! It was completely naked, skinned; the underskin was showing; the tip was a round wound the size of a ten-øre piece. The wound did not hurt at all; it merely radiated white, no, a light lilac—and those cornflower-blue eyes! He looked like a cross between Othello and a deep-water fish!

Trembling, he turned towards the woman, pointed to his nose, said:

"C'est le soleil!"

"Oui," she replied and drew a deep breath, "vous pèlez, Monsieur."

"Oui," he said. (That's taught me a word. It must mean peel. But then what is: I am peeling? Je pèle? I must look it up.)

The woman had gone past him, intending to take his baggage.

He came to.

He darted forward like a falcon and reached the handle of the suitcase a split second before her. She tried to get hold of his rucksack. He was on it like a hawk, ahead of her again.

He was snorting with agitation.

But, she said, frightened, and again at a distance and wide-eyed—shouldn't she take his baggage up to his room?

"Non," he said, panting. A ghastly fear had come over him. Never having stayed in an hotel before, he had the most fantastic ideas of what the bill might amount to. Porters, doormen, page-boys, chamber-maids, he had read about them, they were children of the devil made by God for man's perdition; they seemed so polite and kind and helpful—but only so that afterwards they could hold out a hand, a threatening hand, a claw, demanding a coin, oh, a large coin, perhaps even a note! What might he not have to pay the woman, if he let her carry his baggage up to his room! God knows, there was nothing so dreadful in the whole world as tipping. It's like falling into a sea, like disintegrating! There are no rules! It is a world of arbitrariness.

It is like wanting to go by train, having to go by train; you have had a telegram, are in a hurry, you get to the ticket office, push in the price of the ticket, but no ticket comes, nothing happens, you peer inside, the man in there is reading a newspaper, sitting motionless with his feet on a chair reading a newspaper, and slowly you realize that the system has ceased to exist, you will have to pay, pay extra, and while the clock ticks away you begin slowly to peel off notes, and go on peeling, and this is the nightmare part of it, your nightmare, because you so badly want to reach your destination before it is too late, it is a matter of life and death, and only the train can get you there, and you had thought there were set prices on the railway, but the man in there does not see you, you do not exist, you have begun peeling off notes, but how long have you to go on before the man in there will lay his newspaper aside?—perhaps you will peel off all the notes you own and possess, and slowly, without looking up, the man stretches out a hand and takes them, draws them in through the hatch and you call out "Ticket!" He turns his head hastily and looks at you, with snakey eyes. "Not enough," he says, and picks up his newspaper again. "But how much!" you call. "It has to be enough," he says and goes on reading. "But how much is enough!" you say. He shrugs his shoulders. "That remains to be seen," he says. Again he puts his feet up on the chair, reads. The clock ticks; you are in a world where even everything would not be enough; you will never get there; you are sinking, dying; for man cannot live in a world that does not have definite rules.

*

223

"Non!" he repeated and clung to his baggage. Surely she could not be entitled to a tip, if he carried it up himself? Or would she, even then?

Never again whould he stay in an hotel! Never again would he indulge in foreign travel. When he got back to Norway he would build himself a little log hut in the woods, up on the mountainside, and live there always, all his life, all alone, he would never move from his hut! He would himself carry his suitcase and rucksack inside, would himself fetch the water, himself fetch wood—and once installed he would lie down on the floor, full length, hands clasped under his head, and look up at the timber roof and thank God that he was alone!—thank God that his world was chemically free of doormen, porters and pageboys!

He looked at the woman.

"Non," he panted, "je le fais moi-même."

She lowered her head.

There we are!—he thought—now she's offended! There is, God knows, nothing so dreadful in the whole world as a hurt face. He felt giddy, weak, for a moment he was on the point of holding it out to her; here, for God's sake! But he hardened his heart. He was not made that way, there was nothing that suited him less than being hard-hearted—but he had to be. He searched for an excuse, a lie that would take the sting out of what he was doing; and as always, when he had to lie, it incensed him. He was about to say: "Dangereux," but if he said his baggage was dangerous it could mean anything from cyanide to dynamite—and then they might turn him out of the hotel! Thrown out onto the street! Alone in Paris!

"C'est personnel, madame!" he said. He said it as if his suitcase was stuffed with MS, musical scores, descriptions of patents; he held the curved palm of his hand over his rucksack, protectively, conjuringly; as if he was an inventor, as if the rucksack contained irreplaceable instruments, precision instruments, clockwork, hydrometers, compasses, thermometers of paper-thin glass, carefully packed and wrapped in tissue paper; he so acted himself into his part that for a moment he believed it himself and shuddered at the thought of the fragile precision instruments of paper-thin glass in his rucksack, he said: "C'est très personnel . . . !"

"Bon," she said and sighed, "Comme vous voulez." She looked at him, then asked him to follow her and she would show him the way to his room.

He bent down to pick up his rucksack and suitcase. But what was lying there? On one of the stairs? A peach?

A peach?

He clapped his hand to his breast pocket. It was empty. So it was his peach! It must have fallen out, when he plunged for his baggage. Surprised, he picked it up, held it in his hand, examined it, was it bruised? He blew the dust off it, put his nose to it, laid his cheek against it, ah, it was his peach, his own peach.

The woman had halted on the stairs, their eyes met. Then her gaze moved aside, she stood there looking straight at the wall. She stood thus for a couple of seconds, her lips moved as if she was praying. Then she drew a deep breath, crossed herself and walked on up the stairs.

The corridor was as dark as the grave. She turned a wall switch. Explained that he must always be careful to switch the light off after him. He was about to ask why, but perhaps electricity was expensive in Paris; they did not have waterfalls. Strange. How did the French get electricity, if they did not have waterfalls?

She poked a long key into a door, turned it, opened the door

"Voilà, Monsieur," she said. "Votre chambre."

"Merci," he said, "merci beaucoup." He bowed to her, stepped with his load across the threshold. It was pitch black in the room. She switched on the light behind him; at the same moment he almost had heat stroke. It could have been 25°C outdoors, but in there in that room it must have been over 30. His suitcase and rucksack with all their precision instruments slipped from his hands and landed with a thud on the floor. Air, he thought, what is air in French? Window, he thought, perhaps I have been given a room without a window?

"La fenêtre," he whispered.

He could feel the perspiration trickling down his forehead, down his neck, he wanted to unbutton the neck of his shirt, but it was already open.

The woman opened the window.

One gasp and he was there, gulping air.

"Oh," he groaned, "merci!"

He remained beside the window while she was talking; he also opened the outside shutters with their horizontal slats and fastened them back with the hook. Yes, that was the washbasin; yes, with hot and cold water; yes, that was the wardrobe; yes, that was the light; yes, he would remember to switch it off when he went out; yes, there was the bell-push for the chamber-maid, if he wanted anything; yes, thank you, thank you.

The great air of Paris penetrated to him as he stood by the window. It was night, dark, hot.

Then the woman was going; he took a step forward and bowed; he happened to touch the left side of his shirt with his hand and an idea struck him, after all she had been nice, she had wanted to carry his baggage for him.

He took the peach and held it out to her:

"Voilà," he said, "vous le voulez?"

"Mais comment!" she said and raised a hand fending it off. He felt puzzled. Oh, perhaps peach was feminine. Yes, it was bound to be feminine. He corrected himself.

"Vous *la* voulez? Oui?"

"Mais non!" she said. "Merci!"

"Une pèche," he said, gaily.

"Mais non!" she said. Her strange tooth glinted. She

was breathing agitatedly. "Je viens de manger!" she said, but he did not understand that.

"Mais si!" he said. "Pour vous!"

"Mais non!" she cried, walking backwards, repeated "mais non!" reached the door, opened it, gave a gasp, stepped backwards through it, shut it hurriedly; then all was still.

Valemon stood there thinking. Strange people, the French. What had he done wrong?

Well, well, if she did not want the peach. . . .

He put it carefully down on the chest of drawers. It was a broad chest of drawers and above it was a broad, oval mirror. Good God, what a sight he was. Perhaps the woman had thought he was making advances? That he was *trying it on* with the peach? That the moment she took his peach, he would fling himself upon her and growling like some member of the bear family, rape her on the floor? At the thought of that, the face in the mirror broke into a grin, which showed him his own teeth; they were terrifyingly white; he himself was so frightened that he took a step back.

He looked at the bed. It was enormous. He had not been given a double room, had he? So that he had to pay double? . . . He reassured himself: the price had been mentioned on the first occasion, when Røsok took him there: 12 francs a day, including petit déjeuner, presumably a small breakfast . . . 12 francs, was that cheap? or expensive? He did not know. About one and a half crowns a day, without tips. Tips would bring it up to about two crowns a day.

In Bergen he had a room with breakfast and an evening meal for 80 crowns a month.

Carefully he smoothed the bedspread with his hand and sat down on the edge of the bed.

Now he could allow himself a rest. What a day he had had!

He clasped his hands behind his head and let himself fall back. The bed was even softer than he had thought: it had a dip in the middle, it was like lying in a slack hammock, he crawled up the steep slope with some difficulty and got into a sitting position again. He took off his riding boots.

He lay down on the bed properly, stretched out, hands behind his head; he spread and wiggled his toes; there really are moments when life is good, when life almost vindicates itself. . . .

He lay there feeling the dinner in his body: he relived each course, each taste, each smell; he was like a lover after a meeting, who has to recall every word, every look, every touch, every kiss; who wants to go over it all again from start to finish, but who never reaches the end, because each individual memory fades into dreaming and all the dreams come back with further promise. . . . The radishes; the sardines; a bite of that lovely bread; a mouthful of wine; the sausage, that dangerous wonderful sausage; bread; a mouthful of wine; the bifteck and pommes frites; those golden strips of potato; bread; a mouthful of wine; and tomorrow he would have another such dinner!—God, how good that bread was!—and the wine!—he was far from tipsy, just mellow, nicely mellow; he lay there, hands clasped behind his head, knowing that he had eaten the world's best and richest meal, the perfect meal, from start to finish; it was not just the food itself, but the sequence of the dishes. . . . Suddenly he was able to view his own digestive system as if he had X-ray eyes: the courses lay inside him in layers, as in a silo, the radishes right at the bottom, then the meat and lettuce, and right at the top four red cherries; he felt like a cross-section of a layer cake!—and to crown it all, he did not feel in the least stuffed, not in the least as if he had eaten too much, merely lightly, genially, well. . . .

Just lightly, genially, well. . . .

All at once, he felt that he had to go.

Had to.

He removed his hands from behind his head and sat up.

He had to go that moment. Well, perhaps not exactly that moment. It felt as if he had perhaps a minute in hand, but he would have to then.

Hurriedly he seized his riding boots and pulled them on. He walked across to the door and opened it. The corridor was in utter darkness. Had the woman said anything about the lavatory? Ah, she had said something about a bell for service, he went into his room again, there it was, he pressed it. He waited. Nothing happened. He went out into the corridor, switched on the light, hoped there might be a sign somewhere in the corridor, he went from door to door, what would he not have given for a board with W.C. on it! Anyway, what was it in French? Good God, he had been a whole year at the Commercial College in Bergen, he could write a business letter in perfect French, he could with utmost fluency say: "Je vous prie, Messieurs, de bien vouloir accepter l'assurance de mes sentiments les plus distingués," which means "Yours faithfully"—but had anyone ever told him what loo was? Could he say W.C.? Water closet? But that was English!

He ran back into his room, dancing, and pressed the bell again. He looked round the room in terror; in dire necessity.... There was the basin. But what was that low porcelain affair on the floor beside it? He took a step towards it, surveyed it; it was like a low washbasin, pear-shaped, and in the middle of it was a spout, a kind of water sprinkler, what could it be?

At that moment he heard sounds in the corridor and stormed out. Towards him, but infinitely slowly, came a black, unkempt, shuffling female figure. It was a young girl in a dark, shiny, deep violet, almost black, hotel overall, baggy, with something tied round the waist for a belt. She was young and actually quite pretty, but her hair was uncombed and straggly, she looked broken, more dead than alive, her gait was heavy and apathetic, her breasts pendant, her body seemed composed of bags of flour; she had a long-handled broom in her hand and smelled of sour floor cloths. Her expression was one of utter indifference and apathy.

She held the broom in front of her, leaned on it; he could see that her hands were wet with water, she looked at the wall and said tonelessly:

"Oui, Monsieur?"

For an instant he stood dumbly in front of this young demon of slovenliness. Then he cried:

"Une toilette? Vous avez une toilette ici?"

"Mais oui," she said, raising her eyebrows very slightly.

"Où." he called. "Où?"

Third door on the left, she explained; then she turned and went. He watched her for a moment. She had low, down-trodden shoes; she had no stockings. He shuddered.

"Merci," he called.

One, two, three. It must be here. On the door was "Lavabos". Lavabos? Had that a connection with laver? To wash?

"Lavabos?" he called to the woman in the corridor, loudly, interrogatively.

"Oui, Monsieur, c'est ça," came the reply from the distance.

The place was in darkness. He switched on the light. The room was of concrete, rectangular, about three foot six either way. It was empty. There was no pan or seat, neither of porcelain nor wood; there was nothing. The floor was quite bare. There was, though, a hole in the floor, about eight inches in diameter, and up under the ceiling was what looked like a cistern, with a chain hanging from it. The room was either a pissoir or a shower. Yes, this was where you had a shower, washed. That was why it was called lavabos.

He was in the corridor again. The woman had disappeared. He could not see any other doors. He stormed off in the direction in which the girl had gone.

"Mademoiselle!" he called. "Mademoiselle!"

Slowly she emerged out of the gloom, a ghost, reluctant, supine, lifeless.

"Alors?" she said, brushing the hair from her forehead.

"C'est faux!" he groaned.

"Non pas un pissoir," he was dancing, "mais une toilette! Vous savez—une toilette!"

He took the plunge and risked the English word.

"Un W.C.—vous comprenez?"

"Mais c'est ça," she said.

He looked at her. Then he seized her by the arm and hauled her along with him to the door he had opened. They stood together looking into the concrete room. She looked straight in front of her, unmoved, insensitive; she said:

"Mais c'est ça, Monsieur." She nodded her head towards the little room.

"C'est ça?"

"Oui, Monsieur. C'est ça."

For a brief moment she stood there, then she turned and walked off down the corridor.

He was left standing there, defeated, helpless. He took a step into the room. Looked at the cement floor. Stepped out into the corridor again, was about to call for the woman, abandoned the idea. Went back into the room again. Bent suspiciously over the hole in the floor. It looked like a waste pipe in a laundry. Could that really be for doing big jobs in? If so, you would have to squat? And true enough: in front of the hole, on the floor, were two slabs of cement like big foot-rests. He thought of Hollywood, where it was said, the leading women film stars were asked to put the print of their feet in wet cement, which then hardened and became immortal evidence. But those Hollywood impressions are of pretty, small, bare women's feet, these cement foot-rests were enormous; they were like foot-prints of a flat-footed soldier, of an Alpini with hobnails in his boots. The toes of the foot-rests faced the door, indicating the way in which you had to squat; they stood up an inch above the rest of the floor, with an empty space between them, presumably so that the water could flow round without one's feet getting wet.

The minute was up. It was a sort of pang, like the

beginning of a tremendous orgasm; it had occurred to him that he must have been holding it back all across the Continent, out of apprehension of the three days in Germany that were coming; he got the little bolt on the inside of the door pushed shut, wrenched his belt undone, took aim and squatted, in the very nick of time. He felt as if he was splitting; he felt tears of cramp, enjoyment, relief, festivity, spurt from his eyes; for a second he thought, having a baby must be like this; momentarily he thought that it was a stroke of genius on God's part to make necessity so full of sensual pleasure. . . .

After a while his thighs began to ache; after another while it felt as if his knees were going to break. He tried to ease his position by leaning forward, thought for a moment of supporting himself with his hands, but decided he did not want to touch the floor. Ridiculous, he thought. This is the most ridiculous system I have ever seen. Even in the army—well, I have not been in that, but I have been in a work camp in Norway, up in the mountains one summer— and the first thing we did was to lay a tree trunk horizontally across two low trestles in the wood behind the camp; that's elementary.

Paper.

He had not had time to investigate the roll on the wall.

He pulled off one small piece—and that was all! It was the end of the roll. There he squatted groaning with the pain of it, thinking hard and intently. He removed the empty cardboard cylinder from the holder. It was made up of a number of layers. He tore it apart, divided it into suitable bits. If I am economical, he thought, perhaps it will be enough. . . .

Here am I, he thought, squatting, in the great city of Paris famed for its light and its beauty, wiping my arse with cardboard.

He rose to his feet, trembling and exhausted, reached for the chain hanging from the cistern, pulled.

232

The room filled with a noise like the Last Trump. It reminded him of his confirmation. That had been in a cathedral, this was a concrete closet; those church bells overhead sounding as if they had got loose and were falling onto his head; the organ down below—he looked down, the abyss had opened, a flood was rising! He saw, but did not understand what he saw. He thought that he must have pulled too hard, that he had broken through the pipe, even pulled a hole in the actual main, that he was disrupting the whole of Paris; he shut his eyes, was convinced he was about to drown; the door would not open, he leaped into the air; the door would not open; he squeezed into a corner, and stood there on tip-toe, with head averted, while a flood raged across the whole of the cement floor; he clawed in panic for a hold on the lintel so that he could pull himself up; for in his inner eye he could see his own great turds swirling in the flood, soon to reach him, spinning round and round, heavy, hyperdangerous, and hit him in the face like boomerangs; he would be the man who was drowned; the man who was knocked dead by his own turds.

He stood for a while looking down at the floor; the waves had subsided and now it was just seething; the cistern gave a last gurgle.

Indeed, he thought with pounding heart, indeed France too is a dangerous country; I shall have to be on my guard.

Back in the corridor, he stopped in front of a door that was standing open. Fancy leaving the door of your room open, he thought. He could see right in, right on to the bed, he saw a chest of drawers, he saw a suitcase standing on the floor, he saw a rucksack. But this is my room, he thought.

So the chamber-maid. ... When she left me back there by the lavabos, she must have walked past here. She must have seen my door standing open, yet she did not shut it.

He went inside, pulled the door firmly shut and locked

it. Queer kind of keys they had in France. Long, thin and black. The lock itself was pretty peculiar too: the keyhole was so large and wide, the key rattled in it.

At the bottom of the door, down by the floor, was a gap, an inch deep. Strange. Wouldn't there be an awful draught? Ah, he though, that's for pushing letters in through.

He had seen that on a film. It was fearfully exciting seeing the corner of an envelope appear on the floor and come in, in little jerks. An oblong envelope, with a gold monogram on it.

The letter.

He stared spellbound at the promising gap under the door.

Strange, but standing there he suddenly knew that a letter is the finest and most precious thing there is. The richest gift a person can receive: a letter.

The letter.

It does not need to be from Voltaire; nor from the Academy; nor from La Duchesse. The envelope does not need to be of the finest hand-made paper; it does not have to have a gold monogram, nor a waxen seal; but perhaps it may be enriched with some beautiful little embellishments, arabesques, drawings; it does not need to be brought in by a footman wearing silk stockings and shoes with silver buckles; it can just as well come by post, with an ordinary stamp on it; but all the same the envelope must have a certain substance, weigh a little on your hand; when the letter arrives, the writing on it will be clear and firm and neat; the address will be carefully spaced; every little detail will bear witness to thought and strength, be evidence of smiling assurance, evidence of laughter; when the letter comes and you turn the envelope this way and that, the flap will not be half open; the sender will have carefully licked each of the gummed edges, twice; the sender will have made sure that the letter is well sealed; none but you shall be able to read it; it will be closed, closed even to you; when

234

this letter comes, it cannot be an ordinary letter; even though there is nothing sensational about the envelope, it will stand out immediately; the sender has not let it be one that might risk lying unread for days, or perhaps be put un-opened into the waste-paper basket; this letter insists on its rights; it glows; it shines; calmly, quietly, authoritatively it says: "Here I am!"; when this letter comes one day, you will know it the moment you see it; there will be laughter hidden in it, as if even the envelope was saying: "You idiot, didn't you know? Haven't you known the whole time . . .?"

The letter.

He was standing in front of the oval mirror.

He had intended to change, to put on his suit and shoes; but when he saw how crumpled his light grey trousers had become from being in the suitcase he had to give up the idea. Perhaps the hotel had an iron? He did not dare ask for one; it might cost extra. But he knew another way, familiar to students the world over, which has the ad-vantage of costing nothing. Before you go to bed you put your trousers, well smoothed and stretched, between the mattress and the bottom sheet; then you lie full length on top of the sheet, acting as your own iron. There is only one condition, if you are to get a good result. You must lie quite still, must not move all night. If you toss and turn in your sleep, or are otherwise restless, in the morn-ing, your trousers will probably look like a pleated skirt.

While he was dealing with the bed, he remembered, shuddering, a story from Bergen. A student there had in-vented a way of getting an especially sharp crease in his trousers. Every evening before he put them under the sheet, he carefully rubbed the edge with a piece of dry toilet soap. For two months the chap went about with the finest creases in Bergen. But one evening there was a ball, in the Logesal itself, and there it happened. His trouser legs split. First one, then the other. They opened, like pea pods. There must be a slow acting acid in toilet soap. Instead of dancing in two trouser legs, he was suddenly dancing in four long flaps of cloth, and he had red suspenders for his socks.

The fellow had been a dandy; and that finished him. After that they called him kiltie; some called him Carmen; he had to leave Bergen; it was said he had gone to live in Hamar; a horrible story.

*

He saw himself in the mirror. In his riding boots, breeches, grey woollen sweater and red-checked sports shirt with the collar outside, with his fair, curly hair and dark brown face, he thought he looked quite presentable. If only his nose hadn't been . . .

He leaned towards the mirror. It was adjustable; it was on two supports, one on either side of the chest of drawers; it brought a quick memory of the chest of drawers and mirror that his parents had had in their bedroom when he was a child. He scrutinized the tip of his nose; picked at it cautiously. A flake fell off. The patch was now the size of a 25-øre piece, the bared underskin glowed like a pale wood-violet, corpse-like.

Could you get cancer from the sun?

I must buy a tin of vaseline tomorrow, he thought.

He saw the peach. It was still there on the chest of drawers. Carefully he picked it up, weighed it in his hand; he touched its skin.

His first evening in Paris.

His eyes fell on his sponge bag that he had put on the chest of drawers. He had been thinking of it all day. In it were tooth brush, tooth paste, razor, strop, shaving brush, soap. But it also had a private, gallant little compartment. What if the German customs man at Flensburg had made him turn out his sponge bag! "Kinder, Küche, Kirche." In Germany, they were bound to shove you in prison, if they caught you with a french letter on you!

He had been thinking of the sponge bag all day.

236

"My peach and my son," he suddenly heard himself say.

The words surprised him. . . .

It's a question of politeness, he thought. I was polite that time, the first night; it's over three years ago. Hm. "Take that *thing* off," she said; I felt it would be tactless to ask why; thought a mature woman knew about that sort of thing; so I took it off. Yes, little Viggo, my son. I had not seen the woman before that evening; in the middle of the night I found myself in bed with her. Life is utterly blind. A man thinks he has a little sense, a bit of intelligence, that he is able to choose, that he can plot his future. Then, hey presto, he's caught.

Politeness is lethal.

But, is it? My politeness at least gave *you* life, little Viggo. When I die, you shall be the first in the throng, the right of the first-born will be yours, I have nothing else to leave you—you shall stand out in front of all who point the finger at my coffin, you shall lead the cry.

Do you know what?

Now, as I stand beside this chest of drawers, about to sally forth into the city, Paris, La Ville Lumière, when I really am armed to the *teeth*! Viggo!—you know: not even *now* can I bring myself to take one with me! It would be discourteous to the women of Paris. . . .

An insult. . . .

Cry it *twice*, my small son whom I have never seen, when you and the others are standing beside my coffin:

"This man died of politeness."

Slowly he put the peach down. Ran the comb through his hair a last time. Went to the door.

He stopped, turned, surveyed the room. The lino on the floor was worn, had holes in it; the big iron bedstead with brass knobs on its four posts had an aged mattress that sagged in the middle; there was no hot water in the tap, so how was he going to shave in the morning? The paper on the walls was torn and covered with stains; when he had lain on the bed mentally chewing the cud of his dinner, he had looked up at the room's only source of light, a naked bulb, speckled with fly-spot, hanging on a wire from the ceiling; on the window sill—he had run his finger across it, as he stood there listening to the sounds of the city—was a thick layer of dust; when he had opened the wardrobe to hang up his jacket, the door had half fallen out, the top hinge having rusted through so that the door was being held in place by just the lock and the bottom hinge.

He felt like a king.

This was his room.

He turned the key, opened the door, held the long key in his hand. It was a sort of finer edition of a Norwegian *stabbur* key.

The key to Paris.

On the way down, half-way down the stairs, he was overcome by emotion and the pounding of his heart. Paris by night. For a moment he was on the point of turning and going back to his room. Could he exhibit himself in Paris with a nose like that?

He tried to find an attitude that would allow him to keep his right hand in front of his face, without appearing so peculiar that people would wonder what he was hiding under it; perhaps a sort of philsopher's attitude, slightly pensive, the knuckle of his thumb nonchalantly resting on his chin, while his index finger seemingly played with the tip of his nose, at the same time hiding it.

He walked hurriedly through the hall, bowed sideways to the woman in the desk, he heard her call: "Votre clef, Monsieur!" and he called back that yes, thank you, he had his key. He actually had it in his left hand trouser-pocket, and there he intended it to stay; he was taking no chances; Paris was swarming with hotel thieves.

And with apaches! He was out on the steps; he pressed his hand quickly over his left-hand hip pocket, where his passport was; then quickly over his right-hand pocket, where his pocket book was; yes, both buttons were properly done up. Apaches. First they stick a knife into you and then take your money. If only they would be content with murder.

Paris by night. . . .

He was standing on the pavement: stunned.

*

He stood there stunned by the lights, by the white lights, by the red lights, but most by the shimmering white ones; stunned by the quiet roar of the street, by the people, by the warmth of the night, by the smell of Paris, by the city's strength, by its immense power.

With unseeing eyes, he was gazing at a picture of delights, a description he had read in an old book, and the vision momentarily paralysed him.

"*Moulin Rouge*, (The Red Mill) which is the particular haunt of foreigners and cocottes, comprises a garden, a music hall and a ballroom with a restaurant. There is dancing every evening, a late night on Saturday and a matinée on Sunday. The can-can is danced every hour. The orchestra plays a certain call and above the buzz of sound in the ballroom the cry "La Quadrille!" is heard. Then the foreigner sees to his surprise how the ladies lift their skirts to their waists, and—in order to get their legs going—knock the hats off the heads of the gentlemen nearest them with the points of their toes. The music plays and in the middle of the swirling confusion quadrilles form, made up only of ladies, who are paid to entertain the public with their dancing.

"All the beauties at once raise their skirts and underclothes up to the level of their heads displaying their lower limbs, which are covered only with some semi-opaque material. The music from the orchestra becomes wilder and wilder, and the can-canning ladies are carried away by it, until they are like furies. With foam at the corners of their mouths they dash about furiously, spin

239

round on one leg, scratch themselves behind their ear with the other foot, fall and utter wild shrieks, while their lace skirts swirl round their steaming bodies like white wreaths of foam."

Why should he have remembered that picture just at that moment?

That picture of force, of savagery, of lithe animal resilience, of elastic suppleness beyond conception—it overwhelmed him. It became for him a picture of the city itself. Paris. . . .

And all at once he remembered Thor; the god; Thor with his hammer. The strongest of the gods. . . .

Had not Thor once stood in Utgard as the student now stood in a street in Paris, come to show what he could do.

Utgard.

He had never before heard the resonance of that word.

Thor was put to the test in Utgard. He had to have an eating race with a man called Loge; and Thor lost. He had to run a race with a little fellow called Huge; and Thor lost. He had to drain a drinking horn; and he did not manage it. He had to wrestle with an old woman called Elle; and Thor lost; she forced him to his knees!

(You see Loge was fire, Huge was thought; the drinking horn was the sea; and Elle was old age . . .)

It suddenly struck Valemon how wise that old parable was.

There was one other test that awaited Thor in Utgard.

"Our young lads amuse themselves," Loke of Utgard said, "by lifting my *cat* off the ground. It is only a trifle, and I would not have suggested that you do it, had I not seen that you are not nearly as mighty as I had thought." A grey, fairly large cat then appeared on the floor of the great hall. Thor went up to it, put one hand under its belly, in the middle, and raised it up; but the more Thor raised his hand, the more the cat arched its back, and when Thor had raised his hand as high as he could, the cat had only one foot off the ground. So Thor had to admit defeat in that game too.

The cat was the snake of Midgard, that lies coiled round all the lands.

The coil of strength, of sin, of can-can, of unbreakable lithe resilience, of elastic suppleness, yielding; you can place your hand under the soft belly of the cat and raise it, O Jesus, but can you lift it up?

*

In imagination one had dreamed of conquering Paris. How queer. Conquer Paris. One knew now, standing there, that Paris could not be conquered. He was not even able to cope with the Moulin Rouge. If the place existed. . . . He did not know where it was. He did not even know where in Paris he was. . . .

He had taken the bearings of his hotel: there was a small illuminated sign on it: "Hotel"; but he did not know the name of the street. . . . He must be careful not to go too far; not to get himself lost. So, Jesus, one discards the idea of the Moulin Rouge, even though you did say once: "that ye resist not evil." Evil ought to be taken in small doses.

The cat was larger than one had thought.

The World Cat.

He had taken refuge on the other pavement. It was darker there. There were awnings with shadows under them, or at least shadows between them, and he felt more sheltered. He lit himself a cigarette. It was a Norwegian cigarette, one of the last. Tomorrow, he thought, I must buy some French ones; they are supposed to be cheap, but not particularly good. Anyway, I can hide my nose better, if I have a cigarette in my hand. Nobody will wonder if there's anything under it then.

Slowly, holding the cigarette well in front of him, he ventured a few steps along the pavement.

Where were the grisettes?

Where were the midinettes?

He had dreamed that when he got to Paris, they would be paraded for him, in two ranks, gay, seductive, lovely, two beautiful ranks, grisettes in one, midinettes in the other and that he would walk along between them on red carpet put down in his honour, he would inspect them and they would curtsey to him; he would pat a blushing cheek here, chuck a soft chin there. A little click of his fingers, perhaps a slight nod, would indicate his favour and his choice; like a king. Paris would consider it an honour to serve him; the two ranks would be trembling slightly with eagerness and grace; grisettes and midinettes curtseying deeply to him ... the sound of a thousand starched lace petticoats softly brushing the paving stones. ...

He passed a pavement café. From behind his cigarette smoke he looked at the little tables, the chairs; he also caught a glimpse of the inside; there was a curved counter with coffee machines of glowing copper and ice-cream machines of shiny silver; there were shelves of glasses, and a row of differently-coloured bottles; there were waiters with white aprons, hurriedly edging to and fro with trays balanced on the palms of their hands; they gave brief orders, smiled. I wonder, he thought, looking at the people seated at the tables, I wonder what it would cost to sit down and have a glass of something?

Byrrh?

He walked on, cautiously, close to the wall. He came to an open shop, a grocer's. The goods were displayed on the pavement, in front of the window. He passed a table with vegetables and fruit; he saw carrots and cabbages and bananas, the bananas were smaller than in Norway; below, on the pavement level, was a row of bottles of wine, all of different appearance, with different labels, obviously for sale; there was a big, open sack of coffee beans, brown, glistening; by the door was an enormous glass demi-john in a wicker basket, filled with red wine; customers could

242

come with their own empty bottles and buy wine by the litre; he read: "Vin ordinaire. 40 centimes le litre." He tried to work that out, it made less than 50 øre a litre. There were price tickets on all the goods displayed; the prices were written in white chalk on little pieces of black board. Elegant writing. Beautiful, regular handwriting always impressed him; his own was loose and irregular; he did not have the art of writing horizontally, he could not write evenly. The first four lines were all right; but then he forgot and his hand went off on its own. He disliked his handwriting. The few times in his life he had really enjoyed writing were when he had a typewriter at his disposal. Then there had been real accord between what he thought and wrote. Horizontal lines; letters of equal size. Order.

He noticed that all the figure 4's were written differently to the Norwegian way. A french 4 has a loop on the left; what in Norway is pointed, in France is looped. He suddenly felt how utterly foreign it all was. You might consider it a small thing, call such a loop on the left-hand side of a 4 a bagatelle, but this bagatelle, sent him suddenly running through time; he was then twenty-three, but it sent him hurtling back to the time he was seven and had just gone to school, when he had to sit at a desk in the primary school, with his head on one side and the tip of his tongue thrust into his left cheek, when he used to sit with a red pen-holder, his first, a red pen-holder with a nib, and the ink in the inkwell was a wonderful light blue, sky blue, water-sky blue, a colour he would never forget—to the time he was seven and was sitting there about to write his first 4.

And ever since one had gone on writing 4 that way. One had gone on with it through childhood and youth, so that the Norwegian 4 was with him for ever, his hand accustomed to it. It was not a thing one thought about; it was something that one's body had learned.

That is why the sight of a French 4 sent him tumbling so strangely far; it was different; it had a loop on the left; one could not do that; one would never be able to. One had come to it sixteen years too late. If one had begun as a child, if one had gone to a primary school in France, it would have gone all right. One had had a year at the Commercial College in Bergen, but that was no help; not even a year at the Sorbonne in Paris would have helped.

A visitor.

Never, he thought—I shall never know France.

He had gone a little beyond the grocer's shop. He was standing at the corner of another street.

The women.

He had seen them the whole time.

They were walking and strolling about, handbags gently swinging; most of them wore blouses and skirts, the top button of their blouses was left undone; their skirts were short, only going down to the knee. Their blouses were close fitting; their skirts were close fitting. Their mouths were red; their high-heeled shoes were of black patent leather; they sauntered along the pavement, handbags gently swinging. One of them came to the bit of wall where he was standing; she put her bag behind her back, against the wall, leaned back on it. She had a wide patent leather belt round her waist. Patent leather is so cold. He knew what a girl's patent leather belt feels like under one's hand. Slowly she turned her head towards him in the dark. At that he walked away.

He walked back quickly, back to the grocer's shop. . . . He stopped in the doorway, wondered if he dare go in; plucked up his courage and took a cautious step inside, his heart was in his mouth.

How good, and safe, it smelled inside there. There was the owner; there too was the owner's wife; yes, even two medium-sized children, presumably their own, lending a hand?—but this was a whole family; friendly, cheerful, keen, hard-working. Family, he thought, can you think of anything more lovely in the wide world than a family? The one I come from, was not a family; a father who is always hard with his sons does not create a family; not that I got a whipping from him so very often, but I remember every time I did; he made me take down my trousers; not only was I to be punished, but I was to present myself for it; I was four years old; I was five, I was six, I was seven, I was eight, I was nine; the last time that I had a whipping and had to take down my trousers, I was ten; after that he stopped. He stopped whipping me; instead he used to pull my ear; he used to take hold of the lobe, pull it as though to lift me up by it; I had to go on tiptoe to avoid having it torn off; but the whippings when I was small were the worst; not because I was beaten, but because I had to take down my trousers. I had to undo my buttons, bare myself and present my bottom to him, to be whipped. He broke something in me. I have often thought that what he destroyed in me was the ability to defend myself.... Family? He writes to me occasionally; I have had a couple of letters from him since I have been in Bergen. Always I am told, plaintively "You are not much of a letter writer...." What does he want me to say? To thank him for the good childhood he gave me, for all the fine memories I have? I never write to him. I cannot talk to him either. Whenever we two are left alone in a room, it becomes suddenly still, and cold. Conversation stops; my heart stops; my mouth becomes dry; I try to think of an excuse for getting up. If I was even able to have a cigarette. But I cannot. He won't accept that I smoke. I am twenty-three; I am also married, and have a child; yet if I am sitting in the same room as my father, I dare not light up a cigarette. I haven't the courage. I am reminded of my humiliation, of my convulsive weeping; how he forced me to undress, to take my trousers down, bare myself. That was shame beyond comprehension. I wonder if I shall ever be able to lift my head? Be human? Get the filthiness of it washed away? How long must I live, and what victories must I celebrate before I can feel myself a man? Before I know that I have a right to my own trousers?

A happy family, a family where they all stick together—

father, mother, children; eager, efficient, working together; one bumps into another with a box, yet they just smile to each other. Good God, he thought, God in heaven; give me a warm and smiling family.

Wasn't it a philosopher who wished for a fixed point? And said that if he had one, he would be able to move the whole world? Exactly! A fixed and safe, and kindly point! A family!

"Vous désirez, Monsieur?"

The owner wiped the palms of his hands on his apron, bowed and smiled at the student, white teeth showing.

Valemon became embarrassed.

"Rien," he said. "Je voudrais seulement...." What on earth was look round, have a look, in French?

"... regarder," he said.

"Si vous permettez," he added, bowing.

And, you see, the owner did not mind in the least, quite the contrary, do, please; you're a foreigner perhaps? a tourist? There, now, of course, one must look round, see everything; aha? Norwegian? please, he was to look round as much as he liked; one had heard of Norway, a beautiful country, a free country, a pretty country; one would not mind living there; you in Norway have something France lacks; do you know what it is?—no?—well, in Norway you have socialism and a King! (was she still standing there, against the wall?) it is a perfect combination, an example to be followed; it should be the same every-where: socialism *and* monarchy! (her mouth was red like a wound)—he took a step to one side, because the owner's wife wanted to get past with a box; "Pardon, Monsieur," she bobbed and smiled with white teeth; what do you reply in French, when someone says "Pardon" to you?—he was on the point of saying "Voilà," but could hear that it would be wrong, so he contented himself with smiling back dumbly; he thought: one day I'll discover that, one day in ten years.

He could see carrots, cabbage, red cabbage, cherries, apples, huge apples, cauliflowers; the smell of hot, ripe

Paris was all round him; he saw a peculiar fruit or vegetable, greeny-grey, yellowy-grey, with scales, was it related to the pineapple?—he asked what it was called; (she must have gone now); "Artichaut," said the owner, perhaps they didn't grow in Norway?—no, Valemon replied, feeling strangely grateful to this man who knew of Norway's existence, who had thought about it and decided that Norway had the best constitution in the world, and who now to crown it all, was interested in vegetable growing in Norway—he asked if artichokes were nice?—"Oh là!" said the man, licking his lips, patting his stomach, you really must try them one day!—Valemon looked at the others, they smiled and nodded, nodded in complete agreement with their father; but Valemon had his doubts, he thought it looked like a prehistoric tuber, a cross between a tree-fern and a lizard. He moved restlessly towards the door; he could not spend the entire evening in a shop. Wonder how long they stayed open? It was after ten o'clock already.

Well, he mustn't take up their time any longer. He thanked them for their kindness, bowed in the doorway. "Merci," he said.

"Au revoir, Monsieur!"
"Au revoir, Monsieur!"
"Au revoir, Monsieur!"
"Au revoir, Monsieur!"

The owner bowed, his wife bowed, the son bowed, the daughter bowed. Glitter of friendly faces and teeth.

Was she still standing there, with her handbag in the small of her back?

He walked across the street without looking to see. He walked along the other pavement, quickly. He came to the next street, but instead of looking left he turned abruptly and walked off to the right. He looked at his watch as he did so, a mere gesture, to make it look as if he had an important appointment.

It was darker there. A narrower street. There were trees in the pavement. He stopped under one. It must have been a kind of willow, he could see the shape of its gently drooping branches in the darkness. His heart was thumping.

This is too cheap, he thought.

It lacked romance.

Going straight to the dish. . . . There must be a round-about way. The difference between animal and human is that humans won't go straight at it.

Oh, I know: I did wish for a girl and no commitment; a girl whom one could have and remain gloriously un-involved. I did. But not like this.

Cheap. Yes. But not *too* cheap.

You cannot buy romance.

It's like good strawberry places in the woods, when you are a child.

Either you find them.

Or—you don't.

He stood there under the willow, in the darkness, shy, still, glancing down at the main street. He stood there like an animal on the fringe of the forest, motionless, quiver-ing, snuffing in the direction of the lights, of what was strange and dangerous.

What was it that old book he had once read, said:

"Yes, health and physique are consumed in the Moulin Rouge; and as the night progresses, shameful lusts that smoulder beneath the ashes, inflame the senses into a last dreadful conflagration. When prostitutes and liber-tines, absinthe-drinkers, ether-swallowers stream away from the ballroom in the flickering half-light, and when the excited throng has filled the nocturnal taverns, then man's primal manifestations of life are suffocated in the unhealthy vapours that billow across this the ugliest of all snake-pits: Paris by night."

Not I, he whispered. I want to preserve my body.

All at once he went rigid. Hadn't he heard something prowling behind the trees? His hand moved towards his belt—fancy forgetting his sheath-knife of all things on a journey! All he had was a miserable pen-knife in his hip pocket. Who was moving there in the darkness? A can-can dancing cocotte, standing on one leg scratching herself behind her ear with the other foot? A ponce?—a murderer? —an apache?—an absinthe-drinker?—an ether-swallower? His hair stood on end.

He withdrew further up the street; now it had become like a sunken road. Behind him was a rock face, or perhaps it was a wall. On the other side of the street he could make out more stone walls, iron railings. He was standing in a sort of dell, a broad, tilted dell that sloped from right to left. For some reason or other he was to remember distinctly how the street where he then stood, sloped from right to left.

Those cocottes who danced the can-can. . . . If you were sitting at a table, close to the dance floor, smoking your cigar, presumably the nearest would only be a yard or so only away. Only a yard away; there you would be sitting drinking champagne and there she would be standing on one leg scratching herself behind her ear with her other foot . . . Perhaps you would be sitting so close to her that you would be able to see a dark hair or two curling out from the lace of her knickers. Perhaps you could lay down your cigar and give her short hairs a loving tweak. Perhaps she did not even notice; after all she had to think of what she was doing. So you gave another tweak, an affectionate, man-of-the-world tweak, and cried "La Quadrille!" and she would notice that and scratch behind her ear with one foot and hop on the other and answer ecstatically: "La Quadrille, Monsieur!"

He had to change feet in the darkness.

For one hurried moment he thought of Her.

In his hip pocket, in his pocket book, he had a sheet of

paper with some addresses on it. Among them that of a certain Dupois, manufacturer of fine colours, colours that were not made in Norway, colours used in making artificial flowers. He was rather proud of his little commission. . . . He was to do a little business for Her. In Paris. "De la part de Mademoiselle Borck." Tomorrow, or the day after, he would ring up Monsieur Dupois.

Her hand, so small, so soft, so strong. A craftman's hand. There was nothing he admired so much as a craftsman. Creating. Creating something, out of nothing. The beginning is absolutely nothing: a piece of white material, 1 x 2 metres, silk perhaps, perhaps cotton, which she fastened to a frame and painted with something, stiffening no doubt, to make it taut. What happened then, he had no idea. But the end was mysterious in its creative multiplicity; on her work-table lie rows of the loveliest anemonies, lily-of-the-valley, roses. . . . Carefully, yet with wonderful assurance, she would pack a certain number into a big cardboard box, with tissue paper in between. Thirty young revolutionary students, socialists, as red as the devil, who from soap boxes proclaimed the need for society to switch to mechanization and mass production, here, in front of her work-table, would stand silent and respectful, looking at a handmade white camelia.

That evening in the park, after the ball. Do you remember? But then I was unable to take your hand. Wouldn't it have been an idea, if you had taken mine? Strange. I would not have been standing here, in a side-street in Paris, if you had taken my hand that evening. . . .

Hm. Here. 3,000 kilometres from love, here I can talk to you.

A family. . . .

Don't misunderstand. That is the sort of thing one says, when one does not understand a thing oneself. Don't misunderstand. My hunger for that cocotte was genuine, the one who stood on one leg and scratched herself behind her ear with the other foot. I think it would have been a magnificent sight. I am a lecherous man; an ecstatically lecherous man. Let that be said, from this distance of 3,000 kilometres, so that there shall be no misunderstanding. Yet the next day, and the day after that, I would have had no desire for any such Quadrille. . . .

On the other hand—if you and I had founded a family, Runa, I would desire it, desire your smiling face, every day, every day, all my life. . . .

He realized that he must pull himself together; he must keep his feet on the ground. When it came to the point, Runa was a young woman, pretty, gentle, with big blue eyes, and with smile-crinkles on just one side of her nose; she was an angel; she was one of those wonderful persons who always radiate warmth and lovability; to whom people always gravitate—but she was still flesh and blood. She smoked cigarettes. She ate food. She went to the lav every day. When I am on the point of taking off from earth out of longing for the divine Runa, I must try to remember that every day she sits on the lav and has a good shit.

Not that that is much of a help. I can't make myself shudder that way. I yearn for her just the same. I yearn for her silently.

Or—shall we be honest?—for someone like her. Someone *like* her. Someone to fill my life. To encompass me. Be my mate. Not having a mate, I don't feel as if I am alive, not properly alive.

I throw no shadow. . . .

Someone I can talk to. Strange. I have never thought of that before. But that is what I want: to have someone to talk to. But can two people talk properly to each other without having known each other? If so, then sex is really necessary. . . . A lovely necessity; a necessity with a rainbow above it; but still a necessity!

He thought: if I am ever going to be able to talk with Her, I shall have to *seduce* her first. . . .

Almighty God—I, who did not even dare touch her hand!

He had a wife. Tapeta, the Paper-hanger, he called her to himself, because once, after she became pregnant, she had hinted that they might marry. She had heard of a little apartment that was vacant. He, Valemon, being so clever at business, could get an office job in the Iron Works; the apartment was an old one and would have to be done up, the walls needed re-papering.... She had got no further. She had seen the look in his eye. She never mentioned the flat again.

Every time he thought of the Paperhanger it gave him claustrophobia. He is a clerk in the Iron Works, or was it Lead Works. He never gets promotion because there is nothing to promote him for. He is a clerk. Year after year. Every morning, at eight o'clock, he goes to the office; in rain, in snow; every day he sits for seven hours poking at a little calculating machine, pling-ling, pling-ling, every day. He can guess at the way the others round him smile to themselves; he just bends over his little calculating machine, every year his back becomes a little more bowed. "Our Mr. Gristvåg" they laugh. "Look, sitting over there; he's the one who put Tapeta in pod. What thousands hadn't been able to do, he managed. He even married her. Good old Gristvåg." Then every afternoon at five o'clock he goes home, in rain, in snow. He reaches the little apartment; there is a smell of rissole in the corridor; rissole every day; it is the only dish she can cook; the gramophone is playing; he hears "A Little Ring of Gold", she loves that song; she is singing it too, she is singing "A Little Ring of Gold" he can tell from her voice that she has been drinking; she drinks every day; actually there are two people singing; she has a woman friend with her; every day the friend comes to see her; the woman also drinks, they break off for a moment and laugh shrilly; they are telling each other about the student from Hammerfest who had been a year

252

in Oslo, and what he studied there, they slap each other's thighs, great slaps on the inside of the thigh; and on a pot on the floor sits his child, Viggo, half-naked, numb with cold, with a red bottom, and a cold, eating lumps of sugar that he picks off the linoleum; every day, when her friend arrives, she puts the boy on his pot and empties a packet of sugar lumps over the kitchen floor, so that the two of them are left in peace to sing and slap.

*

But she did have an amusing side to her, he thought, amazed. He was 3,000 miles away from her now, safe, he was in Paris, it was a warm, mild night. How he had run; there wasn't a man in the world could have beaten him over those 400 metres; he had run to catch the mail boat; he had run for his life.... Their marriage had lasted half an hour. He had escaped!

She really had a sense of fun, he thought. I think I'll make her name a bit better. Give it a touch of Hawaii. With all that long raven-black hair she deserves it.

Tapeeta.

After my father there's no one who has humiliated me like Tapeeta. Of course, there is a parallel. *She caught me with my trousers down.*

When she suggested that I marry her and live for the rest of my life in a tiny, sour-smelling apartment up near the North Pole—did she not understand?

We could have been friends today, he thought. If she had said: "You must go away. This is no place for you. And I'm not the woman for you. You go. It was fine while it lasted. It has never been so good with anyone as with you. Did you know that?" "Yes, I have felt it. And may I return the compliment." "Do you mean that?" "Yes. Your body smells like a shieling. Freshly scrubbed, with juniper on the floor." "You certainly know how to talk. Get away from here. Do something with a bang. Don't stick in the mud here. I shall always be able to manage. I shall be able to manage for the kid too. It can't be all that difficult. And you think of me a little, now and again, and perhaps send me a little money—when you achieve fame and glory? You know, money does mean something." "I know." "Money isn't everything, as the man said, but, darn me, it isn't far off it...." "You are good." "And no farewell kiss, either." "No. Fini, c'est fini." "Is that something rude?" "It's French, it means: what's over is over." "There you see, find yourself someone who knows this foreign stuf. All the best, Valemon." "All the best, Tapeeta."

("Oh..." "What?" "The kid. When it grows up, it'll be able to come and see you, won't it? Now and again?" "Yes; now and again." "When it's big enough to travel by train alone?" "Yes. Fine." "All the best, Valemon. Good luck." "Luck, Tapeeta.")

That's how it could have been. Simple. Decent. Calm. Two people of the world.

What hadn't there been instead?

He started, looked round in the darkness.

But what was a Paris apache, an ether-swallower, compared to a Norwegian maintenance order!

Suddenly, as at the wave of a wand, the picture changed. If...

If she had been calm, decent, noble, wouldn't I that time when I set up the world record for 400 metres, wouldn't I have stopped after ten metres and scratched the back of my neck? Instead of running to the mail boat, wouldn't I have turned? Could I have abandoned such a woman of the world? She would have been just the woman for me! The woman in my life! I would have married her readily! I would have gone panting back to her; "Forgive me!"I would have knelt in her hall. "Forgive me! My wife! I have come to stay! With you! For ever!"

All of a sudden he was thanking her, from the depths of his heart, for being what she was: for not being superior, not being noble, not being a woman of the world. Because she was as she was, she had hustled him out. Indeed, she had lent him wings.... Thanks, Tapeeta, he suddenly whispered. You didn't know what you were doing. I shall send you a case of champagne, a boat load of gin, a train full of gramophone records, I shall present you with a bedstead of solid gold; one day I shall make you immortal; you will never die; a whole world shall hum your name; Tapeeta....

One day.

Meanwhile, she is a stewardess on the mail boat; making beds, emptying vomit bowls. Meanwhile, I am a student standing in a cul-de-sac; looking at life in the distance; thinking of those unhealthy vapours that billow about the ugliest of all snake-pits: Paris by night.

He lit a new cigarette in the darkness. Took a long pull. His thoughts were turned towards the lovely and the enticing.

In which street, he wondered, did La Duchesse live? Now he was thinking of her; her salon, her boudoir, her silver hand looking-glass—or was it tortoiseshell? Hadn't he, too, dreamed once of Estelle? Her twin sister? He was thinking of her now; the slight back of her seventeen-year-old neck, her horn-rimmed spectacles, her short hair, her bob—or was it a shingle?

He had better go back to the hotel soon. There was no point in standing there.

Again he could smell the far-away, mature, hairy, warm smell of Paris.

"God," he suddenly said in the dark. "God, couldn't you perhaps conjure one up for me. I am so horribly shy

255

and self-conscious. When I was little, my mother said to me, and her face was fearfully serious: "It's horrid to beg." That's why I can't. When I was small and wanted to hold out my hand, my father used to stop me, he took hold of my hand, dreadfully hard, and said: "Wait till you're given it." That sort of thing sticks, God. I simply cannot beg; can't hold out my hand. It's not my fault. It's not yours either, of course. It just is so.

"If you could arrange the contact, God. I haven't much courage where women are concerned. I haven't the gift of the gab. Just a heart that pounds. I'm embarrassed and that's not much of a help. So I thought that perhaps you could get me one. A woman. Work a miracle; one of your miracles. Of course I am scared. But I am even more scared of having to go back to the hotel, without the experience. ... That perhaps sounds odd to you, but I am under pressure. There are people who expect things of me. They actually demand that when I am in Paris, to talk to the cobbler, I should get a little wax to put on my needle. They are standing behind me, urging me on. Show yourself what you can do!—they call. And show *us*! It's fearful, God, but it's a fact. Take the Commercial College. There are fifty in my class. And with those in the other class it makes a hundred. Am I to go back to them and tell them that nothing came of it? A hundred Norwegian students stand thumping me on the back. Hallo, Valemon, they call. That's no joke, God. Besides, everyone I know, *everybody*, expects the same. Tapeeta, I can see her smile. Runa, yes, as true as I stand here, I can see her smile. Yes, even my father, my mother—they wouldn't admit it—but in their heart of hearts they are nudging me. It feels as if the whole of Norway.... You can be glad, God, you don't have the whole of Norway after you...."

"Anyway, it would be dull, pretty dull and wretched to have to go back to the hotel. It's such a warm lovely evening. You've arranged a real velvet night. And what with one thing and another.... Besides, I imagine that you, God, are better at French than I am.

"You could perhaps conjure up a Parisienne for me. Not one that attaches herself to you like a boa constrictor. No. And not a terribly superior one with unapproachable remoteness in her gaze. No. It must be one who comes up to me of her own accord. A miracle. One who is affectionate. One who is ... Not that I want to lecture you, that would not be fitting, after all you know everything. But, say, a woman who is good, soft, warm, affectionate. Easy. Thanks, God."

"Bon soir, Monsieur," he heard, close to his ear.

Quiet footsteps had reached him; someone had stopped beside him; someone was standing beside him in the darkness.

He felt a gentle tingle up his spine. Was it God standing by his side in the dark?

It was a low, intimate voice, addressed exclusively to him; it had whispered, yet it was extremely distinct. It was a pleasant, friendly voice. Almost humble. He felt the cigarette quiver between his lips. He turned his head, slowly.

Gracious, he thought, was God a woman?

He gulped.

A short, elderly woman was standing beside him. She was bare-headed and had a dark coloured, fringed shawl round her shoulders. She stood with her arms under her shawl: she had crossed them on her bosom, or perhaps was holding them over her stomach; she was stoutish. It was as though she was using the shawl to hide her old body. She had curtseyed to him and was now standing half turned away, round shouldered, head bowed.

Poor woman, he thought, a beggar. He moved a foot, wanting to go; yet remained cautiously standing there.

"Bon soir," she said softly, hesitantly.

"Monsieur?" she whispered; her voice was amazingly cultured; she moved a little closer; he still had not seen her face; she stood the whole time with it half averted; she spoke without looking at him.

"Oui," he whispered.

Again she made a little movement like a curtsey in the dark; she was standing almost under him now, with her back to him; she had a slight stoop, was a tiny bit stout; she looked up at him quickly as she spoke again, for the first time showing him a little of her face; he got a sort of glimpse of her profile, and that made him think momentarily of his own mother.

"Voulez-vous me faire le grand plaisir, Monsieur," the woman said in a low, soft voice, bowing her head, "de passer cette nuit avec moi?"

He blinked in the dark. Gave a little cough. For a moment he thought she had no place to sleep. Then he understood.

He felt a throbbing in his ear-drums. He tried to swallow, but it was as if he had received a blow on his larynx. An old woman of fifty. He glanced down at her, looked away again. An old woman, like his mother; she should have been indoors, in a home, sitting in a chair crotcheting under a standard lamp; yet here she was walking about in the dark under the trees, and ... and ... It made him feel sick. It was outrageous. As a socialist, he could not acquiesce in such a thing. It was revolting. Poor old woman. Having to go about offering herself, for money. In a dark alley, well back from the traffic, in the dark, on the fringe, where no one could see how old she was. Perhaps she was a widow. Perhaps she had children. It was swinish.

He was filled with vehement sadness. Sadness for her—and a sadness for himself. There you are, he thought, God has answered my prayer. God answers all my prayers. In every detail. That's the dreadful thing about God. What was it I prayed for? One who would come to me? Affectionate, good, warm, soft? Here she is. Exactly what I prayed for. It's dreadful. I shall stop praying.

And deep inside him there was a river running, a river

258

of tears, a river of honey. He thought: that is the most beautiful thing a woman has ever said to me. An aged whore, with a stoop, fat, broken down; but all the same she spoke like a queen. She spoke clearly, calmly, without a stammer, she curtseyed to me, she said: "Will you do me the great pleasure, sir, of spending this night with me?" Where, on earth or in heaven, could a man have anything more beautiful said to him?

If he had had a three-cornered hat, he would have doffed it and swept her a deep bow.

"Non," he said. Now his brain was working violently to find words that would do as well as a nobleman's bow; and he found them. "Vous êtes très aimable," he said and was thankful that the words had come to him. He was trembling, wanted to go.

"Pourquoi?" she asked, her voice soft, meek, gentle.

He suddenly felt on the point of collapse. His veins were throbbing thunderously. It was warm and dark and confined there under the trees. He had caught the faint smell of scent in the darkness. He had a violent erection. He wriggled his body, but did not dare use his hand; she might see his state.

"Non," he whispered.

"Non?" she said, making herself meek below him.

"Non," he said, gasping for air.

"Je suis étudiant," he said, and had to shift it with his hand, saw that she had discovered it. He drew a groaning breath. "Je suis étudiant norvègien!" he said, as if that would help him. "Je suis très pauvre, madame. Je n'ai pas d'argent!" He almost shouted it. Oh, his politeness! He would not hurt the woman for anything in the world. Not for anything would he have told her that he had no desire for her!

But why then was his body trembling?

His teeth had begun to chatter.

It does not have to be for the whole night, she said humbly. She had shot a swift glance at his groin. It could be for as long or as short as Monsieur wished.

259

"Non," he said.

The ground seemed to be rocking under his feet; he had a feeling of nausea, like seasickness.

He was afraid. And, suddenly, he told her so.

"J'ai peur. Je n'ose pas."

Now, his whole body was trembling. He remembered feeling this once before. And in a similar situation. When he was at High School. In Trondhjem. He was eighteen. There had been he and another boy. It was night. In a street down by the harbour. An elderly, painted woman; her breath smelt of methylated spirit. The red line of lip-stick was crooked on her broad mouth. They stood in a doorway and struck a bargain with her. The other boy went up into the house with her. He was up there an hour. Meanwhile Valemon stood in the entrance downstairs. It was dark there; the floor was made of old, cracked boards; there was a strong smell of cat piss. For an hour he stood there waiting, stood there trembling, shaking as if he had a fever, trembling and unable to stop; his teeth were chattering and he had to lean against the wall; on the inside of the street door was an iron rod, a fastening, that ran from the door to the wall; he tried draping him-self over it to lessen his trembling; he stood and trembled for an hour, trembled uninterruptedly for an hour, could not stop it. Then his friend came down. Then they went. His friend hadn't managed anything. Valemon was glad about that! So glad that, when they got up into the town, he had stooped and kissed a street lamp! Climbed up and kissed its curved glass!

That strange trembling. It had come again. His body was going like a chaff-cutter. Why? What's the point of shaking like that? In nature everything has a purpose. His body was shaking as if he had a fever. Ah, he thought, perhaps this is Nature trying to tell me that I am ill. That what I have embarked on is wrong. Go into reverse, God is saying. He groped with his hand for a tree trunk in order to support his body; he had to stand bent foward.

"Vous avez peur," she said gently, calmly, "de maladies?"

He could see a slight smile on her face. The calm way she was able to say it! Yes, he was afraid of disease. He was mortally afraid of a certain kind of disease. He had promised himself that he would never get one of them. Mercury, syringes, dorsal tabes, red-hot instruments up the urinary canal, lunacy, never. Things might have been a bit different, if she had belonged to a "house"; in those, he had heard, they had regular medical examinations; but she was just a street walker, on her own, a woman trying to attract a man....

"Oui," he said.

She blinked her eyes.

"Je ne suis pas malade," she said.

He did not know what to say; it was so difficult to stand up to a woman. So difficult to rebuff.

"Eh," he said.

"Je vous assure," she said, quietly.

It was so difficult to have to maintain a suspicion; so difficult to accuse.

"Eh," he said. "Pardon," he added. He whispered: "Pardonnez-moi." For a moment he thought perhaps he ought to produce a franc, or two, and give her them? Or would that be an insult.... God, he thought, you haven't made life easy for your children. Wasn't it I who, once, wished myself someone and no commitment? It's beginning to dawn on me that there are commitments in all relationships; even here; even in the lowest....

"Vous savez," she said, meek once more, quiet once more. What was he supposed to know? A note of intimacy, of fervour had come into her voice; and yet in some extraordinary way she retained her regal distance. You do not have to faire l'amour in just the one way, she said; if Monsieur is afraid, I can give him satisfaction in another way....

She looked at him as she said that, and her eyes were clear, pure, motherly; then she looked away. The night was dark. She was standing close to him; he could smell her scent; she was standing, head bowed, listening, submissive.

He felt as if he was going mad. As if he must burst; into tears, or out laughing. Other ways. Baby tricks. Did she think he was a kid. Of course there were other ways; but they were just like spices for the ordinary way. Trimmings! He was a grown man. He had had girls in Bergen; super girls; not one of them had ever suggested that one could do it in *other* ways. Perhaps fiddle with each other? Do it with your fingers? Blow on each other? Ha! At that moment he was filled with a violent longing for the good, clean girls of Bergen. How pretty they were! When he thought about it, he had not yet seen one pretty girl in Paris!

Other ways? What unheard-of, sweet, disgusting tricks did this woman know? He glanced down at her in the darkness. She must be a witch! A filthy pig! He looked at her round back, her fringed shawl, her bent neck and was suddenly filled with a feeling he had never known before. I could do what I liked with her, he thought. He was filled with a violent terror, terror of an abyss he had not previously known about, an abyss within himself. She would let me do what I liked with her, he thought. It was a tremendous, giddy-making, intoxicating feeling; more evil than any he had ever had before. For a moment his heart stopped beating. He raised his hand.

Now he remembered. That one time. He had been twelve or thirteen. A boy. But something had begun to stir in him. They had a maid servant in the house; she was fifteen or sixteen. She was short, meek, had brown hair, a reddish patchy complexion. There was something poverty-stricken about her; her parents lived up on Byåsen; her father was probably a navvy; she was nice, but not particularly gifted; there was something sorrowful, something broken, in her face; it was not much fun having a miserable face perpetually about the place. A face that seemed always on the point of tears. She was shorter than he; but three years older. As his mother served in the shop every day, this girl had to cook for Valemon, his sister and his little brother. For a year he had had to see her ruddy, small, unintelligent, weak, always sorrowful face. One day, it was summer, he had gone to the woods to look for something to make a bow. He had been lucky, he had found some dog-briar, three long, slender stems, springy, greeny-brown. He bore them home with him. What a find! They pricked his hand, he was quivering with joy at the thought of what he was going to make. When he reached home, the sun was shining; all was still; flies were buzzing; it was hot. The girl came walking across the yard from the kitchen. She stopped in front of him. She said something to him; but he did not remember what. He just looked at that head in front of him: at that small, red, sorrowful, despondent, reproachful face; in a flash he had taken in the whole atmosphere: knew that there was no one at home, no one in the kitchen. Yes, he did remember what she said: "Who gave you permission for this?" she said, looking at the severed branches in his hand. He had been on the point of letting go of them. But at that he tightened his grasp. Then suddenly it happened. He struck her across the face with the thorny branches, with inexplicable force. He struck back-handedly. He hit her right in the face. She shrank. She clapped her hands to her face, but did not move; only her head dropped. He lashed out again, across her ear and her hand, and once again. If only she had defended herself, gone for him like a cat! But she stood there small, bowed, with round, poor shoulders. She didn't say a word. She buried her face in her hands; only her narrow shoulders showed that she was sobbing, quietly, noiselessly, brokenly. Then the thorny branches fell from his hand, to the ground. He felt his own tears coming; he felt violent remorse; he turned, ran out through the gate, up the street, like one pursued, up to the woods, came to a field; there he flung himself down, buried his face in the earth, wished he could drown, in the black earth. There he lay for an hour, gasping with remorse and terror, he prayed

263

to God for forgiveness, prayed that he had not harmed the girl, that he had missed her eyes, he prayed to God that she would not tell his parents; for an hour he lay convulsively sobbing in the dark; then slowly he got to his feet, his face grimy, earth in his mouth and green on his trousers; he sniffed, blew his nose; all at once he knew: she was not going to tell: she would not dare. When he got home, he walked across the yard and into the kitchen. He did not look at her. She did not look at him. "Here you are," she said, tonelessly, setting a plate of fruit-soup on the table in front of him. "Thanks," he said. Three days later she left. His mother told him that she had said that her parents needed her back. He never saw her again.

But there was no broken face here, no face that quivered with pent-in tears. A poor woman? Perhaps. Yet she was a queen. I could do what I liked with her.

She glanced quickly up at him, as if aware what he was thinking, as if she had guessed. Her eyes were wise, clever, knowing slits. Had he not also seen the hint of a grin, fleeting, a glint of white teeth? A queen's grin. Ready. Ready to officiate.

Ready to submit. It felt as if she had gone on all fours for him there in the dark. Other ways. Whatever he liked. But—*what* did he want? He could not envisage it!

"C'est tout près d'ici," she said meekly, politely, "que j'habite."

She pointed across the street, towards a house. She lived there. But what did that imply, when a woman like her said she lived there?

Did she have an apartment there? One room? Husband? Children? He looked across the street. He saw a black iron railing, he saw an iron gateway in wrought iron pattern, the gate hanging slightly awry on its hinges. He strained his eyes, there was a little drive, a path, leading from the gate through a garden, up to a dark brick building; he could see a faint light there, perhaps over the door, perhaps the glow from a hall light; he really thought he could smell a kitchen smell, smell of washing-up, and could he not also hear a faint wail as from an infant?

"Non," he said.

That decided it. His whole body was shaking, he was ready to drop, he had to stand bowed because of his lust; but the matter was decided.

She stood for a moment. She did not seem to be looking at him. Her gaze was directed at the street. Lightly she shrugged her shoulders.

"Tant pis," she said. "Tant pis pour vous."

There, he thought, now I've hurt her. There's nothing in the world so dreadful as hurting a woman. I'm sure she meant well, he thought. No one has ever spoken so beautifully to me, or with such distinction. The way she could discuss even what was deepest and most dangerous in me, my subterranean self, with a calm, regal smile. That woman is Hitler's match. Perhaps she is God after all. It is not she who had done anything wrong. It is I who am the idiot. I asked for something that, when it came to the point, I did not really want. Or for something that I am too green for. How wise she is, he thought. How fine. I don't want to make her sad.

His teeth chattered in the darkness.

"Peut-être. . . ." he said.

"Oui?" she said; looking out at the street.

"Peut-être d-d-demain. . . ." he said, gulping.

He knew privately, that he was lying. There would be no tomorrow.

"Où?" she said; it struck him that she was looking at the street.

"Ici?" he said.

"Bon. A quelle heure, Monsieur?" She threw him a hurried glance, looked back at the street.

He tried to consult his wrist-watch, but his hand was shaking, and it was too dark; anyway there was no need to consult his watch.

"A neuf heures?"

"C'est entendu, Monsieur. Ici demain soir, à neuf heures." She said it lightly, sweetly, without commitment. She pulled back her shoulders, drew herself erect; she was still a plump little woman, but now there was go about her. She adjusted the shawl round her shoulders, straightened it, took hold of each corner in front and pulled it in little jerks from side to side; he thought: I use that movement when I have a bath, when I've finished and am drying my back with the towel.

Is she going now? he thought.

He suddenly felt profoundly sorry.

"Au revoir, Monsieur," she said, curtseyed, shot him a fleeting glance that was half ironical, half indulgent, and went.

He tried to walk away too, but walking was too awkward. Also he felt a strange curiosity, a cruel curiosity; he wanted to see where she went!

Cautiously he stepped towards the street with the traffic, out from the shadow of the trees. He saw her. She was over on the other pavement, which was better lit. She was walking lightly, almost tripping along, waggling her behind. She wore low heels; he could see that the material of her dress, under her black fringed shawl, was dark green, moss green. She was quite stout; she was as old as his mother. Yet she was a lady light-of-foot. He felt himself wondering: why, he thought, why should I feel such a violent revulsion, such horror of the thought of sleeping with an old woman? Actually it's ridiculous, he thought. But I couldn't do it. I could not do it.

"Au revoir, Madame," he whispered and gulped.

Now he could see.

She had gone into the street with the traffic. She was going straight to a man who was walking along there. She gave him a slight curtsey, bent her head. Now she was saying something. *He knew what she was saying.* But the man shook his head, abruptly, walked round her; he was a middle-aged man, wearing a dark brown suit and brown, well polished shoes, a younger pillar of society, strong, broad chested, purposeful, with a fat, pigskin briefcase in his hand, he might be an engineer on his way home from the office. That's the way to do it, Valemon thought. A curt no. Temptation is there to be cut short. Gone round. To work.

She shot a glance after the man; lightly shrugged her shoulders. Might she not quickly have stuck out her tongue?

Again she was waddling along the pavement. Ah, there came another man. He was a small, dried-up, elderly man, about sixty, slight, refined, with a little goatee beard, wearing a grey suit, a light ash grey, rather elegant; he was bare-headed; he was wearing pince-nez; he might have been a man of private means, a librarian; he was out with his dog, a small white poodle, taking it for a walk. She bobbed to him. She was saying something. *He knew what she was saying!* The man stooped, turned an ear towards her, as if he was a bit hard of hearing. Then he raised his head and shook it, shaking his little goatee beard. He tugged crossly at the poodle's lead and walked on. She followed. She was saying something. *He knew what she was saying.* Again the man stopped. He leaned an ear over towards her, listened. He shook his head crossly. She touched his arm. He stopped again, listened. He removed his glasses, held them between the tip of his thumb and his ring finger, he blinked, looked up at the sky, stopped, cleared his throat, looked at his dog, looked at the woman. He set his head on one side, wrinkled his yellow forehead, fixed his pince-nez back in place, took them off again, stood there, peering at her. He did not walk on.

Then Valemon went.

He did not want to see it.

He was jealous! Torn with jealousy! She was his woman. His creation. To other people she might be a whore, to him she was a queen. *His* queen. She had made him rich. God had sent her to him, in his hour of loneliness. She had curtseyed to him, in the darkness, to *him*; it was to *him* she had said the most beautiful, sweetest words in the world:

267

"Voulez-vous me faire le grand plaisir, Monsieur, de passer cette nuit avec moi?"

She's an artist, he thought.

To start with he had felt sorry for her. There had been a moment, in the dark, when he had thought she was a piece of discarded humanity, human wreckage, some forlorn woman; and he had wanted to lay his hand on her shoulder.

(Had he not had the same impulse, momentarily, when parting from the man Røsok? When he saw him shuffling off round the corner in his old jacket and frayed trousers, without a hat? Going back to the store? Had he not wanted to go after him and touch his threadbare shoulder? But he had not done it. The truth is a private matter. And besides: there had been a private, Sunnmørian vigour about the soles of those pigeon-toed feet, as the man spurted round the corner and vanished.)

Now, he saw the artist in her. Indifference to the personal element; attention to the professional. The way she had been standing, as their conversation petered out and it was obvious that he was not a client; the way she had stood there in the dark looking out of the corner of her eye at the street and listening. Courteous to him, of course, courteous to the very last; but first and last her profession, the task in hand, the street. Indeed, she reminded him exactly of the waitress, the wagtail woman; the same ability to divide her attention; the same readiness to act; difficulties do not exist; a shrug of the shoulders if something does not turn out as it should; "Tant pis"; on again; no tears; always on again; always jolly. A client? Coming!

"Vous desirez, Monsieur?"

"Voulez-vous, Monsieur?"

There was nothing poor about her as she walked off down the side street, away from him, crossing one pavement to the other, in her dark-green dress, waggling her behind,

with her black-fringed shawl round her shoulders, waddling; she was a butterfly of the night; a Shakespeare of the
streets. Perhaps she was God.

As you like it.

There are many ways pour faire l'amour.

As *you* like it.

*

What I envy in these people, he thought, is their in-
vulnerability.

Their smoothness.

They have a sort of armour. A shell, that everything
bounces off. Some substance in their organism. What's the
name of the horny stuff in the shells of insects and beetles?
Chitin? A flea can bear five hundred times its own weight.

Funny.

Insects have their softness inside and their hardness out.
People have inner hardness and outer softness.

Man is an insect inside out. . . .

I take everything in earnest. Everything goes in, where
I am concerned. It all goes in. Like harpoons into my
heart. Everything. Now she's ensconced in my heart, for
all time; there's weeping in my heart. . . . Give me a helping of chitin, God, a good, big helping. So that I can grow a
shield. Like a flea. Make me a . . .

He stopped.

Stamped his riding boots on the pavement.

No more praying.

God fulfilled all his prayers.

A flea!

He hurried through the streets. Was he going the right
way? The streets suddenly all seemed alike. . . . He hurried
along with great strides, he could not take any more ex-
periences. He no longer thought about keeping his hand
in front of his nose; he had enough to do hiding the other

269

thing that glowed and bumped against the hotel key in his trousers pocket. He walked bowed. His trembling had not stopped, it had got a grip on him.

He stopped for a moment facing a pavement café. It was all lit up and the most glorious smell was coming from it; actually he was quite hungry; no, mostly thirsty; a beer, he thought, a cup of coffee; a glass of Byrrh; to wash away the taste in his mouth. He was about to cross over, when the thought suddenly struck him: the glass. He is given it. Takes it. His hand is shaking like an old man's. He tries to put it up to his mouth, but every shake sends some of the contents slopping over; the waitress and the other customers are all watching; in his convulsions he spills everything on the floor, there isn't a drop left in the glass. It's no good, he thought, unless I could get a straw to drink it through. A Byrhh, please, with a straw! But no. Even if the glass was on the counter, steady, his head was trembling as much as his hands.

But I've got the peach—he thought, suddenly, happily. It's there on the chest of drawers waiting for me!

As long as the woman at the reception desk hasn't been up and taken it. She had not wanted it, not then, but she might have changed her mind.

Outside the hotel he stopped, halted at the bottom of the steps. Almost instinctively he glanced behind him; as though taking a quick look at the throng of the expectant grisettes and midinettes. Well, he said, twisting his lips, nothing came of that. . . .

From that point of view, I, and the evening, are fiascos.

He rubbed his chin.

But, he thought—weren't there nonetheless, actually— and at that instant it struck him what a remarkable word "actually" is; someone should write a book about it— were there not perhaps a couple of bright spots? A couple of grains of gold in the gravel? Two grammes of honour? Both for him and his country?

In the first place, that evening a young Norwegian had been saved from perdition, lifelong injury, and death. Was that so little? Norway is a lovely country; the loveliest on earth—but it has a small population; there is no surplus of Norwegians; every Norwegian saved is a hymn to the country. He had been balancing a long time on the brink of the abyss, in considerable danger; but look, as the ground began to give under his feet, as the Ginunga chasm opened under him, he had given a heave and swung himself into safety!

And, in the second place, he thought; have I not this evening actually passed my ordeal by fire? Have I not conversed? In French? With a Frenchwoman? I have, indeed.

And not just with anyone. . . .

This evening, June 23, 1939, I, an emissary of Norway, have held a long, diplomatic conversation, without the help of an interpreter—conducting it myself from beginning to end—with the Queen of Paris, about the most delicate subject in the world! I enjoy Her Majesty's favour; I am invited to another audience tomorrow evening at nine o'clock.

He would have liked to have stood a bit straighter and faced Norway, but his state did not permit it. Bowed and still shaking, he walked up the steps to the hotel.

271

AND NOW, his back to her, he had said goodnight to the woman at the reception desk. She had called something about the key, that he must not take it with him when he went out; I've got it all right, he said, and held it up above his shoulder for her to see. When did he wish to be called? Eight o'clock? Yes! Or perhaps he would rather breakfast at nine? One is usually tired after a long journey? Ja! Merci! Bonne nuit, Madame!

And then he had crawled upstairs; he had opened his door, switched on the light; locked the door behind him; he had seen the peach; it was lying on the chest of drawers all right—and all at once he became aware of the stillness.

A new dark patch had appeared on the underside of the peach. Had it been bruised? Or had the patch come from just standing on the chest of drawers?

Was ever fruit so delicate?

Velvet fruit. Heavy, warm, in his hand. When he looked more closely at it, it reminded him of two lovely little buttocks, grown together. A virgin must look like that. He had never experienced a virgin; would he ever do so? The peach was trembling in his hand. He stuck the tip of his tongue into the crack in the peach; licked it. He shut his eyes. Shuddered.

Slowly he took a bite.

It was *too* good. When one is alone. And does not have anyone to share it with.

"My peach and my son," he whispered.

He wiped the juice from his chin with the back of his hand.

He looked at the stone. It was leaping in his hand. It

was peculiar, egg-shaped, light, grooved; the flesh close to it tasted sour. He went to the window. He opened the outer shutter. Suddenly he flung the stone out, down into the yard, a hard throw; he heard it strike the concrete far below in the darkness. He closed the shutter.

His lips were trembling.

And the other that was coming now, that *had to* come if he was to stop that dreadful trembling: if he was not to lie shaking all night on his trousers turning them into a pleated shirt, if he was to get to sleep at all—what should one call it?

The superman's sublime gesture?

The poor man's comfort?

He tried to postpone it. He wanted to avoid it. He wanted to exorcise it. He had promised when he was confirmed. Also he was a socialist. An idealist. He was grown up!

He recalled half-forgotten advice from his youth. Wasn't there something about doing exercises and cold baths? Shaking, he undressed, stood naked.

He turned the tap in the basin, the cold one, though the hot one certainly was as cold. He stood on tip-toe, but could not reach in under the jet; he baled water with his hands, but that did not help. He looked at the pear-shaped china bowl down by the floor, and in which earlier that evening he had washed his riding boots. He squatted over the sprinkler—what was it for? but only got water over his bottom. He dried himself. He was still shaking.

Exercises! He tried a knees bend and groaned with the pain. In his extremity he began to dance. He danced naked on the floor, he hummed, he sang; he danced naked about the floor singing; he had tears in his eyes:

> "Dancing with my shadow,
> feeling kind of blue,
> dancing with my shadow,
> and making believe it's ..."

"Silence!" came in French from the adjacent room; a man's voice; a hand banged on the wall.

He stopped terrified. For a moment he had thought it was God. He managed to think: an hotel ought to have thicker walls. One day I shall build an hotel. A proper hotel. A beautiful hotel. An hotel for lovers. A love-hotel.

And then it was over and done. . . .

He had lost.

He had started to go towards the bed, but his trousers were there being pressed; he had to do it somewhere; at a loss he turned and walked towards the chest of drawers, holding the towel in his left hand; he caught a hurried glimpse of himself in the oval mirror. It was a grotesque sight: an edition of Die Blonde Bestie such as Nietzsche had never imagined. . . . The whole of his long body was white, as white as snow. But the upper extremities: the face and a triangle down from his neck where his shirt had been open on his chest, and both underarms—were dark, almost black. He looked like a faun. Like a polar bear that had had its head in a bed of blackberries and was now rising from the heather, growling, on its hindlegs.

He saw the veins swell under the skin on his hands. A cry was rising in him. What was happening, was happening as it must; there was purpose in it; but what purpose? His hunger, his savage longing, all his stars, his love, his richness and his bewildering surplus—now were all gathered in his bursting flesh; Thor's hammer; God's point; if thy right hand offends thee, cut it off; Norway, freedom, the stars!—he had only to touch his foreskin, he shut his eyes, he had meant to aim at the towel, but it hit the mirror; for one giddy moment the universe was filled with the smell of warm nectar; when he was able to open his eyes again, he saw that he had spattered his own reflection.

274

AND SUDDENLY, suddenly, gravity and seriousness re-turned. For a second, he saw the play-acting; the poverty, the emptiness. The great wave had recoiled, leaving him standing in a vacuum, in an enormous vacuum.

He saw his riding boots, half saw them. They were standing on the floor. The leg of one had gone over at the ankle; it lay flopping and prostrate as if from exhaustion, in embarrassment, in shame. Yes, he whispered. The man who bought himself a motorcycle; who hazarded his life and rode through the whole of Europe; the man who went to Paris; is it not priceless, the man who travelled all the way to Paris, *the city of the fine arts*, in order to . . . just to . . .

The mockery was too great . . . he could not bring himself to call the thing by its name, he felt a gallows laugh mounting in him.

Besides, had not God wished to add injury to insult?

Standing there, he felt a strange fear. It had not even been good! It had been violent, but the pleasure had been merely half! He had felt a hitherto unknown chill in his genitals, as if they were half numb. Was he ill? Had he become infected? He hadn't so much as shaken the woman's hand—or had he? He listened out into space. He had always had a private superstition, that one day in punishment of his sins, he would be struck in the groin. He had read Thomas Wolfe; he had read about Eugene Gant's old father, the stone-cutter, the old man, who had cancer of the bladder and bled to death through his testicles.

He felt as if he was falling through space.

Yes, he thought. I did get a snowball in my groin when I was seven. We were having a snowball fight; I saw one coming through the air, shining, on level flight; that's too low to be dangerous, I thought; I'll take that on my jacket, I thought, my jacket's thick; but it must have been open in

275

front; or perhaps it was short; when the snowball arrived with a thud, really hard, I remember thinking: how queer ...; I dropped, dropped as if I had been shot; I lay in the snow looking up at the blue sky; only I could not see anything, I lay curled up; for half an hour I lay in the snow unable to move; they tried to help me up, but I could not stand; my spine would not support me; I could not breathe, could not even weep; finally I dragged myself home through the snow, on my side, pulling myself along on my elbow; at home I said nothing about it; they might have thought of sending for the doctor, and the doctor would have removed my trousers and examined me; my whole body ached with it for two days; but then the pain went; I have been all right since.

Until today.

He was twenty-three. He was finished. There where a man should feel the utmost sensual rapture, he had felt lifeless.

He had thought that he had out-manoeuvred the enemy; that he had been clever, cunning, slick; that he had side-stepped, disguised himself, gone the cunningest ways round to reach the River; indeed, he really had thought he was across! Not a splendid, imperial crossing, it was true; more a great barbarian's leap at the end of a long run which had landed him on his back in the reeds and mire, gasping, his helmet full of mud; but nonetheless on the other bank—*across*. And then, the moment he staggered to his feet—for a golden helmet can still be emptied, you can wash a golden helmet, a golden helmet is always a golden helmet! —the moment he tottered up the bank, on the other side, that same moment when he thought himself safe and could start his campaign, that very moment the Enemy got him.

From inside.

He could not understand it; he sought an explanation, listening out into the whole of space. That man in Bergen who sold him the motorcycle, what was it he said: "Fifty's your top speed", he had said. "Perhaps she'll need a re-bore when you get to the South of France," he had said. But hadn't he said something else? Wait! He had said: "On a long trip like that you ought really to have a kidney belt." That's what he had said! It did not have to be testicles; it could be kidneys. He had not been able to afford a kidney belt. Now one of his kidneys had become detached, been shaken loose.

Reverence for myself.
My body.
Was it not I swore that I would preserve my body?
"The sign of a true businessman is that he simply no longer has his business where bombs fall."
So, either I'm the world's worst businessman. Or—I have another business....

He thought: they'll take me to hospital tomorrow. If I survive the night. I've heard about French hospitals. They don't use anaesthetics; four men in butcher's aprons hold the patient, while a fifth does the cutting.
At that moment he experienced total fear, total homeless-ness. He suddenly realized that he was in Paris, at an hotel in Paris, and did not even know the name of the street. He did not know the language of the country, he could not make himself understood; he had fleetingly met two people in Paris, one man and one woman, but it was night and he had no idea where either lived. In all France there was not one person he could go to. Was there anyone, in the whole world? He had a father, a mother, a sister, a brother; but did he know them; were they his? He had a wife, a small son; but were they his? He had a girl he was in love with; but was she his? He had a small circle of socialists, comrades; but did he know any of them, were they his? He had a country; but was it his? And, even if

it was, did not Germany lie between him and his country? Had not Hitler built his grim wall that night, that very night?

He had wanted to make a sortie.
But now had he not shut himself out?
Had the copper gates not quietly slipped together, that night, with him on the outside!

He remembered, half-remembered the boy who one autumn morning stood alone on a dark, deserted, pitiless school-yard; all the others had marched in, into the warmth, into the light; only the boy was standing, rooted, in the empty, enormous concrete school-yard, standing looking down the corridor of time. . . .

But there was no concrete beneath his feet now; it felt as if the world was made of glass, that he was standing on a skin of wafer-thin glass. On the one side, that of night, he noticed the shadow of Germany's wall; on the other, that of morning, he thought he could make out the outline of a grey hospital building in France. And had he not read somewhere that Nazism had been a French idea before the Germans took it up? Four men in butcher's overalls and with cigarette ends in the corners of their mouths were to hold him; the fifth had a knife, big, curved, like a scythe, rusty; he had a meat-saw too. The student could not speak French; the surgeon had started on his testicles; the student wanted to say kidney, to suggest kidney, but he did not know what kidney was in French!—he could not talk, he did not even know what help was in French; and when a person has reached the stage of not knowing how to say help, then he is not only outside; he is in total solitude; he is in lunacy; he has reached *beyond the outermost*; a slender note sounds in the universe, a note that seems to come from wafer-thin glass. . . .

He blinked his eyes.

For a moment he had been in the world where Nietzsche once was.... And at that very moment he had managed to think: everybody ... some for many years, some for just a second; but everybody must have known this chilling world; indeed it is common to *all*; it is man's lot, a condition of existence; people *are* completely detached, completely left to themselves; unless they are Siamese twins....

He had blinked his eyes. And, as at the wave of a wand, the picture had changed. He could no longer hear a brittle note as of wafer-thin glass; he could hear, from the street, from the good earth, the distant sound of dulcet motorhorns. He remembered what thirty drivers hanging out of their cabs had shouted at him at that street crossing: "Imbécile"; when exact, an expression never galls; the exact expression is always funny; he could smell something in his room, a delicious smell, the smell of food, to be precise of smoked ham; was it he who had no one to love? —there in his rucksack was that darling little ham of his! It was exactly as if the little pet was lying there *wagging* its tail in the night! Also, he had noticed the gap under the door....

The man who wants to eat cannot be mortally ill; and when a man has an open letter-slot in full view, his great copper gates have not slid shut.

Besides he *did know* what help was in French.

*

It was night.

The night of his first day.

He had put out the lights; he had got into bed; he was lying motionless, on his back, so as not to crumple his trousers that he wanted to press. He lay still with his eyes closed; he could see the highway, endless, it seemed to continue straight into eternity; for a moment he also saw the street like a sunken road; he saw it sloping, unforgettable, from right to left.

It can have had something to do with my having held off so long. That prolonged trembling. Thank God, that at least had stopped. . . .

Later, he had to admit that for a while he had been strongly tempted to take God to task. If God wanted to punish the student—for what?—he should be the first to know that all punishment is a double-edged sword. Yes, he would haul God from the heavenly regions; sit him down in front of life which as we know is a see-saw; caution him, slap the plank with his hand and point; explain to God the elementary fact that when one end of a see-saw goes down, the other goes up.

"Take Beethoven!" he would shout. "Beethoven lost his hearing; Beethoven became deaf. But was that a *loss*, where he was concerned? He avoided having to hear the women's chatter round him; he did not have to hear how out of tune the musicians were who played his symphonies! A loss? A relief! An immense *gain*!"

He had deliberately chosen to use a thunderous voice in order to confuse God, to cover up a certain logical flaw in the argument: namely that ear-drums are not testicles; and also that the student was not Beethoven.

But then there was no need to haul God down; God came of his own accord; there was no wrestling match in front of the see-saw. God was not confused. God was calm. God had a book; a balance book; or a wish book? God had opened the book, fingered through it.

"A flea. . . ." God read.

The student wanted to protest; but at that moment he knew.

"I have it noted down," God said, quietly, business-like one finger pointing to a page. "Not a complete prayer; not a *whole* flea; but I accept bits as well. A small dose of chitin, a tiny one. Wasn't that it? And as it is not practical to have a horny shield outside, actually impossible, I have applied a small dose of insensitivity internally."

There was a lengthy silence.

"I made you slightly—indisposed," God went on, calmly, thoughtfully. God glanced at his book; he said; "some of my sons lack the ability to take things lightly. They elevate every woman to the status of a goddess. There's something here about a rendezvous tomorrow evening at nine o'clock; but there's also a prayer that the arrangement shall not stand. Amen."

"Besides," God said, "there are other sights in Paris. Sometimes I have wondered if it really is so much the women who attract people to Paris."

It was quite still.

The student asked:

"Are wishes always granted?"

God looked at him:

"What else is there to be granted?"

The student opened his mouth; he clasped his hands behind his head and chuckled quietly; he loved a good reply.

Then he grew serious. He had wished, and believed, that this trip was going to be a lucky one. . . . Was that going to be true? Would nothing nasty happen to him?

His heart was thumping. He asked:

"Have I—your protection?"

God gave him a queer, almost offended look; then God lifted his head, turned his face, looked out across Europe, over the world.

God shut the book again; God said:

"All have my protection."

It was night. A June night. 1939. It was warm; dark; still. The foot of a French bed is a strange, peculiar thing; it pinches your toes. He did not have a nice, loose, light eiderdown over him; it was a blanket, thin, rough, like a soldier's blanket. He turned over in the dark, carefully,

281

because of his trousers; lay on his side; that was better. It was a big bed. An enormous bed. Actually it was a double bed. He lay still. Was that a little, hurried, hasty sob coming from the big double bed?

For a moment the man's hand groped in the dark about the empty pillow beside him, as if searching for a beloved head; a little cheek.